CW01660971

Diamond Rock

Paul Weston

www.paulwestonauthor.com

www.paulwestonauthor.com

ISBN: 978-1-9192309-0-0

British Library Cataloguing in Publication Data
A catalogue record for this book is available from the British Library

Cover picture is a detail from 'Cutting out the *Curieux*'
by
Mark Myers

Note:
A glossary is available at www.paulwestonauthor.com

For my sister, Rosemary

Contents

Prologue 1
Chapter 1 – The Song 2
Chapter 2 – Orders 4
Chapter 3 – Légion d'Honneur 7
Chapter 4 – Oleander Heads West 10
Chapter 5 – Squall 15
Chapter 6 - Herault 21
Chapter 7 – Finding the Fleet 25
Chapter 8 – The Dinghy Again 28
Chapter 9 – Grand Cul-de-Sac Marin 32
Chapter 10 – Salt River and the Saintes 36
Chapter 11 – Prince Rupert Bay 39
Chapter 12 – Fort Shirley 43
Chapter 13 – Antigua 48
Chapter 14 – Reconnaissance 50
Chapter 15 – Reunion 53
Chapter 16 – Oleander Heads South 56
Chapter 17 – Columbine's Cruise 60
Chapter 18 – Diamond Rock 65
Chapter 19 – Villeneuve 71
Chapter 20 – Payoff 75
Chapter 21 – Brandywine Creek 78
Chapter 22 – Payoff in the Atlantic 79
Chapter 23 – Villeneuve Arrives 82
Chapter 24 – The Proposal 85
Chapter 25 – Enquiry 87
Chapter 26 – The Descent 89
Chapter 27 – The Yankee 99
Chapter 28 – Return to Molene 104
Chapter 29 – Marigot Bay 109

Chapter 30 – Basse-Terre 115
Chapter 31 – Interlude 120
Chapter 32 – Decisions 122
Chapter 33 – Counter Attack 126
Chapter 34 – Aftermath 135
Chapter 35 – Besieged 146
Chapter 36 – Abandoned 150
Chapter 37 – Baltimore 152
Chapter 38 – Du Pont 156
Chapter 39 – The Dockyard 162
Chapter 40 – The Weary Chase 166
Chapter 41 – Eastwards 167
Chapter 42 – Cape Finisterre 170
Chapter 43 – Respite 175
Chapter 44 – Bermuda 180
Historical and Geographical Notes 182
About the Author 184
Books in This Series 185
Illustrations 186

Prologue

'Those far distant, storm-beaten ships, upon which the Grand Army never looked, stood between it and the dominion of the world'

Alfred Thayer Mahan, *The Influence of Sea Power*

***

'Let us be masters of the Channel for six hours and we are masters of the world'

Napoleon Bonaparte

***

'Is there anything as crazy as the British Navy
Declaring an island's a ship in their fleet?'

Jordan Keyes, *The Island of Diamond Rock (song)*

***

1805

Napoleon, Emperor of France, has assembled a huge army, the *Armée d'Angleterre*, at the port of Boulogne, only thirty miles from the coast of England. He believes that if he can get the army in its invasion barges across the English Channel, Britain will be rapidly defeated. The Royal Navy, which blockades France and keeps the French Navy bottled up in its Atlantic and Mediterranean bases, is determined to stop him. Napoleon devises a plan – his ships will break out of their French bases, Toulon, Brest and Rochefort, cross the Atlantic, and assemble, with their Spanish allies, into a vast fleet which can take command of the Channel and cover Napoleon's invasion.

Admiral Villeneuve, with a French fleet carrying thousands of soldiers, manages to escape from Toulon, evade Nelson, pick up Spanish reinforcements and make his way to Martinique.

Less than a mile off the coast of Martinique, only five miles from the Empress Josephine's birthplace, and commanding the approach to the main French base in the West Indies, is the small precipitous island of Diamond Rock. Through astonishing feats of seamanship, daring and *ad-hoc* engineering, the British under Admiral Hood and the ingenious and determined Lieutenant Maurice have taken possession of the island, fortified it and commissioned it into the navy as HMS *Diamond Rock*.

Napoleon is incensed by this 'impudence' and the failure of an earlier fleet to capture the 'stone frigate'. He orders Villeneuve to take Diamond Rock.

Chapter 1 – The Song

Day after day, Commander Snowden lay in his narrow cot as *Herault*, rolling her trade wind roll, did her best to tip him out of it, while at the same time comforting him with familiar sounds – the wash of the sea along her side, the slatting of sails, the creak of cordage and timber. His thoughts were becoming more coherent, but he just could not remember – anything.

It was the song that did it, jolted him … somewhere on deck, quite distant, a band struck up, a familiar tune, and men began to sing. He tapped out the rhythm with his hand on the side of the cot and started to sing along:

Ah! ça ira, ça ira, ça ira

The band. Fiddles, pipes and drums, a bigger band than …

Ensign Watton's. Watton, with his band on *Oleander*'s deck, off Salé, playing for him as he returned to the ship with the Conde de Premià, playing the tune Watton had learned from the defeated French soldiers in Corsica.

Ah! ça ira, ça ira, ça ira

Ensign Watton, a smile on his boyish face: "Don't know the meaning of the song, Sir, I just like the tune". *Yes, Watton, I believe you*, he had thought, but not said.

Ensign Watton. He remembered, God he remembered. Watton, looking so young, lying lifeless on the bank of the canal. Memory, flooding back, like a spring tide returning over a gently sloping beach.

The hopeless diversion ashore at Maguelone, the explosion, the enormous thump on the back. Watton's body, headache, deafness, the bleak beach, full of enemies, night in the dinghy with the pitiless Mistral blowing, bilge water surging over him, cold, cold.

And *Oleander*? His precious ship? Had she survived? He had last seen her, illuminated by the muzzle flashes of the ambushing gunboats as she closed with the beach at Maguelone, intent on rescuing him.

The cheerful French ship's surgeon visited and, when Snowden told him that his memory seemed to have returned, patted him on the shoulder.

"You will recover, *mon ami*, of that there is no doubt. We will bring you on deck for some sunshine, and feed you up, you will be, to use an English expression 'right as rain'. Allow me to introduce myself. I am Gustave Mercier, Surgeon of *Herault*. You remember your own name now?"

"My name is Snowden, Percy Snowden. I am a commander in the Royal Navy."

The Surgeon, recognising the name, looked keenly at the man lying in the cot. "Are you really Snowden? The man who burnt the Emperor's barges? The name is well known in our navy. You are famous, Commander, and I am pleased to meet you."

The Surgeon stepped back. "Commander Snowden, I must bring the captain to you."

Snowden called out as the man stepped away: "Where are we bound?"

Mercier turned and looked at Snowden "for Martinique, via Guadeloupe, Monsieur."

He felt weak, depressed – captive aboard the French warship that had rescued him from the drifting dinghy in the Mediterranean and was now taking him across the Atlantic, westwards, away from home.

The Surgeon returned, accompanied by another officer, who introduced himself.

"Albert Duval, *capitaine de corvette*, commander of this ship."

"Percy Snowden, commander … "

Duval held up his hand. "We know, Snowden, commander of *Oleander*. There is not a naval man in France who has not heard of you, and in fact I have met you before, or at least tried to, when I was *premier* of *Helene*. We were a little late when you came out of Aber Wrac'h, and that schooner of yours went up to windward and through the Four. If we had arrived a few minutes earlier …"

Snowden nodded, remembering. The French frigates had laid a trap for *Oleander*, in Brittany, and had nearly caught her.

"Where did you go after that?" asked Duval. "It came on to blow very hard."

"Through the Four, and then the Raz," said Snowden, referring to the tide-swept passages around Ushant. "It was not pleasant."

"I am sure it was not. Yes, Snowden, even the Emperor knows of you. Knows! It is more than that! He is quite determined to stop you, so much so that he brought in no less a person than Admiral Morlaix to set up a special command. It seems, from your presence on my ship, destitute, that Morlaix has succeeded."

Morlaix, thought Snowden, and grimaced. He might have guessed. "I know Morlaix," he said, "I have come across him on several occasions. I have even been to his house in Paris. His daughter …" He tailed off, thinking that perhaps he was giving too much away.

"Snowden," said Duval, "I have duties to attend to. It is an honour to have such an officer in my ship. Perhaps you will dine with me as soon as you are able. Good night."

Duval turned and walked to the companionway.

Chapter 2 – Orders

Oleander lay alongside the wharf at Gibraltar. A raft had been rigged under her bowsprit, and men worked on it, making a permanent repair to the bobstay fitting which had been damaged by French fire at Maguelone and temporarily repaired by the ship's carpenter.

Lieutenant Kennedy, watching the repairs from the jetty, was acutely aware that he would soon be parted from the ship. He relished the opportunity that had been given him, to serve on Nelson's staff, but his service in *Oleander* with Snowden had been without doubt the best time of his life. He knew that much of his success was due to Snowden's inspiring leadership, but Kennedy had been tried, severely tried, and had come through.

He started as Pascoe, the young man who had similarly shone under Snowden's leadership, came up to him.

"Nearly complete, Sir," Pascoe said. "Looking forward to the next part of your life? Will you miss us *Oleanders*?"

"I will, Pascoe. She's a fine ship, with a fine crew, it's just a shame ..."

"I know, Sir, but we couldn't have done any different. We had to leave and then come here, when we saw the Frenchies."

Kennedy had been wounded and *Oleander* damaged as the ship stood into a beach in the Gulf of Lions in an attempt to rescue Snowden. They had had to clear out to sea to make temporary repairs, and while hove to had spotted a large French fleet which had slipped past Lord Nelson's blockade of Toulon and was heading west towards the Strait of Gibraltar. Forced to abandon any hope of rescuing Snowden, they had returned to Gibraltar to report what they had seen.

"So I tell myself, but I feel I'm leaving something unfinished."

An unfamiliar lieutenant arrived on the wharf, carrying a package.

"Mr Kennedy," the man said, "may we go to the cabin?"

Pascoe raised an eyebrow and said to no one in particular, "That looks like orders."

Pascoe's surmise had been correct, and in the cabin Kennedy read the orders. When he had finished, he looked up at the lieutenant.

"Well, this is a surprise," he said.

"It is all hands to the pump, presently," said the lieutenant, "with the French breaking out."

"Did he give you any verbal message to pass on?" Kennedy asked, referring to Admiral Jameson.

"No, Mr Kennedy, only the written orders."

"Very well. Will you take a glass?"

"I'd very much like to, but I'm directed to hurry back after delivering the orders."

"I see," said Kennedy, "in that case …"

"On the other hand," said the lieutenant, "I've had a long trip and some refreshment would not go amiss."

When the lieutenant had gone, Kennedy turned to Cox, the steward.

"Have Mr Pascoe and Mr Luciani repair to the cabin, directly, if you please."

When they were sat around the table, Kennedy said, "It seems that Lord Nelson will have to make do without my services for some time."

"How so, Sir?" asked Luciani, *Oleander*'s Corsican Master.

"Orders, Mister, from Admiral Jameson."

Luciani and Pascoe, as though on cue, snorted loudly – Jameson had been responsible for planning the disastrous raid which had led to the loss of a frigate and many men, including Snowden.

Noting Kennedy's disapproving look, Pascoe recovered himself quickly and asked, "What are the orders, Sir?"

"Bermuda, Pascoe."

"Bermuda, Sir?" asked Luciani.

"Yes, we are to take despatches there, presumably to warn that a French fleet is in the Atlantic."

"Keep us out of the way, more like," muttered Pascoe.

"That is quite enough of that, Pascoe," said Kennedy, though the lieutenant carrying the orders had clearly implied that the Admiral was keen to have Kennedy removed from the scene.

"I am sure that never crossed the Admiral's mind, Mr Pascoe," he continued, as Pascoe nodded apologetically. "Now, as to the course we should take."

Pascoe produced a chart, laid it on the table, and set to work with dividers and parallel rule. He looked up. "About 2,900 miles if we go direct, quite a bit longer if we go down to the trade wind. Bermuda's about 32 degrees North, so the Trades would be a considerable diversion, but, let me see."

He set to again and said, half to himself, "If we go down to the trades, say 20 North, off the Cape Verdes, the distance is about 3,500 miles – say three days difference."

He sat in thought for a moment.

"I'd like to consult *Bowditch*" he opened Snowden's frequently consulted copy of Nathanial Bowditch's masterpiece, *American Practical Navigator* "and see what else I can find, but I think I'd be inclined to do the Trades. We don't want to get mixed up with the Azores High – not much wind there."

Luciani looked at Kennedy. "Are you to be in command, Ken?"

"So it seems, Giotto, I don't think they have anyone else on the beach here at short notice. I'm now Commander Kennedy, and you are Lieutenant Pasco, and Acting Lieutenant Luciani."

Pascoe and Luciani looked at each other, smiling. Luciani spoke "That is certainly something, Ken. I hope you're happy, even if you are not to join Nelson's staff. Interest can be a double-edged sword, should your patron fall out of favour or, God forbid, die. Now you have your own ship and a jump in rank," he looked at Pascoe, again absorbed in *American Practical Navigator*, "at least we'll be able to find Bermuda."

Chapter 3 – Légion d'Honneur

"That was quite a climb for your husband, Odile," said the Emperor. "I hope it was worth it."

"I am quite sure it was," replied Odile Morlaix. "He is really very proud, though he tries not to show it. And, Sir, he very much appreciated your gesture."

On the previous day, in the courtyard of Fontainebleau, Napoleon had invested Admiral Morlaix with the Légion d'honneur. Morlaix, missing a leg since the action in St Malo, had had to be assisted by two officers up the stairs of the dais to where Napoleon sat. To the astonishment of the spectators, after the investiture, the Emperor had stood up and helped Morlaix back down the steps.

There was considerable mutual admiration between Odile Morlaix and the Emperor, and they were sitting in Napoleon's private room in the palace, at a table with glasses in front of them.

"Soon, I think later today, Odile, Decrès will make an offer to your husband …"

Odile stiffened and said with some vehemence, "He is not yet ready for the sea. The recent business has exhausted him and …"

"We appreciate that, Odile. I was about to say that we believe that he, and you, may be of great service to France, in a different sphere."

Odile, abashed, nodded as the Emperor continued, "And I have asked you here to make plain that I very much hope that you will be able to accept the service that Decrès will ask of you."

"May I ask what this service will be?"

Napoleon said, with a dismissive hand gesture, "I think it is better if Decrès tells you."

***

Admiral Morlaix was not surprised to be asked to meet Decrès, the Minister of Marine, but he was surprised that the Minister had requested that his wife be present as well.

"Your award, Morlaix - thoroughly deserved, if I may say so. I think that it will be a long time before the English mount any more raids," said Decrès, referring to the trap that Morlaix had successfully set for the English at the Malpas tunnel on the Canal du Midi. He turned to his aide, a smartly dressed senior captain, and continued, "Admiral Morlaix and I go back a long way, Giraud. We were comrades at the Battle of the Saintes."

"I did not know that, Sir," replied the aide. "A bad business, that battle."

"Indeed it was, Giraud."

He turned to Morlaix and Odile. "Your daughter is in America?"

"She is, Decrès," replied Morlaix, in a tone of bewilderment. "Why do you mention that?"

"Because we would like you to visit her."

Morlaix and Odile looked at each other. "Why would you like us to do that?" asked Odile.

"Because, Madame Morlaix, we have a shortage of gunpowder, a considerable shortage, for our navy, and indeed our military in the West Indies. There is little capacity for producing powder in the Islands, and importation from France is difficult. Blockade runners have delivered some American powder, but the quality has been indifferent."

Odile looked at Decrès. "What has that to do with us visiting our daughter?"

She glanced at her husband and saw comprehension starting to dawn on his face as Decrès replied, "Because, Madame, your daughter's husband is an employee of Monsieur du Pont, or more specifically of his firm, E.I. DuPont de Nemours & Company, which manufactures high quality powder on Brandywine Creek, in Delaware."

Odile put her hand on her husband's arm, happiness flooding over her, and when she looked into his eyes she could see that the same was happening to him.

Morlaix turned to Decrès. "What do you want us to do?"

"To visit your daughter and, quietly, inspect Monsieur du Pont's works. If satisfactory, we wish you to arrange for powder to be delivered to our colonies in the Caribbean." He looked at Giraud. "It is Captain Giraud's plan and he will brief you."

"And my present command, the coastal defence?"

"It is the view of the Emperor that the English are unlikely to attempt any more raids on the French mainland for some time. The system of coastal defence you have set up is efficient, and so your presence at Beziers is no longer necessary. He considers the mission to the United States to be of greater importance."

***

They had spent two weeks in Paris. Odile had quickly got back into the swing of life in the capital, Morlaix's recent success had done their reputation no harm, and the house was frequently filled with guests. Now they were at their house in Agen and Odile was sitting in the garden, dozing, when her husband touched her arm.

"Oh, hello, you startled me. I didn't hear you coming."

"It's the leather patch on the wooden leg, helps with the grip as well. Captain Badeau is leaving. Will you come and say goodbye?"

Badeau, until now Morlaix's second in command, was taking his commander's place in charge of the coastal defence force Morlaix had established. When Badeau had departed and they had seated themselves in the garden, Morlaix said, "There's a ship, nearly ready for sea, at Pauillac. I have made arrangements for us to travel aboard her."

"A nice big ship, I hope."

"Not very, Odile, a Yankee schooner." He smiled, "I should think she is probably similar to the cursed *Oleander*." He paused and looked at his wife. "A Yankee ship, *Payoff*."

"Is that ...?"

"Yes it is, it's the ship that took Dominique and Jacques to America! Her Master, Molineux, seems to make a living from running the blockade from the Gironde."

Chapter 4 – Oleander Heads West

A fine levanter, an east wind, was blowing as *Oleander* passed through the Strait of Gibraltar. The setting sun was shining on her sails as Cape Spartel, the north-westerly point of the African continent came abeam, and she turned south-west, into the open Atlantic, making good progress in the strong breeze. On the afternoon of the third day, as the ship rushed along under full sail at eleven knots or so, there was a shout from the masthead: "Land clouds ahead. Fine on the starboard bow."

"That'll be Tenerife," said Pascoe to Luciani as he looked up from his chart. "Giotto, don't even say it!"

Pascoe had developed a habit of saying "just about where I thought we'd be" when *Oleander* made a landfall, and to his outward discomfiture, but secret pride, this had become a source of amusement aboard the ship.

"Of course I won't say it, Pascoe."

Kennedy, who had heard the lookout's shout, appeared on deck, and looked at Pascoe. "Are we just about where you thought we'd be?"

Luciani turned away, chortling, as Kennedy continued. "Tenerife, is it? It certainly generates a lot of cloud."

Tenerife, one of the Canary Islands, had a huge volcano at its centre, about twelve thousand feet high, and the cloud frequently clinging to the mountain made the island visible for an enormous distance.

"Yes, Sir", said Pascoe, smiling, "it'll be Tenerife all right. I'll shoot some stars at dusk with Mr Luciani, but there's not much doubt."

Kennedy considered. "I think we'll pull her in a bit for the night."

"I don't believe there's any need, Sir ..."

At a glance from Kennedy, Pascoe stopped, and Kennedy continued, "I know, Mr Pascoe, but the winds between these high islands are often pretty strong, and flukey."

Kennedy, like all officers commanding schooners, had an abiding fear that there would be an unexpected wind shift and the ship would gybe, sending the great booms crashing across the deck, with potentially serious results. The square topsails and staysails were very much less likely to be taken aback by a wind shift.

"I think we'll snug her down to the square sails and staysails. Mr Luciani!"

"Aye aye, Sir, square sails and staysails."

A whistle blew and barefoot men climbed the ratlines up the masts, while others tailed on ropes. The great fore and mainsails were furled, and the ship became steadier. Pascoe went to the stern, inspected the patent log, and came back to Kennedy.

"Still doing eight knots, Sir."

He was interrupted by another shout from the masthead:

"On deck, I can see the mountain."

And later, as it was getting dark, another call came from the foremast, "Land fine on the port bow."

"Grand Canary," said Pascoe, rather smugly.

There was another shout from the masthead: "Sail, two points on the starboard bow."

"Up and have a look," said Kennedy to Pascoe, "you might be better off with this," holding out the night glass.

A few minutes later, Pascoe, slightly out of breath, came back to the quarterdeck.

"A brig, Sir, I reckon she's for Santa Cruz."

Santa Cruz was the main port of Tenerife, a heavily fortified base of the Spanish navy.

"Get the sails back on her," said Kennedy, "we'll go and have a look."

***

It did not take *Oleander* long to catch up with the ship, a small Portuguese brig. She was a merchantman, no match for *Oleander*, and when the British ship fired a gun, the Portuguese backed his topsails and hove to. The gig was launched, and Luciani, accompanied by Marine Ensign Vause, Watton's replacement, was rowed across the dark sea to the brig. They returned shortly afterwards with a passenger.

"Sir," said Luciani, "this is Captain Alves. He has interesting information, but I think it better if you hear it directly from him."

In the cabin, a glass in front of him, Alves told Kennedy that he had seen a French fleet two days before, south-west of Madeira. A big fleet. He believed there were 18 big ships as well as smaller ones, and they were heading "south of West".

Kennedy's pulse quickened. The French, they must be bound for the West Indies!

"This is very interesting, Captain Alves. If you will excuse me for a moment."

"Of course, *Senhor*, but I must get back to my ship."

"I will not detain you long."

On deck, Kennedy spoke to Luciani and Vause: "The skipper says he saw the French fleet a couple of days ago. That could be very important, but I don't want any mistakes. Go back to the brig and speak to the mate and anyone else you can think of – even the crew – and see if they confirm his story."

Back in the cabin, Kennedy opened his notebook and spoke to the Portuguese skipper.

"Please go over your account again, Sir, from the beginning. You left Funchal on …?"

Vause and Luciani, when they returned from the brig, told Kennedy that the Portuguese crew had confirmed what their skipper had said – they had sighted a big French fleet south of Madeira a few days before, and the fleet was heading south-west.

From the deck, Luciani watched as the Portuguese brig squared her yards and continued her voyage. He expected an order to get the ship underway, and when he did not get one, went to the cabin. Kennedy was seated at the table, on which he'd pinned an Atlantic chart, and was staring fixedly at it, absorbed.

"Orders, Sir?"

Kennedy looked up in surprise. "Not just now, Giotto. I want to think about what we should do with this information."

Kennedy was normally a decisive man, and Luciani, surprised, replied, "Very good, Sir, I'll keep her as she is," and went back out to the deck, meeting quizzical looks with a shake of his head. About an hour later, Cox, the captain's steward, came up and asked Luciani to repair to the cabin.

When Luciani entered, Kennedy was sitting with Pascoe at the table. Without preamble Kennedy said, "We have very important information, vital. The French - Villeneuve - must be headed to the Caribbean, there is no other explanation. Nelson may already know where they're going, but if he does not … No, we have to go back, to Gib. It is possible that Nelson may already be on his way to the Caribbean. If that is the case, we must make every effort to meet him. Explain the plan, Pascoe, if you please."

Pointing to the chart, Pascoe began, "Sir, we have to get back to Gib as soon as possible. However, Nelson may be headed for the Caribbean, and so we must maximise our chances of meeting him. Nelson has the reputation for direct sailing, rather than heading south for the Trades, as we were doing, and then turning west. This means his course is likely to be this," he pointed to the chart, "south of Madeira, and then direct for, let us say, Barbados." He pointed to a series of crosses on the chart, which was based on the Mercator projection, so that the course to Barbados appeared as a curve.

Kennedy nodded and spoke, "Our best bet for meeting any British fleet is to head north from here, towards Madeira, and then turn towards Gib."

Luciani nodded, "Getting up to Madeira will be a flog to windward."

"It will," agreed Kennedy, "but *Oleander* can do it, if any ship can." *Oleander*, Bermuda built with lightweight cedar, and with her extravagant fore and aft sail plan, was, as scientifically determined on her trials, on most points of sailing the fastest ship in the Navy, bettered only by the larger ships on a run directly downwind.

"There is another point to consider," said Kennedy. "In the night, there's a possibility that we could sail straight through the British fleet without realising. To minimise this possibility, we'll heave to during the hours of darkness. Needless to say, we'll keep a very good lookout at all times."

***

Five days later, during which time they had not fallen in with the British fleet, or indeed seen hardly any ships at all, *Oleander* sighted a British frigate, *Dorchester*, patrolling across the Strait of Gibraltar. The two ships hove to close together, and Kennedy went aboard the larger vessel. He delivered his despatch and verbal message to the frigate's commander, Captain Robertson.

"I appreciate the importance of this, Kennedy. Vital stuff. I'll act immediately. Your orders, you say, are for Bermuda?"

"They are, Captain Robertson, but I would like to discuss something with you. The information I have about the French fleet is of extreme importance, as you say, and I believe I should warn the people in the West Indies that the French are heading their way. I'm proposing to call at Antigua en route."

"A very proper course of action, in my opinion, Commander Kennedy."

Confident that *Dorchester*'s captain appreciated the importance of his despatch, and grateful for his support for his decision to head towards Antigua, base of the British Leeward Islands Squadron, Kennedy returned to *Oleander*.

"Change of plan – Antigua," he said to Pascoe on his return to the ship. "You remember the way to Tenerife, I expect!"

***

The dawn of the fourth day out from Gibraltar revealed the towering peak of Tenerife on the starboard quarter and the lower mountains of Grand Canary astern to port. The two high islands funnelled the wind between them, and the night had been quite wild, with only a glimpse of lights on the islands. *Oleander*'s fore and aft sails were still furled, and Kennedy was glad that he had taken them in.

"Shall we try the fore squaresail, Sir?" asked Pascoe.

In Gibraltar, Lieutenant Pascoe, a deep-thinking young man, knowing that a long trade wind passage was imminent, had suggested that a spare mainsail should be modified to work as a square foresail. The ship's sailmaker had finished the sail the day before, and Pascoe was very keen to try it.

"After breakfast", said Kennedy.

It took all morning to get the square foresail bent on and adjusted to Pascoe's satisfaction, but the result was impressive, and soon the ship was surging along at ten knots, heading south-west until she found the north-east trade wind at about 19 degrees North. She turned to starboard, west towards Antigua, more than 2,000 miles distant.

Chapter 5 – Squall

A steward brought food. Snowden, depressed by his memories, had little appetite, but he forced himself to eat, and felt better for it.

He was coming to terms with his memories, and his mood improved. He listened to the sounds of the ship as, with considerable shouting, much more than there ever was in *Oleander*, where a voice was hardly ever raised, sail was reduced, and she was prepared for the long tropical night.

He slept.

***

Herault's commander, Albert Duval, *capitaine de corvette* of the Imperial Navy, sat alone in his cabin, thinking. The man they had rescued from the dinghy in the Mediterranean, injured and near death, was the famous Snowden! He had not captured him in battle, that would have been something, but Snowden, Napoleon's *bête noire*, was here, aboard his ship. He was glad they had rescued him from the little boat – but how had Snowden come to be in it? If his ship, *Oleander*, had sunk, he would not be in its dinghy by himself, with no other people and no wreckage nearby. No, it was a mystery, and he looked forward to another conversation with the English officer.

But first, there was work to do. He stood and went onto the quarterdeck. Lieutenant Cartier, a young, nervous man, saw him approaching in the dim moonlight, and drew himself up.

"Good evening, Cartier."

"Good evening, Sir. Course west by south. Wind from the east, a *jolie brise*, Sir, topsails and staysail only. *Molene* on the port quarter, about a mile distant."

"Squalls?" asked Duval, his eyes scanning the horizon astern of the ship as he spoke. It seemed clear, but it was damned difficult to tell in the dark. He saw the dim blue light of their fellow frigate, *Molene*, but there seemed to be no threatening clouds. How he hated these long tropical nights.

"None visible, Sir."

"Lookouts?"

"Yes, Sir, as attentive as I can make them."

Though *Herault* was a warship, a frigate, she was '*en flûte*', essentially converted into a cargo ship, with a small crew and reduced armament. In Toulon, many of *Herault*'s experienced seamen had been taken from her to bolster the crews of ships that were expected to fight, leaving her with many inexperienced crew members, including a number of landsmen, and this was a constant worry for Duval.

"Ports?"

The weather was warm and humid, and the following wind meant that there was a lack of ventilation in the interior of the ship. The men, some of them ignorant of the consequences of their actions, and one or two of them uncaring, sometimes opened the gun ports, making the heavily laden ship vulnerable to flooding if she heeled in a sudden squall.

"All closed, Sir," Cartier considered. "At least, they were an hour ago."

Duval walked around the ship's upper deck, exchanging pleasantries with the men he encountered, spoke to the quartermaster at the wheel, doffed his hat to Cartier, and went through the door to his cabin. He thought about visiting Snowden, a man who similarly knew the loneliness of command, but he put the thought aside – the hour was late, and the Englishman needed to rest.

He was sleeping, uneasily, when he was awoken by the noise of incredibly heavy rain on the deck above his head. *A squall*, he thought, as he struggled into his coat, *let us hope it's only rain.*

***

Snowden was awakened by shouting above him, "*Rafale, rafale!*" and the sound of torrential rain. A squall, there'd been several so far on this trip across the Atlantic. *Herault*, as far as he could tell by her motion when sailing, was heavy laden, and they'd snugged her down at sunset. She'd be all right, but then ... then, the wind came with a great roar, and the ship staggered awkwardly. Caught aback, he realised, as she heeled violently, flogging sails sending vibrations through the ship's structure. There was a deeper roar followed by splintering noises - guns, breaking free. More shouting, more crashes. Masts and spars, he thought, they're either cutting them away or ... they're just falling. He heard the sound of axes, and then there was an enormous concussion, a deluge of water soaked him, and moonlight trickled into his dark cabin through gaps around a great yard that had fallen through the deck above, narrowly missing him and almost filling the space with the sail that it had been supporting. The ship's list was so great now that he was hanging onto the cot, tying to stop himself sliding to leeward, his world turned on its side.

Relieved of her masts, the ship recovered slightly, but the wind shrieked even louder, and she heeled further, to the sounds of cargo shifting in her hold and more guns breaking free.

The ship was almost on her beam ends now. In the moonlight, as he clung onto his cot, his back supported by what, when the ship was level, had been its side, he saw water surging below him. She was going, he realised, and despite his weakness, tried to make his way past the sail and yard blocking his path to the companionway. With a sick feeling, he knew he was trapped. He shouted, shouted, and shouted again, but his voice was weak with disuse, and there was no response. He tore at the heavy canvas, but it was stiff and wet, roped at its edges, incredibly strong, and he knew it was hopeless. If only he had a knife ...

***

As went onto the deck, Duval heard the wind coming, shrieking, saw a line of foam on the sea's surface advancing, and then, as the gust hit the ship, she staggered, heeling, her sails shaking, before they were blown violently aback and shredded. Yards crashed to the deck. He heard the sound of guns and cargo shifting as the ship heeled almost onto her beam ends.

A time of unbelievable horror - the ship's list was so great that Duval knew that the only chance of righting her was to cut away the rigging in the hope that the masts would go by the board and the ship would right herself sufficiently so that the pumps could be manned. With the officers and men, those that were uninjured and able to work, labouring in darkness and flying spray mixed with rain, he struggled to cut away the masts as the ship lay almost horizontal, rigging and spars trailing alongside her, but, as dawn broke, he realised that it was hopeless, the ship would not right herself. She lay helpless, lolling broadside to the waves whose crests broke and surged against her.

The sun rose, suddenly as it does in the tropics, and the wind, which had been easing for some time, changed from a malevolent monster into a steady trade wind. Ahead, he could see the dark clouds of the squall as it headed westward, away from the ship. The crew, wet through, cold and exhausted, turned their faces to the sun, feeling its warmth. They had done well, he thought, the landsmen, the fleet rejects. Some of them, it was true, had found wine somewhere, and a few were obviously dead drunk, but they had done all they could. The ship was clearly doomed, sinking gradually deeper into the sea. His first ship, a total loss. Would it have been any different if he had a full warship's crew, made up of prime seamen? He started to make his way across the almost vertical deck towards the remains of the ship's boats, and was joined by Lieutenant Cartier, a serious gash in his head, and the Boatswain, a man of perhaps sixty, almost the only professional seaman in the crew, his face looking grey and old despite the sunshine.

"The ship is going, Captain," he said. "She's dead in the water. I don't know how long we ..."

His point was emphasised by a loud noise as one of the masts floating alongside gave the ship's hull a mighty blow. The Boatswain gestured to the boats, which had been neatly chocked down and stacked when the ship had left France but were now hanging from their lashings, their appearance closer to a pile of firewood than finely worked products of the *Arsenal de Rochefort*. The only boat that seemed to have escaped damage was the small one at the top of the stack – the dinghy in which they had found the Englishman.

"These boats, it doesn't look promising," he began, "unless we can all fit into the English dinghy." He paused, thinking. "Perhaps we can make something of the longboat ..."

There was a shout, and then a ragged cheer from the crew, and Duval and his companions looked up. Cartier pointed, making inarticulate sounds in his throat, and grabbed Duval's coat, more, the captain thought, for support than emphasis. Emerging from the black squall ahead, the rising sun starkly illuminating the stumps of her masts and a chaos of fallen rigging and sails, but indisputably upright and floating, was a ship.

"My God, *Molene*," said the Bosun, his voice made hoarse by exhaustion and salt water.

"So it is, by God," said Duval, as the ship lurched again. "I've never seen a finer sight. They've seen us – they're launching a boat!"

A wave, larger than the rest, washed over the ship. There was a cry, and Duval saw that it had taken two men overboard. The men were being carried to leeward by the wind and waves, away from the waterlogged ship. One of them was attempting to support the other, but they were clearly in distress, unable to swim back to the ship. Duval, almost without thinking, removed his jacket and grabbed an oar, which was protruding from the wreckage of one of the boats.

The Boatswain, seeing what he was about to do, shouted "No, Captain," and lunged at him, but Duval, holding onto the oar, was already sliding down the sloping deck, which met the water in a welter of foam. He stepped from the deck into the warm water, much as he would have done from a steeply shelving beach.

The oar was big, perhaps fifteen feet long, and heavy, and though it was difficult to push it through the water, it gave good buoyancy, which was just as well, as the sea was rough, with occasional breaking crests. To the swimming Duval, the waves seemed enormous, and after a few yards, the ship was only visible when he was on the top of a swell. From time to time, he could see the men in the water, and he made his way towards them as quickly as he could, holding onto the oar with one hand and propelling himself along with his feet and other arm.

As he drew closer to the men, he could see that they were still alive, with one gallantly supporting the other. He shouted, but his voice was inaudible over the sound of wind and waves, and the men had no notion of his presence until the blade of the oar hit the man who was supporting the other in the back. The man looked round in surprise, and Duval recognised him as Vincent, one of the landsmen, but a man who had worked tirelessly to save the ship.

"Captain! Thank you."

The three men clung onto the oar, and when they were lifted on a wave, Duval looked back towards the ship, which was by now at quite a distance. To his satisfaction, he saw that three of *Molene*'s boats had arrived. One had put her bow against *Herault*'s listing deck and men were clambering aboard, and the other two were standing a few yards off, wary of the floating spars, waiting their turn. The man who Vincent had been supporting, Duval could not remember his name, was listless, perhaps drunk, and from time to time Vincent spoke to him, encouragingly.

"Don't worry, my friend, they'll come for us soon. The captain has brought you this splendid oar, hang tight onto it."

***

The deck of *Molene* felt wonderful under Duval's feet, even if his legs were rubbery, and the ship's motion was so quick with only stumps of masts left that it was necessary to hang on tightly.

"Thank you, Morel," he said to *Molene*'s commander as he shook his fellow *capitaine de corvette*'s hand.

"Bad luck, Duval," said Morel, "but for the grace of God …"

He gestured to the chaos of *Molene*'s deck, encumbered with the tangled wreckage of spars, rigging and sails. "We were lucky – although lucky is perhaps not the right word – the masts fell immediately, and she did not get knocked down. We didn't lose a single man."

Duval gripped the rail and nodded as Morel continued, "Hull's sound enough, no leaking. We're trying to get something on that foremast stump." He gestured towards where men were working.

"Give me a few minutes and I'll get back up here and help," said Duval.

He went down the companionway to the gun deck. His men, the men from *Herault*, were sitting, braced against *Molene*'s roll, eating. Some were injured, all looked hollow-eyed from exhaustion. Lieutenant Cartier was there, his head bandaged, and between them they established who the survivors were, questioning the men about what had happened to those who were missing. A few men were assuredly dead, or missing, which amounted to the same thing, but Duval felt that thanks to the prompt action of *Molene*'s commander in sending boats, things were not as bad as they might have been. But for him, to lose his first ship, without even seeing an enemy!

"Did anyone see the Englishman?" he asked.

There was a general shaking of heads. The Boatswain said, "The main topsail yard went down on top of his bunk, Sir. If he'd survived he'd have come out on deck. The door wasn't locked."

Such a shame, thought Duval. The famous Snowden, killed by a stupid trade wind squall. He turned back to the men: "Those of you who can, get on deck when you've finished eating. We must get *Molene* underway. We don't want to be hanging around here with no sails! There's always the chance of an English ship, and we'd be sitting ducks."

One of the men stirred and looked around. "Thank you, Sir, for rescuing Vincent and Arnoud. I think I speak for all of the crew when I say it was a brave effort."

Chapter 6 - Herault

Trapped! Snowden was trapped below by the yard and sail which had crashed through the deck and was now filling most of the room. Trapped, with the ship sinking.

It was almost completely dark in the cabin, only a little faint light filtering through the gaps between the splintered deck and the fallen yard. Driven almost by panic, he had pushed and pulled desperately at the sail which blocked his exit, but the heavy canvas was immovable. He shouted again, as loud as he could, but although he could hear the sounds of men nearby, his voice was weak, and there was no response to his calls.

He must have a knife. He recalled that his coat had been hanging from a hook near his cot. He searched through the pockets – no knife. He put the coat on – the earlier soaking had made him chilly. Suddenly, he remembered the dinner he had eaten. There was a knife on the tray, perhaps not much of a knife, but he remembered that its blade was pointed and serrated. It would do – if he could find it in the gloom. He thought – *where would his dinner tray have ended up?* The stool that the tray had been resting on was on its side, prevented from falling further by the side of his cot, but there was no sign of the tray itself. In the dim light, he traced what he thought must have been the tray's path as it fell when the ship heeled, and realised that the knife was somewhere under the water which had accumulated against the side of the ship, and which surged unattractively as the ship moved in the waves.

The noise of the wind had almost vanished, but though the waves still broke against the ship, he could hear shouting on deck, and even what he thought was a cheer. He called out, again and again, as loudly as he could, but there was no reply, and as the shouting from the deck diminished and then stopped, he realised what had happened – the ship had been abandoned, and he was alone.

Snowden did not much like confined spaces, and his heart was beating quickly as he half climbed and half slid down the sloping cabin sole to the side of the ship. Bracing himself against her side, he put his right arm into the water and began feeling for the knife, not an easy process as the moveable contents of the room had obeyed the call of gravity and were now either floating or submerged under the water. Eventually, just before he was about to give up, his fingers felt something sharp – the knife!

He climbed back up the cabin sole, over the cot, and began to cut at the sail. The knife was better than he had expected and before long he had cut a length of cloth away from the yard, making a space sufficient for him to crawl through. He tucked the knife into his belt and, with difficulty, made his way through the sail and to the door. In the topsy-turvy world of the listing ship, the handle was at the top of the door, and when he reached up for it, it turned easily enough, but the door did not move, probably trapped by some distortion of the ship's structure. He braced his knees against the bulkhead and, driven to desperation by his fear of entrapment in the enclosed space, pulled with maniacal strength on the handle.

It did not budge. Panting and near to panic, he forced himself to calm down. He took the knife from his belt and gradually worked it into the gap between the door and its frame. When it had penetrated a good distance, he used the door frame as a fulcrum to lever against the door. It moved, slightly. Breathing deeply, he repeated the process, and the door moved a little more. On the fourth or fifth attempt, to Snowden's enormous relief, with a violent bang, the door swung open. Light flooded in and, just beyond the door opening, he could see the companionway that led to the deck. The door opening was partly blocked by a gun carriage and other debris that had come to rest there, but, driven by fear, Snowden clambered to the companionway and pulled himself up its handrail to the deck.

The scene before him was one of desolation, though the sun shone brightly. The ship was just awash, a tangle of spars and rigging trailing beside her. From time to time one or other of the spars would rise up in a wave and deliver a blow to the ship's hull. He saw the wreckage of the boats, but the ship seemed to be deserted. The crew had surely been rescued, so there must be another ship nearby. He was looking round the horizon for it when he felt raindrops. He looked to windward, saw a line of foam advancing and, within seconds, the rain had turned into a torrent and the wind into an almost living thing that plucked at his clothes, although the rain was so heavy that the sea became smooth. Wet through, he began to shiver and realised that he had to get out of the weather. He saw that the door on the starboard side of the break of the poop was open, and he climbed up the deck and went through it.

Just inside was a table, fastened to the deck, with a chart pinned onto it – the master's chart, they would call it on a British ship. It was of the whole of the North Atlantic in an unfamiliar projection, but the line of bold crosses, annotated with dates, marching across it from the Strait of Gibraltar was clear enough. Noon positions. Snowden peered closely at the chart. *Herault* was clearly a fast sailer – it was only eighteen days since she had left the Strait. She had steered almost south, and then turned to the west and had sailed down the Trade to her present position. He looked at the last faint cross on the chart, marked NE – *navigation estimée*, dead reckoning in English – and saw with a start that the ship was only about sixty miles east of Guadeloupe.

Sixty miles, he thought – it might as well as have been six thousand. The ship was barely afloat, buffeted by the squall, and before long she would sink, a matter of a few hours, at most.

It was lonely by himself on the wreck of *Herault*, surrounded by the vast indifferent ocean. Bleak, noisy, the unceasing wind whistling over her hull, her timbers groaning and creaking like a living thing in distress, and the breaking wave crests slapping against her. Her motion was dreadful, ominous, lolling in the swells like a waterlogged tree trunk.

He looked through the doorway at the desolation on deck. The boats, stacked just forward of him, were a sorry sight, barely recognisable – except, except – he saw a hint of bright blue at the top of the pile. Could it be? Heedless of the wind and rain, he clawed along the starboard rail and looked down. Yes, it was *Oleander*'s dinghy! From where he was it looked pretty intact, in fact the only boat that still looked recognisably like a boat. Its position, almost completely inside what was probably the captain's gig, had protected it. Carefully, hardly daring to hope, he made his way to it and climbed over the other boats until his head was level with its gunwhale. The starboard sheer strake, the plank just below the gunwhale, was stove in, but that was well above the waterline. The oars were stowed neatly in it, as was the short mast and sail. Astonishingly, he could see sand on the bottom boards – it must have come from the beach at Maguelone! Cheered by the sight of something connected with *Oleander*, hope rose within him, but he was becoming seriously cold in the rain and wind, and his teeth were chattering.

He went back through the doorway and into the accommodation, thinking. There was a door at the end of the alleyway, hanging on its hinges, and he went through it into the captain's cabin. He looked out of the stern gallery. Some of the windows were broken and about one-third of them were underwater. A large desk, clearly bolted to the floor, was in the middle of the room, positioned so that the ship's commander would have a view through the windows as he worked at it. He slid down to it, and, with only a vague idea of what he was looking for, opened the drawers one by one. A polished box. He opened it and saw a pair of pistols, new looking, marked 'XIII', and then, to his great joy, found a bag of tacks, perhaps intended to secure charts to the table.

The wind was weakening – the squall was clearly moving past the ship – and the rain had stopped. He went outside, and made his way over to the fallen yard, the lower part of which had nearly trapped him below, and attacked the sail with his knife, cutting out a rough square of canvas of about two feet on the side. He went back to the boats, and climbed up until he was standing so that his shoulders were level with the gunwhale of *Oleander*'s dinghy. With the tacks, using a pistol butt as a hammer, he fixed the square of canvas over the stove-in plank. It was a rough job and the tacks were too short to be really effective, but he managed to get a lot of them in, though his fingers took considerable punishment from the pistol butt. He was satisfied that he had improved the dinghy's seaworthiness, but although he was in a desperate hurry to get off the ship before she sank, he knew that he could not make a trip of any length in the boat without some supplies, and he decided he must return to the accommodation.

As he reached the alleyway, he was thrown off balance by the ship plunging into a wave, and for a sickening moment before she recovered, he thought she would continue to the bottom and he would be trapped below decks. In a small pantry off the alleyway he found a stone jar with liquid in it – water he presumed – and biscuit, which he stuffed into his coat pockets. Enough for a day or so, he thought. Picking up a cooking pan as he left the pantry, suppressing his urge to get out of the confines of the accommodation, he went back into the captain's cabin, an idea forming in his mind, and made his way to the desk. There was a large door set into it, and he tried the handle. It was locked. The ship gave a lurch and he almost gave it up, but he smashed at the wood with the pistol, once, twice, three times, until at last the timber yielded and the door opened. Inside, as he knew there would be, was an oilskin bag, curiously heavy because of the lead weights sewn into it. He could see by the level of water in the cabin that the ship was settling rapidly, and pausing only to collect the captain's boat cloak and hat, hanging from a hook in the door at a ridiculous angle, Snowden went outside and climbed back up to the dinghy.

He put his new possessions into the boat, under the little sail, and thought rapidly. He had to get the dinghy off the stack of boats and down the sloping deck so that he could launch it. There was not much time. He took the boat's painter and turned it round a belaying pin on the ship's rail. Holding the painter in his left hand, he hacked at the boat's lashings with the knife in his right hand. The knife was getting rather blunt, but eventually the last lashing let go and he was able to use the painter to lower the boat down the deck, in a reasonably controlled manner. The dinghy, quite close to vertical, entered the sea stern on and shipped some water over her transom, but she floated well enough, though she banged alarmingly against the ship as she rose and fell on the waves.

Snowden slid down the deck and scrambled into the dinghy. He used an oar to push off, and suddenly the little boat was floating on the rough Atlantic, the ship awash astern with waves breaking against her hull like a half-tide rock. He shipped the oars and got the dinghy stern onto the waves. Pushed by the trade wind, she moved quickly, and when she had travelled about for about half a mile, Snowden rested on his oars and looked astern in horrified fascination as *Herault*, as though tired of life, slipped serenely below the waves.

Chapter 7 – Finding the Fleet

Captain Robertson of the frigate *Dorchester* was an anxious man. He appreciated the gravity of his mission, to get Kennedy's despatches about the French fleet to Nelson, and he had driven his ship as hard as he could to Gibraltar, and almost immediately back out again, eastwards, into the Mediterranean, in search of the British fleet. It was confidently expected at Gibraltar that Nelson would be heading west out of the Mediterranean towards the Atlantic, in pursuit of the French under Admiral Villeneuve, but in his apprehension, Robertson was not so sure. They had been looking for several days now, slowly drawing away from Gibraltar, and they had seen nothing. *What if*, he thought, *what if*? He didn't want to go down in history as the man who had missed Nelson.

He heard the cry from the masthead, a shuffling of feet, and then another cry. Forcing himself to stay in his cabin, he waited, hardly daring to breathe, for the knock on the door. A midshipman.

"It's them!" the lad shouted, and, before Robertson had a chance to remonstrate with him for his lack of formality, or even basic politeness, turned on his heel and went back through the door. With hardly less speed, Robertson went after him. The First Lieutenant saw him, nodded and smiled broadly.

"It's them all right, Sir."

Nelson, thought Robertson, *thank God*.

***

Robertson would never forget his meeting with Nelson and, according to his wife and children, would never tire of telling of it. He sat with Nelson and *Victory*'s captain, Hardy, in the ship's great cabin. Robertson had not met the Admiral before and was shocked at his gaunt appearance, although, as Nelson read the despatch from *Oleander* and Gibraltar, his expression became much more cheerful.

"Seems as though Villeneuve is for the West Indies, Hardy," he said, passing the despatch from *Oleander* across the table to the captain. Hardy read quickly, stood and marked positions off on an Atlantic chart. Nelson looked at the chart and nodded.

"Thank you, Captain Robertson, you have done a great service. *Oleander* is well known to us, is she not, Hardy?"

"Indeed she is, Sir, I well remember the trip into Toulon."

Snowden had taken Nelson and several other officers aboard *Oleander* into Toulon harbour.

Nelson smiled, "And that Corsican woman! Tell me, Robertson, how was Snowden?"

"Snowden was not aboard, Your Lordship. Kennedy had her."

"Ah yes, Kennedy. An able man, I was hoping to make use of his services. Where was Snowden?"

"Snowden is missing, Your Lordship, presumed dead."

Nelson grimaced. "Do you know the circumstances?"

"Not exactly. Kennedy and I were both anxious to get our ships underway and so time was limited, but ..."

Robertson thought carefully about what he should say, as Kennedy had been scathing about the raid that Admiral Jameson had planned, and opinion in Gibraltar had been similarly unfavourable. It was quite likely that Nelson, who had been blockading Toulon, had not heard of the raid.

"There was a raid on the French coast, and it seems that the French were expecting such a thing and had set a trap. *Oleander* was making a diversion, somewhere near Sète."

"A raid?" Nelson looked at Hardy. "We were not aware of this. Was Snowden the instigator?"

"No, Your Lordship, it was not Snowden's idea." He cleared his throat. "It was organised at a higher level."

Nelson looked at Robertson: "Jameson?" he said, and Robertson nodded. The Admiral looked at Hardy and then said to Robertson. "Please continue, Captain."

"As I said, Your Lordship, *Oleander* was only a diversion."

"You said the French had set a trap. Were there any other losses?"

Robertson swallowed hard. "Yes, Your Lordship, I am afraid so. *Pegasus* was lost, captured by the French, Captain Clasby killed, the crew all taken prisoner. The soldiers ... well, they didn't return."

"Clasby! Clasby killed! A finer frigate captain I never knew and a fine man. And *Pegasus!* He spent all of his money on her, you know, Robertson, *'Clasby's Yacht'*, they called her."

"I know they did, Your Lordship, she was his pride and joy."

Nelson looked again at Hardy, "A bad business, Hardy – Clasby and perhaps Snowden."

Hardy nodded, "So it seems, My Lord."

"Jameson," said Nelson, "Jameson," and then collecting himself, "Please continue, Robertson."

"My Lord, Kennedy said that when Snowden was ashore, *Oleander* was attacked and damaged. She got away, but they saw Villeneuve's ships and went to Gib to report them."

"A proper course of action. And now *Oleander* is on her way to Antigua."

"Yes, Your Lordship."

"Thank you, Robertson, you have done well. It seems, Hardy, as though we must follow our elusive Frenchman to the West Indies."

Hardy accompanied Robertson across the deck. "Damn that man," he said under his breath.

"That man, Captain Hardy?"

"Jameson. I know I'm speaking out of turn, Robertson, but Jameson ..."

"I know, Captain Hardy. Clasby was my friend."

As the pipes struck up, Hardy shook Robertson's hand.

"Well, back to your patrol, and best of luck."

Chapter 8 – The Dinghy Again

The dinghy was about twelve feet long, and to Snowden it seemed pitifully small in the Atlantic swells. He remembered the prayer Captain Berthou had recited, in Breton, when *Penfret* had been hove to in a gale in Quiberon Bay:

'Lord, protect me
My ship is so small,
And your sea is so big.'

Though the sun shone brightly from a sky scattered with fluffy clouds, the trade wind blew relentlessly from the east, producing breaking crests which occasionally sent spray into the boat, requiring Snowden to bail with the cooking pan. The wind on her hull blew the boat slowly along, and to start with Snowden kept the boat before the wind by backwatering occasionally with the oars. It was tiring work, but he put one of the oars into the pocket in the boat's transom and steered with that.

The small clouds gave little protection from the sun and, to avoid sunburn, Snowden put the hat on and draped the boat cloak over him. He kept a good watch astern for approaching squalls, but the horizon remained clear, and he saw no ships.

The last position marked on *Herault*'s chart was about sixty miles off the French island of Guadeloupe. Since the cross had been made, she had sailed some distance, and after her capsize the Equatorial Current must have pushed her west and north. Perhaps, he thought, he was fifty miles from Guadeloupe. The trade wind was probably giving the boat a knot and a half, and the current might add another knot, two and a half or three knots total, say sixteen or twenty hours to the island.

His main worry was that he could miss the island altogether. The trade wind and current would accelerate in the channel between Guadeloupe and Monserrat, and he knew that if he failed to get ashore, he would have no chance of sailing or rowing to the east, and South America was a long way away. No, he would have only one chance. He had to get the boat ashore on Guadeloupe. Sixteen hours!

Darkness came quickly, relieved only by the brilliant canopy of stars which was enough to show the horizon, and the phosphorescence in the water. He became very tired, the weariness like an irresistible force, and frequently woke with a start to find himself resting on the steering oar, the boat sometimes broadside on to the waves, in danger of capsize. Eventually, he realised that he was doing more harm than good at the steering oar, so he took it in and laid down in the bottom of the boat (again, he thought) and, allowing the boat to do as she pleased, slept. Rain on his face woke him, but fatigue lay on him like a physical force holding him down, and he was unable to rise, even though the wind had increased, and he pulled the boat cloak over his face and went back to sleep.

When he awoke, overjoyed that there was a sliver of moon, he stood up as high as he could in the boat and looked around him. In the west – was that a dark line on the horizon? He was not sure. He ate some biscuit and drank from the flagon – not water as he had expected, but beer. He busied himself about the boat, bailing her out with the cooking pan and in the process discovering that the water in the bilge was almost fresh. He drank as much as he could and refilled the flagon. He re-shipped the steering oar, securing it in its notch with a piece of the boat's painter, and got the boat pointed downwind again.

The moon and stars progressed across the sky, and the band of darkness on the horizon gradually became more distinct. Snowden was in no doubt now, it was land, and that land could only be Guadeloupe. As far as he could remember – it was a long time since he had been in the Caribbean – Guadeloupe looked like a butterfly on the chart, almost two separate islands, the eastern part low, the western one higher. He was probably too far north, he thought, and shuddered at the thought of being blown straight past the island. When it was light he would have to try the sail, despite the difficulties of shipping the mast.

***

The sky lightened, and almost instantly, it seemed, the sun had risen, revealing the low coast of Guadeloupe, quite close, but the boat was further north, more distant from the land than he liked. He looked around the horizon, straining his eyes when the boat lifted on a swell. Yes, to the north, there was a dark smudge – Antigua, probably - forty miles away. Antigua was British, friendly and safe, with a naval base and dockyard. Snowden had spent time there in his youth, and had fond memories of it. *Oleander* could have got him there in a few hours, but the passage to windward was impossible for the dinghy. He could just about see, very distant, another island, Monserrat, but that was across the wind as well. No, it would have to be Guadeloupe, but at this rate he would be swept past it, and rowing would not make much difference to the dinghy's course in the wind and waves.

The sail was his only chance, but stepping the mast and getting the sail up in the open Atlantic would be a desperate business. The mast, it wasn't very long, was laid in the bottom of the boat, with the sail wrapped round it. He couldn't remember ever seeing the dinghy being sailed, but Snowden had spent much of his life in small boats, and it was not difficult to see how the rig worked.

The lower part of the mast fitted through a hole in the forward thwart. There was a socket attached to the bottom of the boat, into which the squared off heel of the mast fitted. This arrangement meant that the little mast was self-supporting – there were no stays. The sail had a small yard at its top, which was raised by a thin halyard.

The dinghy had spent several days buried under the beach of Maguelone in the Gulf of Lions, and sand fell from the sail as Snowden unwrapped it from the mast. Trying not to rush, he carefully sorted out the yard and the ropes. Crouching on the bottom boards, the mast over his shoulder, he looked round at the waves, trying to judge his moment. A breaking crest passed, and he stood carefully up until the mast was nearly vertical and with surprising ease guided its heel through the hole in the thwart until it was resting in the keel socket. The motion of the boat suddenly became less violent, and he collapsed back onto the bottom boards, resting. That was the worst part over, but Guadeloupe was starting to slide past alarmingly, and he got back up almost immediately and raised the sail.

It flogged once or twice, but when he pulled in the sheet the boat came alive. He had forgotten what it was like to sail in the Caribbean – the warm water, the steady wind! No Mistral! With a feeling almost of exhilaration he pointed the boat at the north-eastern extremity of Guadeloupe, making generous allowance for leeway and current. No time for finesse, he thought, just concentrate on not being swept past the island. Gradually, as the land drew closer, his fear of missing the island altogether reduced and he brought the boat round to starboard so that it would pass the point – he could not remember its name – well to port. "*Very well* to port," he said to himself, then audibly, "you know how nasty the ends of the Caribbean islands are."

By the afternoon, he had passed the point and was in the lee of the land, the sea much calmer, though the wind still blew strongly. His fear of being swept past the island was replaced by the dread of capture and imprisonment, and he wondered what he should do.

Antigua was inaccessible to him in the dinghy. Dominica was British, about twenty miles from the southern tip of Guadeloupe, but getting there would involve a lengthy trip along the lee side of the island, past populous towns. A route close to the coast of Guadeloupe would almost certainly result in capture, an offshore route in being blown away to leeward.

It was all too much for him. He was in the last stages of exhaustion, holding conversations with himself, occasionally hallucinating. The boat slid along the coast, a couple of miles offshore, and then Snowden steered her through a passage between coral heads on which the ocean swell was breaking, into calmer water. He saw a small village and occasionally little boats with low sails, looking much like his, but nobody took any notice of him. He was in an enormous enclosed bay, sheltered, surrounded by low land, fringed with mangroves. From time to time he fell asleep over the steering oar, loudly admonishing himself when he woke up.

He had to rest. He turned the boat, pointed her into the land, and when the wind dropped he furled the sail and rowed through calm water until the bow pushed into a mangrove bush, disturbing the crabs that had been climbing on it. He tied the painter onto a branch, lay down in the bottom of the boat, and slept.

Chapter 9 – Grand Cul-de-Sac Marin

Snowden was woken by the rising sun. Every part of his body was sore, and his head ached so much that he had to pull the boat cloak over it to shade his eyes from the light. Under its cover he drank from his flagon, and ate the – by now rather soggy – biscuit he had acquired from *Herault*. The pain in his head gradually subsided to a dull ache, and by stages he removed the cloak from his head and considered his position.

The boat was gently scraping against the mangroves, still held by the painter he had attached to a branch the evening before. Turning his head, he started. About fifty yards away was a very small boat, hardly bigger than the man in it. The man, who was black and quite young, was watching Snowden intently. He saw Snowden move, lifted his hat, and then paddled towards the dinghy. He did not seem hostile, and when the boat, which was a small dugout canoe, was nearly alongside he again lifted his hat and spoke.

Snowden could not recognise the language and shrugged his shoulders. "Not understand," he said, wishing his headache would go away.

The man spoke again, and Snowden realised that the language he was using was something akin to French. "*Lentement, s'il vous plait.*"

The man nodded in understanding and said slowly in French, "Where have you come from?"

Snowden thought for the right word for wreck – '*naufrage*' – and pointed out to sea.

The man nodded, considering. "Are you French?"

"No," said Snowden, and then, knowing that he was in no condition to devise or maintain subterfuge, "*Anglais.*"

The man raised his eyebrows and replied in heavily accented English, an accent that to Snowden sounded like *Oleander's* Bermudians "You are English?"

"Yes, my ship was wrecked."

"Where are the others?"

"They were in other boats."

The man brought his canoe closer. A cutlass was clearly visible in the bottom of the canoe, and Snowden tensed – he was completely unarmed, pistols but no powder - and was in no state to defend himself if the man decided to rob him.

Snowden gestured towards the open sea. "I expect the others will arrive soon."

The man sat in the canoe, seemingly absorbed in thought, and asked, "Your ship – she English?"

Snowden did not know how much he should tell this man, but knew that he was presently unable to think logically enough to maintain a lie.

"No, I was in a French ship."

"Prisoner?"

"Yes. The ship was sunk by the wind. The French were rescued by another ship, but they left me behind."

The man sat still, his huge hat shading his face. "French bastards!" he said, and then "Are you in the English Navy?"

"Yes, I am." On impulse Snowden held out his hand. "Percy Snowden."

The man shook his hand. "Oliver. You are an officer?"

"Yes, I am, a commander."

The man paused and then said: "And you want to go back to the English Navy?"

"Yes, I do."

"I can help you. Wait here for me."

Oliver took up his paddle and was soon lost to sight behind the mangroves.

That afternoon, lying on the bottom boards of the boat, still tied to the mangroves, surrounded by dazzling, light-blue water, with darker patches of coral, waves breaking on the ones further out to sea, Snowden thought about his situation. Give himself up to the French? That would mean imprisonment and an uncertain future, and given the notoriety of his actions ashore in France, perhaps even being treated as a spy. Find the English? He was still physically weak, hungry, and his time in the boat had not helped his health.

By himself he couldn't get to Antigua, and he couldn't get to Dominica. He might as well see what Oliver was proposing. In the meantime, he would sleep. He moved the mast and sail to one side, to act as a better pillow, and saw the weighted bag that he had taken from the captain's desk on *Herault*. Despite his aching head and desire to sleep, he opened it, seeing that it contained a number of letters.

Using his knife, he opened the seal of the first one and read: '*We, by the grace of God, Napoleon I, Emperor of the French, to …*'

He sat up suddenly, causing a wave of pain to run through his head, but he ignored it and read on, gradually realising that he now had no choice. No choice at all. He could not give himself up, he had to try to get the French documents to a British ship or base.

***

It was afternoon when he heard the splash of paddles, and roused himself from his reverie and looked up. Two little canoes were approaching, each carrying a single paddler. They bumped alongside, and Oliver gestured to his companion.

"Andre," he said. The man nodded. "He speaks only a little English," continued Oliver. "I will tell you of our plan."

"Please do," said Snowden, though he had little hope that Oliver and Andre could help him.

"Snowden, Andre and I are sailors. We have sailed on schooners, but they sent us to work on a farm. We escaped, and joined other people – the Maroons."

Snowden nodded and Andre said, "Join Navy."

Snowden asked, bewildered, "Join the Navy?"

Oliver nodded vigorously and as though to clear up any misunderstanding added "We would like to join the English Navy."

"Really?" He was just about ask why when he realised that the answer was obvious, and listened as Oliver continued.

"It is terrible here. The French are cruel. They freed us, but now they have made us slaves again. There are a few of us Maroons that have escaped from the farms. We live in the woods over there, but there is no rest for us, and sometimes they try to recapture us. Some men have gone off to join the English Army or Navy. We would be good men for the navy, after our experience in schooners."

Naval or indeed army life was hard, but it was undoubtedly better than that of a runaway slave. He thought of his *Oleander* with its Bermudians, good men, and knew that British ships, chronically undermanned, would welcome such recruits. He recalled hearing that there was a British Army regiment in the West Indies composed entirely of former slaves.

The men had a choice – it was plain that, apart from the boat and the pistols, Snowden had little that was worth stealing. True, gold had been sewn into his coat before his shore expeditions in Europe, but the Maroons did not know of that. Alive, he might be worth something – a passport to a life as a British seaman. Turning Snowden over to the French might bring a reward, but it could also expose Oliver and Andre to capture.

"If I helped you to return to the English, would they reward me?" asked Oliver

"I would reward you myself."

"You have money?"

"If I can return to the English Navy I will have money, and if you wish I will find you a place on a ship, not my own ship, she's in Europe, but you will have a place."

Oliver smiled. "We will help you."

Snowden, momentarily elated at having allies, suddenly felt drained.

"How? Antigua is a long way away, to windward. This boat …"

"She would never get there," agreed Oliver. "We must go to Dominica."

Snowden pictured the chart in his head.

"That will not work. We will have to go round Guadeloupe. It's a long way. The French would see us. For me, perhaps it would not be so bad, but for you …" He thought further. "And we would lose quite a bit of ground to the west. No …"

Oliver held up his hand and Snowden stopped talking.

"We do not have to go round Guadeloupe." He saw Snowden's puzzlement. "We go through it, along the Salt River."

"The Salt River?" and then Snowden remembered - Guadeloupe was almost two separate islands, joined by a strip of low-lying land. Through this swampy land ran the Salt River, not really a river, but a narrow channel of sea joining the bay in the north, the Grand Cul-de-Sac Marin, with the southern bay, the Petit Cul-de-Sac Marin.

His erstwhile companions were proposing to go through this channel to the southern shore of Guadeloupe and from there sail to Dominica. On the face of it, this made sense, but …

He tried to visualise the chart – there was a town: "The Salt River it runs through a port doesn't it, a French town?"

"Yeah, man, Pitre, we have to be very quiet."

Chapter 10 – Salt River and the Saintes

Snowden's command was not a prestigious one, but he welcomed his crew aboard with some formality, shaking their hands as they climbed over the gunwhale. Although Oliver and Andre were not large men, and their baggage, no doubt all they possessed, was scanty, the dinghy was heavily laden.

It was late afternoon when they pushed off from the beach where they had left the canoes. They set the little sail, and the dinghy surged ahead in the north-east trade wind, with Andre at the steering oar, sailing southward over the almost smooth water of the Grand Cul-de-Sac Marin. In some ways, it reminded Snowden of Poole Harbour in England, although it was shut off from the sea by coral reefs, rather than a sandy peninsular, and the bay was fringed with mangroves rather than heathland and fields. Snowden could see little sign of settlement, and there were only a few small boats, probably fishing, he thought. To starboard, the high hills of western Guadeloupe were visible, but to port the land was low.

They made good progress, and as the sun went down and the stars came out Snowden could see that they were approaching a dark low shoreline. There were quiet discussions between the two Maroons and Andre made some small course corrections, but before long the dinghy was sailing along a narrow channel, the Salt River, which led through mangroves to the south of Guadeloupe.

When the wind dropped in the shelter of the land, they furled the sail and Oliver unshipped the steering oar from the dinghy's stern.

"We will row," he said.

Snowden took one oar and Andre the other as Oliver conned them through the narrowing channel, tapping one gunwhale or another and gesturing to direct the oarsmen to row faster or slower. The boat slid between the banks, and occasionally there were lights ashore and Snowden heard snatches of song. He realised with relief that both members of his crew were competent boatmen, and they were cheerful companions, seemingly undaunted by what they were about to do.

"We come to the town now," said Oliver, "Pitre," and Snowden looked over his shoulder as he rowed, to see dimly illuminated streets close to the port side of the dinghy, with a wharf with small ships and boats lying alongside. As the town came abeam, Snowden felt a stab of emotion as he saw a sudden gleam of light and watched the door of a large church open and people spill out into a square. So neat, so peaceful, he thought as he rowed, so different from the situation of himself and his companions – fugitives setting out on an uncertain and dangerous journey.

They were not challenged as they rowed gently along, and before the town was very far astern they were sailing again, listening to the sound of waves breaking on rocks to starboard and seeing the occasional white flash of surf.

"Petite Cul-de-Sac," said Oliver as he steered the boat, a little east of south, Snowden thought, judging as well as he could by the stars. Higher land was visible to the west, but after an hour or so the land to the east fell away and the sea became rough and unpleasant. Water came into the boat from breaking crests. Snowden was in a state of near collapse, sitting on the bottom boards with his back against the side of the boat, as Oliver steered and Andre bailed, joking between themselves, seemingly completely unconcerned by their situation. *Able seaman*, thought Snowden to himself again, as he drifted into sleep.

He was woken with a start by rough hands lifting him and moving him around. He thought briefly that his companions had decided to throw him overboard and was immensely relieved when Oliver spoke to him over the noise of the wind and sea.

"I think you are sick. You will get wet if you sit there. Lie down in your cloak and we will take care of the crossing. We have done it many times."

When he next woke and sat up, stiff and cold, the moon was illuminating a rough sea. The dinghy, *the blessed dinghy*, thought Snowden, though he hoped very much that this was his last night aboard, was sailing well with her scrap of canvas, and Andre sat at the steering oar with his eyes moving between the waves and the sail, from time to time luffing up or bearing away from a breaking crest. Snowden realised that the sea had gone down.

Oliver saw that he was awake and pointed to the west, where Snowden could make out a high island, a few miles distant.

"Saintes," he said, "Terre de Haut." He turned and pointed to the east. "Marie-Galante is over there. Flat but it gives us shelter."

With difficulty, Snowden concentrated and recalled the chart. They must be half way to Dominica.

"Why are you sick?" asked Oliver.

Snowden thought before replying. "My head. I have had many wounds to my head. I was in France, ashore, not on my ship. We set an explosion, but it went off too soon and I was caught in it. I was alone. Many French soldiers and boats were looking for me, but we had hidden this dinghy," he patted the boat's wooden side, "the dinghy of my ship, on the beach, and I was able to get her into the water, away from the French."

"But you were in a French ship, the one that sank?"

"I was – it picked me up. I could remember nothing. Eventually the French ship sank, and here I am. I hope that this will be my last night in the dinghy!"

"Dominica," said Andre from the steering oar, pointing ahead. Snowden looked and saw a looming blackness against the background of stars. He slept again, and when he awoke the sun was just rising. Ahead, perhaps three miles away, he saw a mountainous island, intensely green with a shadow of rain in its interior, and grey cliffs against which the white surf broke. Instantly recognisable – Dominica!

Chapter 11 – Prince Rupert Bay

On a headland near the northern cape of Dominica, Snowden could see a tall flagstaff, and with a start he realised that the Union Flag was flying from it. He touched Andre's elbow and pointed – Andre nodded. Oliver, at the steering oar, saw the exchange and pointed to the sea ahead.

"I will go a little further out, the waves are breaking there."

Snowden saw there was indeed a good deal of disturbed water near the point. He knew that the trade wind tended to funnel around the extremities of the West Indian islands, giving rise to sudden gusts, and there were frequently tidal streams as well as the ocean currents.

He watched Oliver turn the boat away from the land, not too soon, as for a few minutes the sea became rough and Andre became busy with the bailer. As suddenly as it had arisen, the wind died away almost to nothing, and behind the boat Snowden could see that there was a distinct line on the sea where the wind ended.

Ahead they could see Cabrits headland, with its distinctive dual peaks and high cliffs. The British had strongly fortified the headland – they called it Fort Shirley – and behind it lay the protected roadstead of Prince Rupert Bay, a windy place but sheltered from the waves and one of the best anchorages in the Lesser Antilles.

They shipped the oars, and Snowden conned the boat while the two Maroons rowed. He kept the dinghy close inshore and they crept along the coast. Vegetation tumbled down the slopes to the shore, where boulders gave way to sandy beaches and mangroves, and then they coasted around the headland, fortifications visible high above them, with gun muzzles pointing in every direction. As they rounded the point, Prince Rupert Bay opened before them with a small town at its head. On the boat's port side he saw stone-built military buildings at the head of a jetty, to which a small ship was made fast, discharging her cargo.

A British frigate lay at anchor, one of the *Hebe* class, Snowden realised. A boat came out from the jetty, a young midshipman in the sternsheets, obviously intending to intercept them. Snowden gestured and Oliver and Andre stopped rowing and rested on their oars. They were clearly nervous, as well they might be – their whole future relied on their acceptance by the Navy. Snowden thought how he could best help them.

The other boat stopped quite close to the dinghy, but the midshipman used a speaking trumpet to shout, "What boat, who are you, and where are you going?"

Snowden had been wearing his hat, but, at the midshipman's hail, removed it, to the youngster's obvious discomfiture – he had clearly not expected to see a white man in the small boat.

"Good morning, Midshipman. I am Commander Snowden, Royal Navy. My ship is *Oleander*, and this is her dinghy. We're going to that ship over there," he pointed to the frigate.

The boats had drifted closer together and Snowden could see that the midshipman was nonplussed by his reply. The lad gave an order and his boat moved so that the oars of the two boats were almost touching. The midshipman looked closely at Snowden, taking in his tattered clothes.

"Snowden, Sir?" he asked, "Boney's barges and all that?" and then, "*Oleander*, Sir, where ...?"

"Midshipman ...?"

"Sorry, Sir – Fisher."

"Thank you, Fisher. I left *Oleander* in the Med, and I expect she's still there. The French Navy was good enough to bring me here."

"Um ... Welcome to Dominica, Sir. I'll lead the way to *Columbine*."

***

Snowden climbed aboard the frigate, followed by Oliver and Andre, and shortly afterwards by Midshipman Fisher, who ran ahead. Snowden waited and in a few minutes a young lieutenant, a large man, came on deck, followed by a party of marines who formed into a line, muskets at the slope.

The lieutenant spoke: "Sir, Mr Fisher here informs me that you are Commander Snowden. I'm Lieutenant Baker, first lieutenant of *Columbine*. Welcome aboard, Sir. I'm sorry that our commanding officer is presently indisposed, but perhaps you'll follow me to the cabin." He looked at Oliver and Andre. "Your, er, your companions, Sir?"

"Andre and Oliver, Lieutenant Baker. I don't know their other names, but they're prime seamen, and probably recruits. Please ensure they're well taken care of and fed."

"Aye aye, Sir. See to it, Mr Fisher."

"Go with the Midshipman," Snowden said to the two men, who were clearly very relieved that Snowden really was a British officer. "Thank you very much for your help. I will see you later."

He watched as the slaves, former slaves now he supposed, went forward with Midshipman Fisher, and then he turned back to Lieutenant Baker, who held out his hand.

"Shall I take your things, Sir? The bag?"

Snowden recoiled involuntarily and Baker, taking the hint, led the way to the cabin.

"May I offer you refreshment, Commander? Some food, Sir?"

He looked at Snowden, "And perhaps, Sir, you might wish to borrow some clothes?"

A feeling of unreality washed over Snowden, as he heard himself say, "Thank you, Lieutenant, that would be most welcome, but we must hurry. The bag contains French despatches and speed is of the essence."

As he ate and drank rapidly, he asked Baker, "The ship's commander, Lieutenant, is he aboard?"

"Yes, Sir, but, as I said, Captain Thorneycroft is indisposed, he ..."

A door crashed open and a dishevelled figure staggered into the room. Lieutenant Baker stood up.

"Sir," he said, "perhaps it would be better ..."

Snowden saw that the man who had just entered was in uniform and realised he must be the frigate's commander.

"Don't tell me what's for the best, Baker," he boomed, and, looking at Snowden, "Who is this? He looks like a tramp!"

"Sir, I really think ..."

"Damn you, shut up!"

He turned to Snowden. "What are you doing in my cabin, in my ship? Who are you?"

"Sir," Baker tried again, "you must ..."

"DAMN YOU, BAKER, SHUT UP!"

Snowden stood and held out his hand. "Percy Snowden, Commander, RN. HMS *Oleander*."

As his hand was ignored, Snowden felt the anger rise within him, but he remembered his father, drinking to forget, and steadied himself.

"And you are ..., Sir?" asked Snowden, "apart from being damnably drunk early in the morning."

"Sir, this is Commander Snowden," stammered Baker "you know – *the* Snowden. Sir, I think you had better ..."

"Sentry," shouted the commander, and when the redcoat appeared, "show this gentleman off the ship."

The man paled. "Sir, I am not, I can't …"

Snowden held up his hand. "Don't worry, corporal, I'll come with you."

Snowden, the marine and Baker went out onto the deck.

"Sir," said the marine and Baker, almost in unison.

Snowden, despite himself, smiled. "Thank you, corporal," he said. "Fetch your officer, if you please, and also the Second Lieutenant."

"What is happening with your captain?" Snowden asked Lieutenant Baker.

"It's obvious, isn't it, Sir? The man's a drunkard."

"How long?" asked Snowden.

"Since I've been in the ship, Sir, but he's getting much worse. I don't know how to put this politely, but he's a bastard when he's sober, and when he's drunk, well, Sir, when he's drunk he's …," the man searched for words, "a *complete* bastard, Sir."

A marine officer arrived and saluted Snowden, shortly followed by a naval officer.

"Captain Ferrier, 93rd Foot, Commander Snowden. I am very pleased to make your acquaintance, Sir."

"West, Sir, Second Lieutenant. Likewise, Sir."

Snowden nodded. "Ferrier, West, I have to repair ashore, urgently. The ship is not to leave Prince Rupert Bay until I or another senior officer gives permission." He looked at the two men, "Is that clear? The ship stays here. If necessary, as a last resort, you will detain the captain."

"Aye aye, Sir," said West, with the trace of a smile, "the ship is not to leave the Bay."

Snowden turned to Baker, "Let us go ashore."

Chapter 12 – Fort Shirley

"Who is the commanding officer here?" Snowden asked Baker as they were rowed across the bay towards the wharf. He felt slightly ridiculous in his salt-stained coat and the shirt and trousers he'd borrowed from Baker, who was a much bigger man than he.

"Major Nunn, Sir, 46th Regiment. There are not many of the 46th here now, most of the soldiers are black men from the 1st West Indies. Rupert's a damned unhealthy place for white men."

"What is Nunn like?"

"Well, Sir, I should think he's a man after your own heart. When the French came, under Admiral Missiessy, a few months ago, Nunn defended Roseau, that's the main town, near the southern end of the island. When it burned down, though he was wounded, he brought a large body of men over the island – it is unbelievably difficult country, Sir, mountainous and thick jungle – to Rupert."

"He stiffened the governor's nerve – that was General Prevost, now departed – and the French thought better of attacking Fort Shirley and cleared off. Dominica has had a hard time of it in the last few years, with the French and the mutiny."

Snowden remembered being told of the mutiny of a West India regiment at Fort Shirley some years earlier. Over the objections of the planters on the island, to whom the idea of trained black soldiers was anathema, the British Army, alarmed at the number of white troops dying of disease, and in its heart realising that the islands were of little importance compared with the defence of Britain, had recruited regiments of black men. The troops had become discontented, and the resulting mutiny had to be put down with grapeshot from a British warship. Lessons had been learned, and the West Indies regiments were now better led.

"Who is the governor now?" asked Snowden

"There is not really one presently, Sir, Roseau is still in ruins. Major Nunn is effectively in charge."

The boat tied up to the wharf, and Snowden and Baker were accompanied by soldiers as they set out along a paved road. At the start of a steep hill Snowden realised he could go no further, and sat suddenly on tree stump. "Sorry, Fisher, I can't go on."

Eventually, somewhat rested, Snowden was almost carried between two soldiers along the road to the top of the hill, where there was a stone fortification. They went through the gate, onto a flat area, surrounded by ramparts. Guns, including 32 pounders, commanded the bay. They were shown through the door of an elegant stone building, its entrance guarded by two small Carrons, and into a beautifully panelled office. Behind a desk sat an army officer, who looked closely at Snowden.

"Take a chair, Sir, you look like you're about to collapse." The soldiers deposited Snowden in a chair and withdrew.

"Hello Baker," said the army officer cheerfully, and turned to Snowden. "Excuse me if I don't stand in the presence of the Navy, Sir, but my wound makes me very sedentary." He gestured to his bandaged left leg. "Major Nunn, 46th Regiment of Foot."

He reached his hand across the desk, and Snowden shook it. "Commander Snowden, late of *Oleander*."

"Late?"

"Yes, about a month ago I was doing some work ashore, in the Med, near the mouth of the Rhone. I became separated from *Oleander* and the French were kind enough to bring me to the Caribbean, in a frigate, a *flûte*. The ship sank in a storm a few days ago and the crew abandoned ship. I escaped in a small boat and made my way here."

"Ashore, in France – and the rest? That sounds like quite a story, Snowden, but I sense impatience. That bag you're holding …"

"Despatches, Nunn, French. I got them from the French ship, from her captain's desk."

"Did you, by God!" exclaimed Nunn, leaning forward. "Is there anything of import in the documents?"

"There is, Nunn, of prime importance I should say. Do you read French?"

Nunn was not fluent in French, so Snowden read the documents, translating into English.

When he finished, Nunn said, "So that's it. In summary, Villeneuve's heading for Martinique, only a few miles south of here. But the objective is just to make a diversion, noise really, get Nelson after him, and hence leave the Channel wide open. When do you think the French will arrive, Snowden?"

"Quite soon, in fact I wouldn't be surprised if they were there already. The two *flûtes* were to conceal themselves in Guadeloupe until the fleet needed to resupply."

Nunn looked thoughtful. "The French plan, it's bold, but I don't think it'll work."

"Why not?" asked Snowden.

"The French navy, Commander. They were here not two months ago. Five line-of-battle ships, four thousand men, artillery, the whole thing. They tried to take Dominica, but after they burned Roseau, they didn't even have a try at this place. Cabrits is strong, Snowden, but they could have tried much harder. This Villeneuve who's on his way may be a better man than Admiral Missiessy, but they just don't seem to press their advantage. Take Diamond Rock, or should I say HMS *Diamond Rock*! Just off the coast of Martinique, a few miles away from Fort de France, it completely dominates the entrance to their base. Our navy took it a year ago, fortified it, but Missiessy with his five battleships didn't even try to capture it. And this place, not a sign of a French ship. Nelson took Calvi and Bastia, didn't he, on ..."

He stopped, and looked appraisingly at Snowden, "Corsica? You've been there as well, haven't you, Snowden? My God, I thought I recognised the name. And your ship, *Oleander*! Taking on a regiment of chasseurs with a schooner! I read a pamphlet about it ..."

"Yes, that was me," said Snowden, who did not underestimate his own abilities and was not at all averse to recognition. "But I can see why the French would not like to try to take your fort on."

Snowden knew that the French were anxious to take Dominica, situated between their most significant Caribbean islands, Guadeloupe and Martinique, but he was not surprised that the French admiral had not tried to enter Prince Rupert Bay, dominated by the guns he had seen just outside the building they were in. The place was notoriously unhealthy, and a siege of any length would undoubtedly have resulted in the reduction by disease of the attacking force. He thought that some English admirals might have tried to get their ships in, but others would not have attempted it.

"You may be right about their navy, Nunn, but Boney's said he only needs command of the Channel for a few hours and he'll have England. We must get word to the Navy, so that they don't leave the Channel open".

"Of course, we can't have that. We must get these," Nunn gestured to the French documents, "to Antigua." He looked at Baker. "*Columbine's* moored in the bay, she can go. We will be well warned here if the French approach. We have an excellent view, usually, over to the Saints and Guadeloupe from the top of the hill here and the lookout station at Capuchin. There's a semaphore all the way to Scotts Head, right in the south. We won't be caught napping. We saw them approaching Roseau when they attacked us a while ago, but there was confusion as they were flying British colours. Not twice!"

Baker said in a quiet voice, "Um, there is a problem, Major Nunn – our captain."

"Thorneycroft – drunk again, is he? Bastard!"

"Yes, Sir, ranting, and sometimes, well sometimes he's quite mad. He believes frogs, the animals, Sir, are hiding under his bed and will attack him if he goes to sleep."

Nunn shook his head "Commander Snowden …"

Snowden spoke, "I have taken steps to address the problem, Nunn."

"You *are* having a busy time, Snowden. What have you done? No, I won't interfere, it's a Navy matter."

"I was intending to speak to *Columbine*'s surgeon – I haven't met him yet, but Baker here says he's a good man – and let Thorneycroft dry out over a week or so, aboard, but in view of this emergency I think it might be best if Baker here took the ship to Antigua, with me as supernumerary, while Captain Thorneycroft accepted your hospitality and stayed here in the fort. What do you think, Baker?"

"I believe it would be very beneficial to the Captain's health if he were to stay ashore for a few days, Sir, if that could be arranged."

"I think we can arrange that quite easily, Mr Baker," said Nunn.

"And, of course, I would be happy to take *Columbine* to Antigua with you, Sir," added Baker, turning to Snowden.

Nunn looked up. "Before you go, Snowden, I have one question to ask, if you don't mind."

"Of course, Nunn."

"Were you weighed or measured for those clothes?"

As Snowden and Baker laughed, Nunn said, "I'm about your size, Snowden …"

***

Baker was visibly nervous on the way back to the ship, across the windy bay.

"Mutiny," he said, "I could be about to commit mutiny."

Snowden reassured him, "There's no need to worry, Baker. You are acting under my orders, your actions are entirely justified, and you have been given them in writing. You have the support of the military, that is to say Nunn, who is presently also the civil power."

***

In the event, Captain Thorneycroft's removal was an anticlimax. There was a meeting in the gunroom, presided over by Snowden, and then the delegation, if that is how it should be described, went to the cabin, relieved to find Thorneycroft sprawled on the day bed, almost comatose. Snowden read out a short statement, which the captain took no notice of, and marines carried him on deck, where he was put in the sling, lowered into the waiting boat, and taken ashore.

Snowden had insisted, to avoid trouble later, that the crew must be told what was happening and be reassured that it was legal. Even as Thorneycroft was being rowed ashore, the entire crew was assembled. To Snowden, used to *Oleander*'s meagre crew, *Columbine*'s complement, over three hundred men, seemed huge as he addressed them above the noise of the wind in the rigging.

"I will make this short. I am Commander Snowden, late of HMS *Oleander*," there was a stir amongst the men, "and, even later, of her dinghy," the men laughed as he gestured to where the little boat was stacked on deck nearby. "As you know, I came aboard *Columbine* this morning, to find a very poor state of affairs - you are not fools, I am sure, and know the reason for this. I consulted with the military and the civil power and it was decided that as Captain Thorneycroft's indisposition made him incapable of commanding the ship he should be taken ashore to recover, and that Lieutenant Baker should assume command." He turned to Baker.

The lieutenant smiled and, in a confident voice, addressed the men. "Commander Snowden has explained the situation very well. Now, we have urgent despatches for Antigua, and we will depart immediately." He turned to the Second Lieutenant. "Make ready for sea, if you please"

Chapter 13 – Antigua

On the morning of the twelfth day from Tenerife, the lookout at *Oleander's* masthead sighted land ahead, which Pascoe confidently asserted, rightly, was Antigua, and by evening they passed between Fort Berkeley on the northern headland and Horseshoe Battery on the southern side and moored securely in English Harbour.

Kennedy had handed over his despatches earlier, as soon as *Oleander* docked, and was not surprised when a lieutenant arrived aboard to take him to a meeting with the commander of the Leeward Islands Station. Kennedy did not know who the commander was, and said as much to the lieutenant as they walked through the busy dockyard.

"Sir Alexander Cochrane, Mr Kennedy," the Lieutenant said. After a pause he added, "I advise you to be cautious with him."

"Why is that?"

"Well, Kennedy, you're a tarpaulin, ain't you?" he asked. Men who joined the navy as seamen, as Kennedy had, and who worked themselves up by merit were often known as tarpaulins.

"I am, volunteered from a merchantman. Joined as an AB."

"And I've heard that Nelson's taken a particular shine to you."

Kennedy almost blushed. "He offered me a job, yes, after we took him on a little excursion into Toulon harbour."

"I'm not surprised, Kennedy, from what I've heard about *Oleander's* service …"

"Well, Cochrane is an able man, without doubt," the Lieutenant continued, "brave, good with his people and all that, but he's recently been passed over for the East Indies by Pellew, which Cochrane doesn't think is fair as he's an aristocrat and Pellew came up through the hawsehole. He probably knows in his heart that Pellew's the better man, but I fear you may be tarred with the same brush."

Kennedy thought that Cochrane must have a skewed notion of fairness, but said nothing.

They walked on "Look here, Kennedy, there's one other thing. I probably shouldn't say this, but our Admiral has an interest in Trinidad, a plantation there, and sometimes … well sometimes it seems to colour his views."

Despite the lieutenant's warning, Cochrane was by no means unpleasant to Kennedy. He was desperate to know where Villeneuve's fleet was heading, and it seemed to Kennedy that he was unburdening himself, almost thinking out loud.

"It's my view, Kennedy, but God knows it's little more than a guess, that he'll go south, to Trinidad. He can cause enormous destruction there, almost unopposed. He could do that in Jamaica, of course, but that's a long way downwind, and if the whole thing's a diversion ..."

A huge French army waited in Boulogne for an opportunity to invade England. Napoleon was famously supposed to have said

'Let us be masters of the Channel for six hours and we are masters of the world'

Cochrane knew that any French attack on the West Indies, even if on a large scale, could very well be a diversion to try to draw the British fleet away from their supreme task – guarding the English Channel and hence preventing an invasion of England. A diversionary attack on Jamaica, hundreds of miles downwind to the west of Antigua, would put the French fleet at a disadvantage. French ships bound for the English Channel to protect the invasion army would have to claw their way upwind on the first part of their voyage, through the infamous Windward Passage between Hispaniola and Cuba.

Kennedy, who although only a commander, was a clever, thoughtful man, even a cunning one, with an innate grasp of strategy. Snowden realised this, and used it to his advantage, and Nelson himself had appreciated Kennedy's potential. Kennedy had used the long voyage to Antigua to consider the likely destination of the French.

He did not think that, if he was the French admiral, he would head to Trinidad. He would come here, to Antigua, and attack the Royal Navy in its base, with sufficient determination to make a good show, while limiting his losses. If he, Kennedy, was a French admiral, he would fall on Antigua as soon as he crossed the Atlantic, but he expected that Villeneuve would go first to a French stronghold, either Guadeloupe or more likely Martinique, to refit his ships.

Could he say this to the admiral?

He drew a breath, and tried. "Sir, if the French attack is a diversion ..."

To his surprise, Cochrane did not cut him off but listened intently to this very junior man speaking of grand strategy.

"You speak a good deal of sense, Kennedy, and you may well be right, but still ..."

Chapter 14 – Reconnaissance

Lieutenant Baker took the ship out of Prince Rupert Bay competently enough, turning north when they were well clear of Cabrits headland. The wind became flukey in the lee of the cliffs, and progress was slow until they reached the northern tip of the island.

Snowden did not interfere in the running of the ship, but observed discreetly, approving as sail was taken in when the lookout reported the disturbed water ahead that marked the end of the island's wind shadow, so that the ship was not overpowered in the famously rough area near Dominica's northern cape.

Soon *Columbine* was running quickly over sparkling blue seas, lifting to the ocean swell, with the trade wind abeam, and Snowden felt an irresistible wave of tiredness sweep over him. He spoke to Baker, who had taken over the starboard, weather side of the quarterdeck.

"I must rest, Baker. May I use the cabin?"

"Of course, Sir."

"But before I collapse entirely, Baker, could I have a word with you?"

***

Snowden was awoken by the steward gently shaking his shoulder. For what seemed like a long time he could not remember where he was, but gradually came to his senses. *Columbine*'s cabin was spacious and quiet, dark, the motion of the ship much reduced. They were in the lee of Guadeloupe, he realised, and that for the first time, for weeks or perhaps months, he did not have a headache. He smiled and thought, *I've made it!*

The steward spoke, "Sir, Lieutenant Baker would like your presence on deck."

"Very well, tell him I'll be there directly."

On deck, he approached Baker who touched his hat, "Hello, Sir, we are just about there, so I called you as you requested. As far as we could see, there was nothing much in Basse-Terre."

Basse-Terre was the main town of Guadeloupe, a port in the south-west of the island which was sometimes used by the French Navy.

Baker pulled out his watch.

"I'll heave her to, Sir."

"Very well, Baker, please carry on." Snowden realised that he was ravenously hungry. "While you do that, I'm going in search of food."

***

The ship was hove to, and Snowden sat in the cabin with Baker and West, the Second Lieutenant. Snowden looked away from the small chart on the table to the young man, trying to assess his capability.

"The object is, West, just to have a look into this inlet, Anse à la Barque. *Molene* – that's the French *flûte* – her orders were to stay there until her supplies were required by the French fleet, and I want so see if she actually is there. This chart, a sketch plan really, was included in *Herault*'s orders, and we'll sound a few times to confirm its accuracy. We must do everything we can to avoid detection."

"I understand, Sir."

Baker said, "Moon will rise in about an hour."

"We had best be off," said Snowden. "Make sure the boat's crew understand what we are about. Above all, no noise."

Snowden was about to climb over the rail, when a boatswain's mate, a man whose name he did not know, spoke to Baker.

"Excuse me, Sir, Best here would like to speak to you."

"Very well, Best, please speak," said Snowden.

"Begging your pardon, Your Honour. Oliver, the man you brought with you in the little boat, says that he knows the shore here and asks if he should go with you."

"Does he? That could be useful. Please bring him …"

"He's here, Sir."

Oliver stepped forward.

"Sir, are you going to Anse à la Barque?" Snowden nodded, and Oliver continued "I know it well, been there in schooners, and if you want I can pilot the boat in."

"Well, Oliver, thank you. That would be most useful."

***

The frigate's launch, driven by the light wind that had appeared as the sun set, sailed quietly east, the dark outline of the coast of Guadeloupe visible against the lighter sky ahead, the land gaining definition as they drew closer. When the moon rose ahead of them, they saw white flashes of surf breaking against the rocky shore and low headlands on either side of a small bay.

Oliver, sitting beside West in the stern of the boat, pointed ahead.

"Anse à la Barque," whispered West, "we'll start sounding."

Quietly, a lead was lowered over the side as the boat crept forward between the headlands. The leadsman whispered the soundings to a master's mate, who wrote them down on a slate.

West nudged Snowden and pointed: "A light, Sir, on the headland to port."

Snowden looked and glimpsed a dim light above them. "I see it."

Another flash of light on the headland, and they smelt tobacco smoke.

Oliver said, pointing, "There is a jetty over there, ships go alongside. The French ship will be there."

They were well inside the bay when Snowden saw the men in the bow of the boat stir, word was passed aft, and the man sitting at stroke oar whispered, "They've seen a ship, Your Honour."

Snowden peered ahead, and suddenly he saw it as well, tied to a wharf at the end of the bay. A ship, a big one, but with short, stumpy masts, dim light showing in her cabin.

Molene!

"That's the *flûte*, Mr West. Let's get back to *Columbine*."

***

At four o'clock on the following afternoon, *Columbine* was making her way into English Harbour on Antigua, the main British naval base in the Caribbean. Snowden was on deck, watching as Baker conned the ship through the entrance. There were several ships moored in the harbour, which was very secure. Snowden's gaze rested on a pair of raking masts.

Could it be? Impulsively, he grabbed Baker's arm. "Over there, Baker."

Baker, startled, said, "I beg your pardon, Sir, what is it?"

"It's my ship, Baker, my ship!"

"What ship, Sir?"

"*Oleander*!"

As *Columbine* manoeuvred to her mooring, Snowden was scarcely able to keep his excitement under control. *Oleander*, here! She looked good – slightly worn, perhaps, but, to Snowden's eyes, uniquely beautiful.

With *Columbine* secure, Snowden said, "Would you mind, Baker, doing something for me?"

"What is that, Sir?"

"What I want to do is ..."

Chapter 15 – Reunion

Kennedy stood with Luciani and Pascoe on the deck of *Oleander*. They had had a very busy day, but now the ship was almost ready for sea. A frigate made her way into the harbour, and as she moored, one of her bow chasers fired. They watched, fascinated, as a small blue boat was hoisted from her main yardarm until it was ten or more feet above the deck.

"That's unusual, it looks like ...," said Kennedy in wonder, and then, "she's signalling."

Pascoe looked at the signal. "Alphabetical," he said, and then "MISSING A BOAT." He turned in surprise. "What does that ...?"

"Pascoe," interrupted Kennedy, "that's our dinghy. Do you think ...?"

Kennedy gripped the rail, astonished. They watched as the frigate's launch was rowed briskly towards *Oleander*.

Luciani studied it through his telescope. "I think," he said, "the Old Man" – he looked at Kennedy – "the Old Man is in that boat!"

Snowden, with a feeling of unreality, climbed from the launch onto *Oleander*'s deck, so familiar to him. The entire crew, *so many well-remembered faces*, he thought, and then, with relief, *none missing*, was arranged in a rough formation. A pipe shrilled and Kennedy, *dear Ken!*, walked towards him, hand outstretched. As they shook hands, the crew burst into cheers, hats flying. Snowden opened his arms wide and shouted "*Oleanders*!"

Baker, his back against the rail, watched as Snowden, throwing protocol to the wind, walked among his crew, his *Oleanders*, shaking hands, patting shoulders, exchanging words. Snowden saw a red coat and recognised Sergeant Riley, a look of enquiry on his face. Snowden knew what he was thinking and shook his head.

"I'm sorry, Riley," he said softly, "Watton was killed in the explosion ashore."

"So young, Sir ..."

"I know, Riley, not *ça ira*."

***

As Snowden and Kennedy left the deck and went into the cabin, Pascoe saw Baker leaning against the rail and introduced himself: "Good morning, I'm Pascoe of *Oleander*."

"Good morning. Baker, premier of *Columbine*."

"How did Commander Snowden come to be aboard your ship?" asked Pascoe. "The last time we saw him was in the Med. He went ashore with our Marine officer and didn't return. We assumed he'd been killed or captured, and now he turns up in Antigua, with *Oleander*'s dinghy, which we'd left buried on a beach in France! Not even the Old Man could sail the dinghy across the Atlantic."

"It's been a very rushed few days, Pascoe, confusing, I might say, but he arrived in Dominica the day before yesterday, in that blue dinghy, with two black men, ragged as you please. Apparently he'd been rescued, well out to sea in the Med, by a French ship, a *flûte*, which brought him nearly to Guadeloupe, but which foundered in a squall. The crew abandoned her, leaving him behind. He got off in *Oleander*'s dinghy, with the Froggie's despatches, and made his way via Guadeloupe to Prince Rupert, acquiring two slaves along the way. It's just ..."

"It's just Snowden, Baker, just Snowden."

"It becomes even stranger, Pascoe. I was entertaining Commander Snowden in the cabin, and our skipper, Captain Thorneycroft, crashes into the room, dead drunk, abuses Snowden, and within two hours Thorneycroft's ashore 'for his health' but under lock and key, and I'm taking *Columbine* out to sea. Last night, we hove to just off the coast, and Snowden takes the launch into a little bay on Guadeloupe and finds another French *flûte* in there."

He looked at Pascoe. "As I said, Pascoe, a very rushed couple of days."

"So how is he going to get at the *flûte*?"

"He hasn't told me, but – how did you know he'd want to do that?"

"Several years' experience with hardly a dull moment."

"He's behaved very properly, but he acts as though him taking over *Columbine* is a foregone conclusion. Not that I have any objection, quite the reverse."

"I think he'll have *Columbine*, Baker, and you can forget any dreams of a quiet life."

***

In the cabin, Snowden finished his drink and looked at Kennedy.

"So, that's it, Ken, in a nutshell. You've done very well, and I've been remarkably lucky. And what do you want to do now?"

"I don't really know, Perce, this is all so unexpected. I had the offer to go to *Victory*, but that seems to have been overtaken by events."

"I have to tell you, Ken, that I think you should keep *Olly*."

"I believe I'd like that, Perce, but she's your ship."

"She'll be yours, Ken."

"Thank you. And what of you?"

"I'm going to have that damned frigate over there, by hook or by crook. I'll get my 'post' now or have done with the navy."

"Quite right, Perce. If anyone has deserved it, you have."

***

Snowden stood on the quarterdeck of *Columbine*, in full dress uniform. He looked at the crew gathered around – over three hundred of them, so many more than *Oleander* – and read from the unrolled parchment in his hand:

"*... By virtue of the power and authority to me given, I do hereby constitute and appoint you ... willing and requiring you forthwith to repair on board His Majesty's ship* Columbine *and take upon you ...*"

Later he sat in *Columbine*'s cabin, *the Captain*'s *cabin*, he thought, and reflected on the day's events. He had perhaps thrown his weight around somewhat in his interview with Admiral Cochrane, but, as he expected, he was pushing at an open door, and the man really had had no alternative. He had got everything he wanted. A 'post' and a ship, *Columbine.* In theory, the promotion could be reversed by the Admiralty, but he knew the chances were vanishingly remote. And Kennedy had done well – Commander Kennedy - with his own ship.

And now, what was he to do? He called the steward: "Taggart, please give my compliments to Lieutenant Baker and Captain Ferrier and ask them to repair to the cabin."

"Anse à la Barque," he said, when they arrived, pointing to the French sketch plan, now including the soundings they had taken in the night, spread out on the cabin table. "We know *Molene*'s in there, we saw her last night."

"She's en *flûte*, stuffed with stores, stores for Villeneuve's fleet when it arrives here. He's already lost one supply ship, *Herault*, the one I was in, and he will be seriously inconvenienced if he loses another, and of course, gentlemen, we would stand to profit somewhat from her capture."

Baker looked at the sketch plan. "This fort, Sir, the one on the headland. Can we take it on with the ship?"

"That would be a very uncertain thing, Baker, and I hope that can be avoided." Snowden pointed to the plan of the place, "but I think we may be able to be a little more imaginative".

Chapter 16 – Oleander Heads South

As the sun rose, Kennedy stood with Snowden on *Columbine*'s deck, watching as chests and packages were unloaded from one of *Oleander*'s boats, *Rosa*, a craft of distinctly Mediterranean appearance which they had acquired in Gibraltar.

"That's all of your gear, I think, Percy," said Kennedy.

"I didn't realise I'd acquired so much."

"Well, you've been in *Oleander* a long time"

"What's that?" asked Snowden, pointing to a polished wooden box.

"The Berthoud chronometer – Pascoe sent it."

Snowden, touched, said, "That was good of him, his prize possession!"

"Well, a prize, certainly, but not exactly his possession!"

"Well, you must take it back to him. It is more useful to the great navigator than it is to me."

Kennedy pointed to a large wooden case. "And there's something else. Bakers. I bought some, in Gib, and, well, we've got quite a few in *Oleander* already, and you seem to know better than anyone how to make use of them, so I thought …"

The Baker rifle was a much more accurate weapon than the common musket, and *Oleander*'s marines and seamen were well practised in its use. Some were excellent sharpshooters, especially Luciani, the ship's Acting Lieutenant, and Marine Sergeant Riley.

Kennedy saw that Snowden was deeply affected, and to give his former commander time to recover himself, he slowly looked around, inspecting the ship. "It will be a change after the schooner. The people?"

"I don't really know yet, Ken. Baker handled the ship well enough when we came here from Dominica, and West, the Second, was steady enough on our boat expedition."

"Boat expedition? What was that?"

"Well, I was curious about *Molene*, the surviving *flûte*. Her orders were to hide out of the way until Villeneuve's fleet needed her stores."

"Hide, where?"

"In Anse à la Barque. It's a little bay, more of an inlet really, three hundred yards wide perhaps, on the leeward coast of Guadeloupe, about halfway up. On the way here, in the night, we hove to, and I took the launch in with West to see if she was there."

"And was she?"

"She was, Ken."

"I must say, Percy, that you are," Kennedy searched for the right word, "incorrigible. I should think that most men would be content with a bit of quiet after surviving a shipwreck and a dinghy trip like yours."

"Perhaps they would, Ken."

Kennedy looked across the anchorage to where *Oleander* was anchored, her forestaysail flapping in the breeze to indicate her imminent departure.

"We've been together for a long time, Percy, since I came aboard at Bermuda."

"I remember it well, Ken. You joined and almost straightaway we ran into *Blonde*!"

"We got her, though, didn't we, in the end!"

"By God we did, and her cargo," he paused, "and the chronometer."

"And Corsica, and Maguelone … Morocco …"

"Look after her, Ken. She's looked after us, and made our fortunes."

"Sometimes, Percy, it's not the ships but the men in 'em."

***

Oleander stood to the south-east from Antigua, the trade wind blowing briskly, the ship sailing fast over the bright blue waves, under a sky cluttered with small woolly clouds. They ran along Guadeloupe's eastern, windward shore, passing close to the small islands of La Désirade and Terre-de-Bas, before turning south. When the sun rose on the next day, the ship was just off Pointe d'Enfer, the south-east extremity of Martinique. She gybed onto the starboard tack and ran quickly west-north-west towards the high steep island off Martinique's south-western point – Diamond Rock.

"HMS *Diamond Rock*," said Lieutenant Pascoe to Acting Lieutenant Luciani. "Extraordinary sight."

Diamond Rock had been occupied and incorporated into the Royal Navy for over a year now. The Rock, a small precipitous island, its peak rising to more than six hundred feet, was just over a mile from the coast of Martinique and dominated the approach to Fort de France, the main French base in the West Indies. Any ship approaching the main port would have to either run the gauntlet of the 'stone frigate's' guns, or make a detour around it, a wide detour, down wind and current, given the range of the long 24 pounders at the summit.

It was astonishing to Luciani that anyone could have landed on the island, which was extremely steep, never mind fortifying it. "How did they get the guns up there?" he asked.

Pascoe, naturally, knew. "It was Lieutenant Maurice that did it, from *Centaur*. They anchored the ship, and Maurice and some men climbed up with ladders and ropes. Got an eight-inch rope to the top and made it fast to a rock. The other end was on *Centaur*'s mainmast. Slung the guns from a block and hauled them up with the ship's capstan."

"Sounds very easy!"

"I'm sure it was. I hope to meet Maurice ashore."

Oleander hove to just off the island, and Pascoe went ashore in *Liberté*, the longboat. Despite the rough sea, landing was simple at an improvised jetty and Pascoe was met, as he had hoped, by Commander Maurice himself. Pascoe handed him the despatches, which Maurice read eagerly.

"You saw them, then, Villeneuve's fleet, in the Med?" he asked.

"Not me," said Pascoe, "I had a command independent of *Oleander* at the time, and we went straight back to Gib. I must say, Sir, I do admire what you've done here ..."

Pascoe's conversation with the enterprising Commander Maurice was rudely cut short by the sound of a gun fired from *Oleander*. The ship had worked her way very close inshore and Pascoe could see the recall signal flying from the mainmast. No doubt, thought Pascoe, Kennedy had had his telescope trained on him since he'd been ashore.

Maurice smiled, "I think, Mr Pascoe, you'd better return to your ship, your commander seems to be anxious to get away. The next one might have shot in it, and I'm standing right next to you!"

Oleander was underway even before *Liberté* was stowed on deck, heading south. The trade wind was blowing strongly from the north-east, and *Oleander*, under full sail, crossed the St Lucia Channel probably as fast as it had ever been crossed before, anchoring below the guns of Fort Rodney in the north of the island of St Lucia at four in the afternoon.

She left again as the sun was setting, heading directly out to sea to get out of St Lucia's wind shadow as quickly as possible, and, over the next two days, sailing as only *Oleander* could sail, and stopping only briefly in each port, spread word of the imminent arrival of the French fleet to the British Windward Islands, except Barbados, before arriving in Port of Spain, Trinidad.

Except Barbados, thought Kennedy. His orders had explicitly forbidden him from venturing to Barbados, a hundred miles to windward of the other islands, on the grounds that it would take too long to beat up to it. Kennedy knew, and he had briefly attempted to argue the point with Admiral Cochrane, that *Oleander* would not take long on the passage, but Cochrane had been insistent, and his orders had left no room for independent action. *Let's hope it doesn't matter*, he thought.

But it did, because it was Nelson's first port of call after his trip from Gibraltar.

Chapter 17 – Columbine's Cruise

Snowden, at the head of the table in *Columbine*'s cabin, *so much more spacious than* Oleander's, he thought, looked at the ship's officers as they finished their meal. He was no prude, but he was glad to see that none had overindulged in drink.

"Gentlemen, thank you for dining with me," he said, which was slightly ironic, as none of them could have declined the invitation. "I know you've all had a hard day, but, as a result, Mr Baker," he nodded to the First Lieutenant, "tells me that the ship is ready for sea. Now, I'm not much of a one for speeches, but I will just say that I know that *Columbine* has not been a happy ship recently, and I hope we will be able to put that behind us."

He saw heads nodding – he had been afraid he would be greeted with cynicism and that his task would be an uphill one – but that did not seem to be the case.

"You all saw my old ship leave today. I was sad to see her go, but I am very much looking forward to my time in *Columbine*. Thank you."

As the officers rose to leave, Snowden said to the First Lieutenant, "Mr Baker, stay behind if you please."

When they were alone, Snowden thought carefully about what he was about to say.

"Mr Baker, you've been *Columbine*'s First for some time, and, given the circumstances, effectively in command for much of that. And now you've got a new commander …"

"Yes, Sir, I understand what you're alluding to."

"Good … I've arrived and you are no longer your own man."

"I'm very glad of that, Sir."

"How so?"

"The strain, Sir, it has been too much for me. The ship is too big for a first command, and with the Captain still aboard, sometimes sober, it was very difficult. I don't know how I'd have coped without Dawson."

Dawson was the ship's surgeon, an older man, reserved, but probably very competent, Snowden thought.

"So, Sir, it does not feel as though the ship has been taken away from me. There was no chance of me getting *Columbine*, and, well, I spoke at some length to Lieutenant Pascoe earlier."

"Pascoe! I'm going to miss him!"

"Yes, Sir, and he's going to miss you, but I am very much looking forward to continuing as *Columbine*'s First, if you'll have me that is, Sir."

"You can take that as given, Mr Baker. Perhaps you could give me your view of the ship?"

"Well, Sir, she's ready for sea ..."

"I know that, Baker, I would like something more general. You might call it background, perhaps."

"Yes, Sir, I know what you mean, and I'll try to answer. As you can see, the ship is new, only a year old, built at Chatham. Came from Pompey about a year ago, we were supposed to convoy some merchantmen, but we arrived late and so crossed by ourselves. Captain Thorneycroft had not had much success, and we had trouble recruiting. We ended up with quite a few pressed men, and quota men - landsmen mostly, and there were problems. Captain Thorneycroft responded with great firmness ... in fact, Sir, he behaved like a savage. When we stopped at Madeira, quite a few of them ran, and we got very little assistance from the civil power to get them back. I think most signed on to a couple of Yankee merchant ships that were about to depart."

"And after that, Baker?"

"Well," Baker dropped his voice, "there was a deputation from the men, very respectful, outwardly, but I believe Thorneycroft was really frightened, and the punishments stopped immediately. Thorneycroft largely stayed in his cabin, more often drunk than sober. The ship has not done much since we arrived in the West Indies, Sir, short cruises, assembling convoys. I think the Admiral probably had enough problems without dealing with Thorneycroft – he has interest you know – so we've been swinging round the hook more than I'd like, often at Prince Rupert". Baker looked at Snowden, "I'm afraid to say, Sir, that there were some aboard, many probably, that hoped the drink would quickly carry him off." He paused, smiling, "And now he's gone."

"And the people?"

"Well, Sir, surprisingly good. You've met the officers. The warrants are a good bunch. As I said, Dawson, the Surgeon, is a very good man, the Gunner, Forbes is very clever, exceptional, and the men generally do their duty. The ship, thank God, has been largely healthy. We've kept her clean – even taken out the ballast and washed it off, and Dawson's insisted on sea bathing and taking the ship out to sea as often as we can. I really don't know how I would have coped without him."

Snowden thought of the burden the young lieutenant must have borne.

"It does you great credit, Baker, that you managed to run the ship despite all the difficulties."

"Thank you, Sir."

"To practicalities, Baker, this is what I intend to do."

"Sir," said Baker, sitting forward.

***

Snowden took *Columbine* out of English Harbour, with Baker at his side and Lacey, the Master, hovering nearby.

"I'd give her the courses, now, Sir," said the First Lieutenant as they cleared the Pillars of Hercules at the harbour's entrance, and Snowden nodded to the Master, who in his turn nodded to the Bosun. His whistle shrilled, and men scrambled up the ratlines.

As she felt the boisterous trade wind, the ship heeled, seeming to come alive under all plain sail, heading south-south-west, away from Antigua.

"Would you object, Mr Lacey, if I took a brief trick at the helm? Just to get the feel of her."

Lacey smiled, "Of course not, Sir," and spoke to the quartermaster.

Snowden thought, as he experimented at the wheel, the ship, his frigate, heeling to the trade wind and making good speed through the blue waves, that he had never felt more content.

After a while, he relinquished the helm, turned to Baker and said, "Now, Baker, we had better start work."

All that day, and into the night, they worked *Columbine* hard. Snowden spent much of his time with the First Lieutenant and Gunner Forbes, on the gun deck. The men seemed eager enough, crowding round as Snowden, with the assistance of Forbes, demonstrated how he wanted *Columbine*'s main armament to be worked. Later, they threw barrels overboard, worked the ship so that she passed close by, and fired at them, occasionally causing one to disintegrate spectacularly.

Later, when Ferrier's marines were drawn up on deck, Snowden rather theatrically had the boxes containing the rifles brought from the cabin by Harding, the Master at Arms, with the assistance of several seamen. Men craned their necks as Harding opened a box, and Snowden lifted out a rifle. Previously, in the privacy of the cabin, Snowden had given Harding and Forbes an opportunity to familiarise themselves with the rifles.

"In case you are wondering, this is a rifle, a Baker rifle to be exact. Many of you will know of it, but for those that don't, the barrel of the gun has a spiral cut into it. The ball is made to spin as it travels down the barrel, and the result is greater range than an ordinary musket." He pointed to the Marine Corporal who had helped remove Captain Thorneycroft. "Please step this way, Corporal, er …?"

"Corporal Taylor, Your Honour."

"Well, Taylor, please take the rifle ..."

For the next two days, every spare moment was occupied with exercising the crew in the use of small arms, pikes and swords, with Harding often assisted by Snowden himself, who by now had a good deal of practical experience. To his satisfaction, the men responded with enthusiasm, and, despite the lack of battle experience of most of them, he was satisfied that they would fight with confidence when the time came.

***

Snowden invited the Surgeon to dine with him that evening. Dawson was probably forty or so years old, a rather taciturn man with a tendency, outwardly at least, towards cynicism.

After satisfying, or at least assuaging, Dawson's curiosity about his past (Dawson had read the pamphlet by 'British Tar' on Snowden's expedition to Corsica and wanted a first-hand explanation of how Snowden had arrived in the West Indies independently of the ship he commanded), Snowden said, "You're an educated man, I think, Dawson. Quite unusual in the Navy!"

"I'm not sure about that, Sir. The Navy educates officers in its own way," said Dawson, his Scottish accent pleasant to Snowden's ears.

Snowden thought of Pascoe. "A severely practical education is provided by the Service, but sometimes officers educate themselves further."

"They do, Sir. It is true, though," continued Dawson, "that I was more conventionally educated, at what Voltaire called the 'hotbed of genius' – the University of Edinburgh."

"You studied medicine at Edinburgh?" said Snowden, astonished. Edinburgh was perhaps the preeminent medical establishment in the world, and to have one of its alumni as a ship's surgeon, especially on such a small ship, was, to say the least, unusual.

"I did, Sir."

"If you don't mind me asking, Dawson, what are you doing here in a fifth-rate ship?"

"I suppose, Sir, I am running away."

Snowden raised his eyebrows. "How is that?"

"My wife, Sir. She died."

"I'm very sorry to hear that."

"Two years ago. Cholera, there was an outbreak in Edinburgh. I couldn't bear to be in the house where we had lived together, and so I sold my practice, and well, here I am."

"But why the Navy?"

"I'll tell you, Snowden, because I hate the Revolution and the Empire, and the Navy does them the most damage. My wife was French, from a family of, well, not even aristocrats really, from Lyon. She was sent away to Scotland at the start of the Revolution, so she was not in Lyon, thank God, when Monsieur Fouché went there. He murdered her relatives, murdered them in the most horrid circumstances ..."

He stopped, overcome, collected himself and continued.

"Her whole family, Sir, it's inconceivable. It made her miserable, depressed in spirit. Sometimes she stole laudanum from my surgery. When the cholera arrived, she was not strong enough to resist it."

"A dreadful story, Dawson, dreadful, and I'm very sorry to hear it. You spoke of Monsieur Fouché. He glanced at me once, across a room, in Paris, during the Peace. I will never forget the horror I felt, just from a look. He had a particular hatred for the man I was with, Jack Stone. We were warned and got away quickly, but eventually Stone ended up in the Temple."

"In the Temple? My God!"

"Yes," said Snowden, "in the Temple, but he escaped."

Snowden looked thoughtful. "Now, Lieutenant Baker speaks very highly of you, Dawson. He says you helped him greatly when Captain Thorneycroft was indisposed."

"He was a very young man for such a great responsibility. I did what I could to support him."

***

To avoid the island's wind shadow, *Columbine* sailed well to the west of Guadeloupe, and then proceeded into Prince Rupert Bay on Dominica, following her orders to 'water and wood' there, as those commodities were limited in Antigua. Dawson, convinced of the unhealthy nature of the place, was very insistent that the ship be anchored a good way offshore, even if it meant that the task of watering the ship was made somewhat harder.

While the ship lay at anchor, with watering proceeding under Baker's supervision, Snowden, with his unrivalled experience of combined operations, supervised Captain Ferrier as he practised embarking the marines into the ship's boats and in landing on an enemy coast, with some of Major Nunn's troops providing simulated opposition.

It was with a tired but increasingly confident ship's company that *Columbine* departed the Bay and headed north.

Chapter 18 – Diamond Rock

It was a wet ride north in *Oleander*, crashing to windward with the north-east trade wind on her starboard bow, but it was the sort of sailing in which she excelled, and they made good progress, passing to the east of the southern windward islands to avoid wind shadows.

In the morning of the second day, they passed the northern tip of St Lucia, signalling their presence to the British signal station, and bore away for Diamond Rock off the southern coast of Martinique, crossing the twenty miles or so of the St Lucia Channel in a couple of hours.

At Antigua, *Oleander* had embarked stores for the stone frigate and now she anchored just off the landing place. Pascoe took *Liberté* ashore with the first load of stores, and *Oleander*'s other boats were soon following, towing casks of water which had come from Antigua's scarce supply.

Pascoe was soon busily employed in landing the stores and water and was watching, engrossed, as the supplies were hoisted hundreds of feet up the almost sheer side of the rock, when his reverie was interrupted by the voice of Commander Maurice.

"Pascoe, welcome back. I trust you had a pleasant voyage?"

"Oh, hello, Sir. I was just watching your operation here. It is most impressive."

"Thank you. When convenient, I would like to repair aboard *Oleander* for a discussion with your commander … Kennedy, is that it?"

"Yes, Sir, it's Kennedy."

***

Commander Maurice was piped aboard *Oleander* and was met on deck by Kennedy. The ship was swept by the wind and moved uneasily in the swell.

"Not a comfortable anchorage," said Kennedy to Maurice when they were seated in the cabin. He raised his glass and Maurice did likewise.

"*Oleander* certainly moves more in a seaway than my own command, Kennedy!"

"Yours is probably the steadiest ship in the Navy."

"She is. Now, *Oleander* has some experience of combined operations, if I'm not mistaken, Kennedy."

Kennedy smiled. "It is our speciality, I suppose, and I must say, under Commander Snowden, we were most successful at it."

"Ah yes, Corsica – I have read the pamphlet. And more recently, I think, in France and even Morocco."

"That is true, we have done quite well. Do you want something from us?"

"Yes, correctly divined, Kennedy. I would like your help."

"I would be happy to assist, Maurice, as long as it does not contradict my orders."

"I'm sure it will not, and, as you know, great importance is attached to *Diamond Rock.*"

"Please tell me what you have in mind."

"Well, Kennedy, local people come out in pirogues from Martinique to sell us fruit and vegetables, and most welcome it is too, especially as we've picked nearly all the callaloo now."

Kennedy nodded. The inhabitants of the West Indies traded enthusiastically with the Royal Navy.

"*Diamond Rock* is quite resistant to attack from the sea, providing we have sufficient supplies and water. However, we're only just over a mile from the shore of Martinique, and the coast is pretty high, so we'd be quite vulnerable to fire from a large mortar, if it was carefully emplaced."

"I suppose you would," said Kennedy.

"Well, one of the fruit sellers was sold by his English owners to the French – it's a complicated story and I don't fully understand it, but the upshot is, he doesn't like the new owner, and indeed the French in general. This man, Rodriguez – I don't know how he acquired a Spanish name – told us that a French engineer, I think a colonel, arrived to commence survey work for a battery some time ago, and that he has identified a suitable position, and work will commence shortly. The mortar has already arrived."

"That's a worry, Maurice – can anything be done about it?"

"It certainly concerns me, and it could make the *Diamond* untenable. As to whether anything can be done – I think it can. Rodriguez comes from a plantation ashore, and it seems that the French engineer is staying at the plantation house. Rodriguez, in return for being allowed to enlist in the Navy, has offered to lead us to the house. I was thinking, Kennedy, that we might …"

"Do you trust this Rodriguez?" Kennedy asked, excitement rising in him.

"I think we can trust him, Kennedy. He seems to me to be a steady sort of man, and his story was corroborated by the other boatmen. Even so, we'd better keep him on a tight leash."

***

When Maurice left, Kennedy wrestled with the decision. He wanted, desperately, to go ashore himself. *What would Snowden do?* he wondered. Snowden did not hesitate to lead shore parties in person, but usually his expeditions had either been on a large scale or required considerable diplomacy.

The exception was Snowden's last shore excursion, where he had gone ashore at Maguelone accompanied by only one man, on a mission of negligible importance. That had ended in disaster, or near disaster. Kennedy thought he understood why Snowden had gone – he had received a head wound which had depressed his mood, and in his despair he could not bear to order other men to take risks on what he considered to be an act of rank stupidity.

No, he, Kennedy should stay with the ship, especially as the French fleet was bound for Martinique and could arrive at any moment. Acting Lieutenant Giotto Luciani, an experienced guerrilla fighter and who, as a Corsican, could speak French, would be in overall command of the party. Ensign Vause, who would lead the marines, had been in *Oleander* for only a few weeks. Kennedy believed him to be a promising officer, but he was a very young man, and the presence of the veteran Sergeant Riley would steady him if necessary.

Everything depended on Rodriguez, and before anything advanced further, he decided he must meet him and make his own judgement of the man's character. If he had any doubts, no *Oleanders* would take part.

He wanted at least one officer and some men from *Diamond Rock*'s establishment to participate. *Oleander*'s company had hardly been ashore in the West Indies, and he instinctively believed that it was better if Commander Maurice made an investment in the expedition – that he had something to lose.

***

Kennedy interviewed Rodriguez in the presence of Luciani and Pascoe. Kennedy was inclined to agree with Maurice's assessment that the former slave seemed 'to be a steady sort of man' and keen to earn a place in the Royal Navy, but he instructed the landing party to keep a good watch on the man. Rodriguez had no trouble using the chart to point out the location of the plantation house, as well as a suitable landing place and the road into the interior.

Pascoe and Luciani went with Rodriguez to *Diamond Rock.* They were met by Maurice at a gun emplacement just above sea level which Maurice called 'Centaur's Battery'. Eyeing the plane table which Pascoe had improvised, and his other bulky surveying equipment, Maurice gestured upwards to a ledge, perhaps three hundred feet above them from which a gun barrel protruded, and said:

"Hood's Battery - a stiff climb up the rope ladder"

As they craned their necks to look at it, Maurice asked "Would you like to take the Mail Coach?" pointing to a large cask suspended from a block which ran on a line secured at the battery above.

"Rather" said Pascoe, enthusiastically, and the *Oleanders* and their gear were soon pulled up the cliff in the cask by a party of sailors. From the battery, a steep path led to the summit, which had a signal station and a pair of long 24 pounders.

As Pascoe levelled the table, and started his survey with the help of Rodriguez, who pointed out features ashore, Luciani thought about the strategic advantage given by the guns at the summit, some 600 feet above sea level. He wondered, if he was commanding a French ship, whether he would run the risk of fire from the *Diamond*, or accept that he would have to beat back up to Fort de France.

Pascoe's chart was used in the briefing held aboard *Oleander*, as was a sketch that Gunner Trott, a gifted artist, had made of the house with the assistance of Rodriguez. *Diamond Rock*'s contribution to the shore party consisted of an officer, Acting Lieutenant Westcott, and five seamen. At the briefing aboard *Oleander* that afternoon, the querulous Westcott had not impressed Luciani, though the *Rock's* seamen seemed steady enough. Westcott was of equal rank with Luciani, and Westcott might have claimed more say in the expedition's leadership, but so far there had been no dissent. The Corsican, who was already an experienced and confident seaman when he joined *Oleander*, was by now an imposing figure, a powerful, battle-hardened veteran of sea fights and guerilla warfare, a man entirely untroubled by want of self-belief.

***

By seven that evening, after the sun had gone down but before the moon had risen, the boats set off from *Oleander*, which had run in close to the shore and was now lying at anchor. Despite the swell, there had been no difficulty in embarking the shore party in *Rosa* and *Liberté* and, as the moon rose, the boats' keels grated on the sandy beach, and the sailors and marines disembarked. The boats pulled off the beach and waited, *Rosa's* Carron and *Liberté's* swivel gun loaded and ready.

Luciani, with Rodriguez guiding him, led the way to the road, which was no more than a track. At Kennedy's insistence, an *Oleander*, Corporal Simms, stayed close to the former slave. Any attempt at treachery would be swiftly dealt with. Ensign Vause, with Sergeant Riley at his elbow, walked behind the column, alert for any attempt to attack it from the rear.

The walk in the moonlight was not difficult, though the column moved slowly to minimise the noise of their passage. The night was warm, the path sheltered from the trade wind, and Luciani sweated as he walked. It was not the first time – far from the first time – that he had moved around enemy territory at night, but the luxuriant vegetation and the sticky mud underfoot were unfamiliar to him, as was the noise in the woods from the crickets – or were they crickets? Luciani thought that perhaps frogs were the source of the noise.

They walked steadily, the road climbing into the hills. Though they passed several huts, and dogs barked at them, they did not see a single inhabitant. From time to time Luciani stopped the column and walked forward by himself, creeping along in the shadow of the trees, his bayonetted Baker in his hands, alert for an ambush.

They had been moving for over an hour when Rodriguez pulled at Luciani's arm and indicated that they should stop. Luciani went forward by himself and abruptly found himself in a clearing, or lawn, in the middle of which was a large house, a house that Luciani recognised from Gunner Trott's sketch. They had arrived.

The lower floor of the house was lit, quite brightly. Luciani moved cautiously round the house until he was at the back, where there was a paved patio, raised about two feet above the surrounding grass. He crouched behind the patio wall, and looked through glass doors into a well lit room, where several white people were sitting round a table, eating. He watched for several minutes, and then returned to the men who were waiting by the side of the road at the front of the house. Riley and Vause, who had been reconnoitring the outbuildings, returned shortly after Luciani, and reported that there appeared to be troops in one of the buildings, but that their muskets were stored in a nearby shed. There were no sentries.

After a brief whispered conference, Luciani decided that he would lead a party which would enter the house through the patio doors, men under Vause would go in through the front door, and Riley with Lieutenant Westcott from *Diamond Rock* would take a group to secure the French soldiers in the outbuilding.

To Luciani, crouched behind the wall at the base of the patio with a party of seamen and marines from *Oleander*, the men moving around the perimeter of the clearing towards the outbuilding were horribly visible in the moonlight, and at any moment he expected a challenge to be shouted, but there was silence until … a pistol shot, immensely loud in the quiet night, the shot immediately followed by a shout – of pain or anger – Luciani could not tell. Dogs began to bark. Inside the house, the people at the table looked at each other and some stood.

Luciani knew he had to act, quickly. He blew his whistle, watching as the people in the room looked towards the sound, horrified expressions on their faces. As he ran up the steps and across the patio, he heard wood splintering from the front of the house as boarding axes smashed down the front door.

A sailor pushed past Luciani and swung his axe against the patio door, once, twice, and it burst open to the sound of shattering glass and splintering wood. The people in the room watched, transfixed, as Luciani entered, bayonetted rifle in his hands, followed by several men, who halted, raised their rifles and pointed them towards the diners, to be joined almost immediately by the men who had come in through the front door.

"Good evening," said Luciani in French, "the English Navy has come to visit you."

There was more shouting, inside and out, and he could hear the sound of men opening doors inside the house and running upstairs. The noises gradually subsided and Luciani looked at his prisoners. They were about twenty in number, a roughly equal number of well dressed men and women. The men looked shocked and some of the women were in tears.

Some of the men were in uniform, soldiers. He addressed the oldest of them, a tall man, probably in his forties.

"You are the colonel of engineers?"

"It is pointless to deny it, you can see by my uniform that I am," the man answered. "Colonel Lambert, at your service." The man looked at Luciani.

"Giotto Luciani, Lieutenant, Royal Navy."

"By your accent, Lieutenant Luciani, I think you are Corsican."

"You are correct, Frenchman, I am a Corsican."

Vause entered the room, out of breath. "All secure, I believe all of the white people in the house are in this room."

A seaman, one of the Bermudians, entered the room though the remains of the glass doors.

"Sergeant Riley's compliments, Lieutenant Luciani, we've found the mortar. Great bronze thing it is. We're spiking it now and building the bonfire to melt it. We've got fifteen prisoners, no fighting a'tall."

"Thank you, Pirera. Were there any casualties?"

"No, Sir, only that Lieutenant who shot himself."

"Lieutenant Westcott? Is he hurt?"

"Man, his pride be hurt bad, but he good"

Chapter 19 – Villeneuve

They heard nothing from the shore until the moon was past the zenith. Kennedy, anxiously pacing *Oleander*'s deck, heard the call from the foretop: "Boats moving into the beach."

And then: "Men on the beach."

The ship was anchored well inshore, and from the deck, Kennedy, almost beside himself with worry, watched as the boats were rowed across the moonlit sea. With some difficulty, as the sea was rough, they came alongside *Oleander* and men began to clamber aboard, led by Luciani, who, to Kennedy's enormous relief, was smiling broadly.

"We got him, Sir," he called out, and then, in answer to Kennedy's unasked question, "Only Lieutenant Westcott, Sir, wound in his foot, not serious."

A man in the uniform of a senior French officer was helped aboard by a marine. He was about forty years old and, even allowing for the moonlight, looked grey and anxious. He was followed by two other more junior men. The French private soldiers who had been captured had been released on the beach as there was no room for them in the boats, though their muskets were now aboard *Oleander.*

Luciani and Kennedy walked over to the officers and there was an exchange in French between Luciani and the senior man, too fast for Kennedy to follow. Luciani said in English, "This Frenchman is Colonel Lambert, of the engineers."

Kennedy nodded towards the Frenchman. "Commander Kennedy, His Majesty's Ship *Oleander.*"

One of the subalterns started and whispered to Lambert, who thought for a moment and then, in heavily accented English, said, "*Oleander* – we have heard of this ship – she is commanded by the *célèbre* Cochrane."

The subaltern said, "*Non, pas* Cochrane, Snowden."

***

Kennedy wrote a note for Maurice, *Diamond Rock*'s commander, and handed it to Acting Lieutenant Westcott, who was hobbling on his injured foot.

"It doesn't say anything about the accidental discharge, Westcott, it may be wise for you to mention it to Commander Maurice yourself as he's bound to find out about it, but it made no difference to the action."

"Thank you, Sir."

***

Diamond Rock's water tank had cracked, and, with the imminent arrival of the French fleet and the almost certainty of a siege, the stone frigate needed water, as much as it could get.

The closest place for obtaining water was at Rodney Bay in the north of St Lucia, but Commander Maurice was very much against the water from that source, declaring it to be a hazard to health, and so, on leaving *Diamond Rock*, *Oleander* headed north, towards Roseau, in the south of Dominica. The course was not direct, as she sailed a good way off the land to avoid the island's wind shadow, but by evening the ship was anchored as close to the shore as possible, and watering from the fast-flowing river near the town commenced. The barrels were difficult to handle, but they were filled rapidly, and the boats towed them out to the ship, where they were lifted aboard by a tackle from the foreyardarm.

Roseau was the capital of Dominica and had been burned almost completely down during the French attack earlier that year, and reconstruction was taking place slowly. Snowden and Luciani went ashore with the French prisoners. Nunn, commander of Fort Shirley and *pro-tem* governor of Dominica, was in one of the few intact buildings. He rose a little unsteadily to meet *Oleander*'s officers as they entered his room.

"Able to stand up now, thank God," he said. "Pleased to see you again."

He started to read Kennedy's despatch, pausing after some minutes to ring a bell.

A servant entered with a tray, bearing a bottle and glasses.

Nunn finished reading and raised his glass.

"To you, gentlemen. My word, you have been busy."

***

By the next morning, *Oleander* was once again anchored off *Diamond Rock*. The passage south had been slow but exciting. Kennedy had realised that the water casks, some stowed high in the ship or even on deck, would have an effect on *Oleander*'s stability, but he had not expected her to react in the way she had when she left Dominica's wind shadow and was hit by a gust of wind falling downhill along a valley ashore. Despite being snugged down with little sail set, the ship heeled horribly and, for a moment, Kennedy, holding onto the lee shrouds, thought she would not recover, and that *Oleander* would share the same fate as the French ship Snowden had been in.

But the lashings were sound, the casks did not move, and as the sheets were let fly and the helm put down, *Oleander* righted herself, her sails thundering as she came up into the wind.

Kennedy knew that the arrival of the French fleet, Villeneuve's fleet, the one they had seen in the Mediterranean, was imminent, and, with *Oleander* anchored just off *Diamond Rock*, he sent Pascoe with Iris, the Bermudian seaman with the best eyes on the ship, to keep a lookout from the summit.

Pascoe was immensely interested in HMS *Diamond Rock*, and he was full of admiration for Lord Howe, who had the idea of fortifying the island, and Commander Maurice, who had carried it out. A wooden landing stage had been built on the north side, which made transferring men and stores from a boat possible even if a swell was running, which it usually was. A short distance from the landing stage was a battery, 'Queens Battery', equipped with long eighteen pounders, and they walked south behind the 'Covered Way', a stone wall which protected the passage between Queens Battery and the other two low batteries. Further on were the living quarters, established in a huge cave, and which included a hospital. They climbed up to what *Diamond Rock*'s crew referred to as 'Portland Place', a flat area, and from there ascended in the 'Mail Coach', which took them to where a path led to the two upper batteries and the signal station.

From the signal station at the summit, six hundred feet above the sea, they would be easily able to see Villeneuve's fleet as it entered the St Lucia Channel – the twenty-mile-wide strait between St Lucia and Martinique. It would be very much better than keeping watch from *Oleander*'s masts.

From the windswept top of Diamond Rock, Iris, the 'Bye Iris' as he was known aboard *Oleander*, and the possessor of the ship's sharpest eyes, had a spectacular view. To the north about a mile away was Martinique, steep and wooded. The land trended south-east, and Hell Point, the southernmost tip of Martinique, was about twelve miles away, across a bay of brilliant blue sea, flecked with white breaking crests. The Bermudian could just make out the high island of St Lucia, twenty miles south, cloud building above it.

Since Iris had joined *Oleander*, the ship had operated mostly in the Mediterranean. There had been spells in England and northern France, and once they had been to Morocco, but for the bulk of the time it had been the Med, unfamiliar and often harsh. Like many of *Oleander*'s Bermudians, he had worked, almost been brought up in Bermudian sloops which had traded to the West Indies, and the Islands seemed, if not quite home, then familiar territory. He had been happy enough in *Oleander*, knew that he was a valued member of the crew, and prize money had been substantial. But now, the warm blue sea and the exuberant foliage reminded him of what he was missing, and he thought yearningly of home.

He turned his head and scanned the horizon.

***

The *Oleanders* worked hard, watch and watch, as the sun set and the moon rose, to unload the casks onto the rock, and as soon as they were landed, the stone frigate's crew hoisted them aloft. As the sky lightened to the east, the weary men aboard *Oleander* and her boats heard a gun from the rock.

Kennedy looked up and saw a signal break out:

ENEMY IN SIGHT BEARING SOUTH EAST

And then, at intervals of a few minutes,

FIVE SHIPS ... TEN SHIPS ... ELEVEN SHIPS ... DISTANT FIFTEEN MILES

"It's them," he said to Luciani, who had broken off from supervising the discharge of *Oleander*'s cargo.

"Recall?"

"How much longer until all the water is off the ship?"

"Probably two hours," Luciani replied.

Kennedy thought out loud: "Fifteen miles, the wind's blowing strong, so they could be doing say seven knots. That's two hours. We'd be cutting it fine!"

Pascoe subsequently remarked that "There's nothing quite like the imminent arrival of a French fleet to concentrate the mind," and they worked feverishly for the next two hours to finish the watering. As the men worked, Kennedy thought about what he should do – go to Antigua by way of Martinique's west coast, or head east out of the St Lucia Channel and then turn northward along the island's windward side. Sailing eastward was riskier – they would be close to the French fleet, but they could collect information about the size and disposition of the enemy, which could be of critical importance, relying on *Oleander*'s windward performance to avoid destruction or capture.

"Cargo nearly all ashore, Sir. Shall I sound the recall?"

"Yes, Giotto, if you please, sound the recall."

Chapter 20 – Payoff

Admiral and Odile Morlaix sat in the snug bar of the chandlery in Pauillac, across the street from the wharf where *Payoff*, the American schooner, was intermittently visible through the driving rain. They had arrived unaccompanied, and both were plainly dressed.

Odile stretched her arm across the table and gripped her husband's hand. He turned from his inspection of the ship and looked at her.

"Will we ever come back?" she asked.

Surprised, he paused before replying, "I had never thought there might be a possibility of us not returning, Odile, but now that you mention it …"

"I miss Dominique …"

At that moment, the door to the street opened, bringing with it a gust of cold wet air, and a tall thin man entered. He looked around the room and walked over to the Morlaixs' table, where he took off his hat, bowed and said in strongly accented French, "Mr and Mrs Walling, I presume?" The passage had been booked in the names of a fictional American couple. "Captain Molineux, schooner *Payoff*, at your service."

He looked shrewdly at the admiral. "Seafaring man, are you, Mr Walling?"

"I have spent some time at sea, Captain Molineux."

"I thought so, Sir." His gaze moved to Odile and he visibly started. "You very much remind me of someone, Madam, very much."

"And who might that be?" asked Odile.

Molineux smiled, "A deckhand from my ship, Madam, a very unusual deckhand."

"A deckhand, Mr Molineux?"

"Yes, though not a professional sailor. She was at the helm of my ship when we took her downriver, on a night much like this. An unpleasant trip, especially as Lord Cochrane in his *Pallas* was in the Gironde." He turned to the admiral, "As a seaman, Sir, you've perhaps heard of this Cochrane, the 'Sea Wolf'?"

Thomas Cochrane was probably the most daring commander in the Royal Navy, an organisation not short of enterprising men, and his raid deep into the Gironde in HMS *Pallas* still touched a raw nerve in French naval circles.

"I have heard of him, yes."

"Well, some time ago my ship was alongside the wharf over there, flying an American ensign, almost as big as the mizzen. *Pallas* ranged up to us, bold as brass, and backed her topsails, stemming the tide, not half a pistol-shot away.

Never seen a smarter bit of work in my life! And damn me if the ports don't open and she runs out her guns. What a sight!"

"I'm sure it was," said Morlaix dryly.

"Staring down those barrels!" Molineux shook his head, "and Cochrane himself, full uniform and sword, shouts through a speaking trumpet that he knows we're a blockade runner, and that when he catches us at sea, any American aboard will be pressed into the British Navy. Well, most of the men go over the rail and ashore, straight away."

Don't blame them, thought Morlaix.

"About half of 'em didn't return! Well, we were laden with a cargo for Baltimore, fine wines mostly. You get a good price for them now in America, but the ship's making no money, tied up like that. Then we had a stroke of luck. Word came that *Pallas* had run aground and was stuck until the next tide. I knew that was my chance! Well, to cut a long story short, we did get away, with the help of the passengers, including a young woman who took the helm," Molineux continued, "a young woman, Madam, that looked most remarkably like you."

Dominique, thought Odile – how like her daughter to steer a ship down the Gironde! But …

"Excuse me," she said to Molineux, and whispered in her husband's ear, in Breton in case she was overheard: "Did he say all that because he saw a likeness, or has there been a leak?"

"I expect there has been idle talk, Odile, but I don't think it will matter if we can get away quickly," replied her husband quietly, and then, speaking in English to Molineux, "When can we leave?"

"As soon as you like. The Royal Navy is not very attentive in weather like this, and the Sea Wolf is long gone!"

"The tide?" Morlaix knew that the tidal currents in the Gironde were very strong.

Molineux looked at his watch. "Good at about six pm. Carry it nearly all the way, I like it to be slack when we get out to the bar."

Morlaix nodded, "Very nasty out there, wind against the tide."

***

It was the first time that Morlaix had been to sea since his leg was amputated, and he had been dreading that he would be unable to cope. As *Payoff*, the tide under her, sped down the Gironde, the water like liquid mud, he realised to his great joy that his fears had been unfounded.

"Is it a long time since you've been at sea?" asked Molineux, above the roar of the wind.

"Too long," replied Morlaix.

Chapter 21 - Brandywine Creek

Since five o'clock, Jack Stone, formerly Midshipman Stone RN and now an employee of E.I. DuPont de Nemours & Company, had been in the engine shed, where the Watts pattern steam engine was slowly taking shape. Feeling pangs of hunger, he wiped his hands on some cotton waste and took out his watch - seven o'clock - breakfast time. As he walked to his house, he was struck once again by the feeling that he was not in America, but in France. The house of Monsieur du Pont, for example, looked like the residence of a prosperous Parisian businessman, transported from the banks of the Seine to Brandywine Creek.

He sat at breakfast opposite his wife, Dominique, thinking, as usual, about the engine.

"As I've said before, Dom, the key to everything is boring the cylinder ..."

He knew, as soon as he spoke, that by using the word 'boring' he had left himself wide open for a riposte from his wife, and he was surprised when instead she looked at him seriously.

"Jacques," she said - the couple communicated in a mixture of French and English - "*regardez,*" pointing to an article in an English newspaper they had just received in a bundle.

Jack stood and moved round the table to look over her shoulder, reading rapidly:

'*Commander Snowden ...* Oleander *... France ... Lezardrieux ... privateer ...* Blonde *frigate ... cut out ... Kennedy ... loot ... prize*'

Dominique quickly scanned through the rest of the bundle. "Here's another one, Jacques."

She read aloud:

'*Snowden ...* Oleander *... France ... near Montpellier ... Canal du Rhone à Sète ... barges ... Spanish gold ... enormous prize*'

"Well," he said, "it looks as though Percy is making a name for himself. And some money! Back to his favourite target, barges, it seems."

Chapter 22 - Payoff in the Atlantic

Molineux, confident of *Payoff*'s ability to match the speed of most potential foes, which in practice meant the blockading ships of the Royal Navy, took his ship out of the main entrance of the Gironde in driving rain, driven by a blustery south-south-west wind, the spring tide ebbing strongly under her.

Progress was rapid and the ship was at the mouth of the Estuary by ten in the evening. The combination of the outflowing tide running against the wind, coupled with the Atlantic swells piling up in the shallows, made the entrance a forbidding place. Molineux kept a good deal of canvas on her and she rushed along, shipping green water over her decks in the confused seas.

Morlaix sat on a chair lashed to the weather rail, wet through and feeling, it was to be admitted, slightly seasick. Despite the discomfort, he seemed to feel more alive than he had done in years. At sea again!

Rain, driven almost horizontal by the wind, reduced the visibility to only a few yards, and they did not see the Cadouan light. The seas began to die down as the estuary was left behind, but suddenly there was a shout from forward: "Dead ahead! Ship!"

Morlaix tensed and rose from his chair. Molineux shouted, "Up your helm!" and rushed to the wheel, helping the helmsman wind it round spoke by spoke.

The ship came upright as she turned away from the wind, and Morlaix had just time to glimpse the ship that the lookout had spotted - close, impossibly close, so that Morlaix felt that if he stretched his arm out he could touch her. *Payoff* ran under her stern, and Morlaix saw a huge ensign flying from her mizzen and realised she was a British frigate, hove to under reefed topsails. As he read the name on her stern, *Amphion*, the frigate was swallowed up in the rain, as though she had been an apparition rather than a real ship.

Molineux moved over towards Morlaix, visibly shaken.

"I thought they'd all be hiding in the Basque Roads, Mr Walling, this weather," he said.

"Perhaps that's the last of them," replied Morlaix, more in hope than expectation.

***

Despite the prevailing westerly winds of the northern part of the Atlantic, Molineux did not intend to take the southern trade wind route. Instead, he plotted a course - almost direct - which would take *Payoff* well south of Cape Race in Newfoundland, and then to their destination, Cape Henry at the entrance to the Chesapeake. The slight deviation from the direct route enabled the ship to give the Grand Banks and Sable Island a wide berth, and would also avoid a close approach to Halifax, where there was a British base.

Morlaix's seasickness lasted only a couple of days, and he was never completely prostrate, but Odile's ordeal lasted longer, and it was only on the fourth day that she got out of her bunk and nibbled on some biscuit. She quickly recovered and became ravenously hungry, as though to make up for lost time.

For the first few days, the trip across the Atlantic had been hard going, the ship sailing close to the wind, the decks constantly wet with spray. Morlaix gradually became much more agile, and after a week was moving around the ship, determination helping to offset his disability.

One morning after breakfast, he came on deck and saw a tired-looking Molineux speaking to the Mate, who looked equally exhausted.

"A fine morning, Captain Molineux," said Morlaix, above the noise of the wind.

"So it is, Mr Walling, very pleasant to have the wind on the beam for once, though the night was rather hectic."

Morlaix was still referred to as 'Mr Walling', though it was evident that the story of the Morlaixs' true identity was well known aboard.

"I have been thinking, Captain. You know that I have some nautical experience."

"I had guessed as much, Mr Walling, a good deal of experience I'll be bound!"

Morlaix smiled and glanced at the Mate. "I wondered if you would like me to take a watch. I think I'm finding my sea leg, and with the weather as it is I would have no problems."

Molineux looked from Morlaix to the Mate, who was now resting his head on the weather shrouds, as though he did not have the strength to support it.

"That is a very handsome offer, Mr Walling, very handsome and most welcome." He turned to the Mate: "Get yourself below, Mister, I'll show Mr Walling around."

The Mate looked gratefully at Morlaix, turned and went down the companionway.

***

On the eleventh day, the Morlaixs sat at dinner in *Payoff*'s cabin with Captain Molineux.

"Half-way, then," said Odile. "Let's hope the weather is better for the second half of our voyage."

"There always seems to be at least one gale during an Atlantic trip, Mrs Walling, in my experience," said Molineux.

“Now that you mention it, I have never known one without some heavy weather,” said Morlaix. “In the summer it’s bearable, but I would not like to do this trip in winter. Eastbound, possibly, but not this way.”

He looked at Odile before continuing, “Perhaps, Captain, you would like to tell us something of the passage with – we may as well be honest in the confines of this cabin – with our daughter and her husband.”

“Yes, let’s be honest, Admiral Morlaix. That trip! Half the crew frightened off the ship by Cochrane. We had the devil of a time getting out of the Gironde, with Cochrane lurking about in *Pallas.* He spotted us, but fortunately His Lordship seemed not to fancy taking his frigate through the Passe de Grave.”

Morlaix shuddered – he knew the Passe de Grave, a channel into the Gironde which passed perilously between sandbanks and the low shore. He was not surprised that even the ‘Sea Wolf’, Cochrane, had declined to take *Pallas* through it.

“Blowing a gale, a nasty business. It was Jacques that suggested short tacking up to windward to get away from the frigate.” He looked meaningfully at Morlaix. “Seems he’d seen that done before, Admiral Morlaix …”

“He had,” replied Morlaix, smiling. “I once found that a useful tactic.”

“Well,” continued Molineux, “we got through the Passe de Grave without mishap. Your daughter, Madam Morlaix, was at the helm with Jackson, and Jacques was rousting about with the crew, or what there were of them. But, well, we made it, and the rest of the trip was uneventful.”

“And when you got to America?”

“Jacques and Dominique left the ship in high spirits and I didn’t see them again, though I did get a letter from them just before we sailed, thanking me for my help and saying that they were living at Brandywine Creek – that’s some distance from Baltimore.”

Chapter 23 – Villeneuve Arrives

The French ships seemed terribly close when, to his great relief, Pascoe heard a gun fire and saw the recall signal break out on *Oleander*'s mast. The last water cask had been landed, but *Diamond Rock* was a hive of activity as Pascoe and Iris scrambled down to the top of the Mail Coach, where they were winched down to sea level, and embarked in *Liberté, Oleander*'s longboat.

The anchor was aweigh and *Oleander* already forging slowly ahead as *Liberté* came alongside and Iris and Pascoe scrambled aboard.

"Well done, Mr Pascoe," said Kennedy. "I'm minded to take her up to windward, past the French."

"Very well, Sir. There's twelve ships of the line, four frigates and," he looked at his book, "five smaller ships. The battlers are more or less in line ahead, but quite well spread out. I think if we keep her full and bye on the port tack, say south-east, we can give them a bit of distance, and bring her on the wind if any of them show an interest in chasing us."

Kennedy watched as the longboat was lifted aboard and stowed. "I was thinking along the same lines, Pascoe." He turned: "South-east, Lieutenant Luciani, if you please."

From *Oleander*, the French fleet was an impressive sight, but to the experienced eyes of *Oleander*'s officers it did not seem to be quite as ordered as a British fleet would have been. "Slack, all over the place," as Luciani said to Pascoe.

Oleander was not molested, and she shortened sail as the French fleet advanced westward. Soon they heard firing to the west and realised that *Diamond Rock*'s guns were firing on the French. Each ship, as it passed the rock, responded with an impressively noisy cannonade, producing great volumes of smoke which rolled away on the trade wind, but which, as far as they could see, left *Diamond Rock* entirely unscathed.

The entire French fleet had passed her by, without the slightest acknowledgement of her presence, and Kennedy turned *Oleander* to follow them.

"We'll just make sure they're heading north before we leave," said Kennedy, and sometime later, to his great satisfaction, the leading French ship passed Diamond Head and turned to starboard, clearly heading towards Fort de France.

Kennedy and Pascoe were finalising their dispatch as *Oleander*, on the port tack, beat her way out of the St Lucia Channel. They heard a whistle blow and felt the ship come up into the wind with a slatting of sails and, after a pause, settle onto the starboard tack.

Almost immediately there was a knock on the door and a seaman entered the cabin.

"Lieutenant's compliments, Your Honour, but there's sails on the starboard bow."

Snowden and Pascoe were standing up as the seaman added, "Lot of sails, Sir."

Kennedy climbed the foremast ratlines and, at the hounds, looked in the direction indicated by the lookout. He might not have noticed it himself, but just about visible were what could only be the upper sails of ships.

"Well spotted, Bye," he said to Iris, and hurried back down to the deck in the gathering darkness.

"Tack the ship, if you please, Luciani, we'll get up to windward of them in the night."

The ships, now closer, were silhouetted by the rising moon, and during the night *Oleander* was able to manoeuvre so that she was well placed to observe them when the sun rose.

The morning light revealed six ships of the line, heading west, flying Spanish ensigns. Like their French comrades in arms, they seemed to take no notice of *Oleander*.

"I think they are like their friends at Maguelone," said Luciani, thinking of the attitude of the Spanish prisoners they had taken in France, and observing the Spanish ships easy sail and slow rate of progress – "not enthusiasts".

Kennedy had seen enough, and *Oleander* tacked and headed north, towards Antigua.

***

Snowden, on *Columbine*'s deck at the first flush of daylight, saw *Oleander*, signals flying, rush into English Harbour with almost indecent haste and watched as Kennedy, even before the ship had started to moor, jump into *Liberté*, which immediately pulled for the shore.

"Something's up," he said to Baker. "I've a shrewd idea of what it might be."

"What's that Sir?"

"He's seen the French fleet, I'd lay money on it."

You often have laid down money, so I've been told, thought Baker, and then banished the thought as unworthy.

"Kennedy's not usually a one for rushing like that, before the ship's moored, so it must be something important. I think I'll go ashore and see if I can speak to him. Please prepare the gig."

Ashore, Snowden walked towards the Admiral's headquarters and was gratified when he saw Kennedy hurrying along in the opposite direction. "Ken," he shouted, and Kennedy looked up.

"Hello Percy, I saw *Columbine* as we came in." He nodded up the hill: "I've just taken my report to the Admiral."

"The Froggies have arrived, I presume. How have you been doing?"

"A very interesting few days, quite like old times!" He indicated a tavern. "Should we go in here, Perce, and have a chat?"

They sat inside and Kennedy leaned forward and said in a quiet voice, "You're right, Villeneuve, well at least the French fleet, arrived yesterday at Martinique. We spotted them miles off, from the top of *Diamond Rock*. They went into Fort de France. Yesterday we were heading back here, to report, and we saw the Spanish arrive."

"Did you, by God!"

"Yes, six Spanish ships of the line. That means that Villeneuve, if he is the French Admiral, has got eighteen ships of the line altogether."

"Did you do anything else, Ken?"

Kennedy smiled. "Since you ask, Percy, we have been rather busy ..."

Snowden listened to Kennedy's account of *Oleander*'s activities with a great deal of satisfaction, for *Oleander* as a fighting machine was his creation, and Kennedy his protégé, but not, he admitted to himself, without a certain feeling of envy.

When Kennedy finished his narrative, Snowden said, "I've been devising a little scheme, Ken, and I'd welcome your opinion of it. Would you spare me an hour of your time ...?"

***

They sat in *Columbine*'s cabin, the remains of the meal cleared away, the table covered with charts and maps.

"Well, Ken, I think that's about it," said Snowden. "Thanks very much for your contribution. I'm invited to dine with the Admiral tomorrow, and I'll put it to him then."

And that is how the descent on Anse à la Barque was conceived.

Chapter 24 – The Proposal

The dinner aboard *Northumberland*, flagship of the commander of the Leeward Islands Station, had been convivial, and now Snowden sat alone with Admiral Cochrane.

"Your Commander Kennedy has done surprisingly well, Snowden," said Cochrane.

The Admiral's resentment of officers who had been promoted from the lower deck was well known, but Snowden, though he felt himself unreasonably irritated by Cochrane's use of the word 'surprisingly', said nothing.

"He is a fine officer, Sir, and he has done exceptionally well in *Oleander* before and after I left her."

"Indeed – he seems to have almost a knack for finding the French fleet."

"And the Spanish as well" – *now or never*, thought Snowden – adding, "You'll recall, Sir, that the sister ship of the *flûte* that sunk under me is, or at least was, in Anse à la Barque in Guadeloupe?"

"I do, Snowden."

Snowden pulled a document from his pocket.

"Sir, I have been thinking about her and have drawn up a proposal for your …, well, hopefully for your approval."

"Have you, Snowden? Perhaps you could talk me through what you propose."

"I will, Sir. It involves cutting out the *Molene*, that's the *flûte* in Anse à la Barque, and then …"

"A fine prize in itself, no doubt."

"She would be, Sir, and full of stores, stores for the French fleet. Capturing or destroying her would have quite an effect on Admiral Villeneuve's fleet."

"No doubt it would considerably inconvenience Villeneuve."

"There is a small difficulty, Sir – the fort on the northern headland of Anse à la Barque." Snowden retrieved the plan he had obtained from *Herault* before she sank and pointed, "It's marked on the French plan, here."

"Let me see. It looks like, if I can translate properly, 'five thirty-two pounders'. A formidable armament, Snowden."

"Indeed, Sir, I would not like to try to fight past it into Anse à la Barque, but there is another way."

"Is there, Snowden? I don't think I'd listen to it from another junior captain, but with your experience I suppose I should."

I've got him, thought Snowden.

"Well, Sir, we have two West Indians aboard who know Anse à la Barque very well."

"I read your report. I know the ones you mean, you recruited them yourself, in a manner of speaking. As you know, I am very much in favour of local recruitment in this unhealthy climate."

"And some of *Oleander's* men, Bermudians, have been there as well. So, Sir, if I may explain further …"

***

The pipes alerted Kennedy to Snowden's arrival a few seconds before the cabin door flew open.

"He's gone for it, Ken," said Snowden, "he's only gone for it, completely!."

"Well done, Percy. Was it difficult?"

"Pushing at an open door, Ken, an open door. He badly needs a success, and he thinks this could give him one. He'll claim ownership if it goes well, and if it doesn't …"

"When?"

"Soon, very soon. I am to work with Cochrane and his staff to prepare detailed orders, but as soon as that's done we'll be on our way. As you know, there are to be three parts to this attack, and I want you and your *Oleanders* …"

Chapter 25 – Enquiry

Capitaine de corvette Albert Duval, late of the *flûte Herault*, accompanied by his First Lieutenant, Cartier, and *Molene*'s Commander Morel and his First Lieutenant, Garnier, sat in a glum group outside an office within the fort of Basse-Terre, the French headquarters in the south of Guadeloupe. They had arrived by road – it was only about ten miles from Anse à la Barque in a straight line, but the road, which followed the coast, was winding and it had taken most of yesterday to travel to Basse-Terre. The French fort was impressive, strongly fortified, commanding the approach to the roadstead of Basse-Terre and with views stretching miles out to sea. The office belonged to Captain Barcley, the French Naval Commander of Guadeloupe, who was presently, presumably, reading the dispatches and reports which the officers had brought with them.

A secretary came out of the office. "Please accompany me, Monsieur Duval."

Duval stood and Morel gave him an encouraging smile. "Good Luck, Albert," he said.

Barcley, an older man with a wrinkled careworn face, was sitting behind a large desk. He put down the paper he was reading. "Please take a seat, Duval."

When Duval was seated, Barcley continued: "The loss of *Herault* is a grievous blow. Villeneuve has arrived with a fleet," (Duval already knew this – Basse-Terre, where they had stayed last night, was alive with rumour) "and the supplies that were aboard *Herault* were vital for its operation."

"I appreciate that, Sir, I did everything …"

"Yes, Duval, I read your report, and this is an opportunity for you to tell me in your own words what happened. This is not a court martial, you understand, but an attempt to get the true story."

"Well, Sir, I head the rain and …"

When Duval had finished, the other officers were called in, one by one. Eventually, the last one to be called, Cartier, emerged, and the group waited silently for nearly an hour until the secretary called Duval back into the Captain's room, where Barcley was writing at his desk.

Barcley looked up. "Duval, I have written to the commander of the newly arrived fleet, Villeneuve, to the effect that the loss of *Herault* was due to an act of God, despite your seamanlike precautions, and that you did everything you could to save the ship, *with the resources you had available.* Furthermore, I have stated that your conduct in saving the seamen from drowning, and in assisting in the repair of *Molene* was exemplary. I have stated that an efficient officer such as yourself should be found employment in the Admiral's fleet. Well, Duval, don't stand there with your mouth open, bring the others in. I will let them hear this from me."

Later, the officers from the *flûtes* dined with Captain Barcley, a convivial meal, the officers much cheered by the arrival of Villeneuve's fleet. In the morning they were outside the inn, about to set out towards Anse à la Barque, when the Captain's secretary arrived, breathless and agitated. "I am so glad I have caught you, gentlemen, before you set off. I must ask you to immediately return to the Captain's office."

The officers looked at each other in puzzlement and followed the secretary, who was walking quickly up the hill. When they arrived at the fort, they went straight into the Captain's office.

"Gentlemen," the Captain said as they entered the room, where several other naval and military officers were present, "we have just received word from Anse à la Barque, extraordinary news."

"What is that, Sir?" asked Morel, a feeling of dread washing over him.

"I don't know exactly, Morel, but this gentleman here," he indicated a civilian in expensive though rather dirty clothes, "will explain."

The man nodded and said in a cultured voice, "I am Armand Dreyfus, a merchant from Basse-Terre. Last night I was staying with a client at Marigot – that is just south-west of Anse à la Barque – and we, the whole household, were awoken by the sound of guns, heavy guns you understand, and when we went outside – it was raining heavily – we saw the flashes, orange muzzle flashes. We walked up the hill and saw they were coming from a ship firing at the fort on the headland at the Anse. Firing many times, slowly. Occasionally in the flashes I could make out the ship's outline. I believe it was a single decker, a frigate."

Dreyfus paused and looked closely at the officers.

"This morning I walked near to the Anse, and peered over the headland – the one on the south side of the Anse, very cautiously, you understand. I saw that the fort had been damaged, men were working to repair it, and an English flag was flying above it."

"My God!" said Morel, "and the ships, Monsieur? The ships on the jetty?"

"The two ships are still there."

"What flags do they fly?"

"The schooner has the Stars and Stripes, the frigate the *Tricolore*."

Chapter 26 – The Descent

Oleander, *Columbine* and Cochrane's flagship *Northumberland*, a 74, sailed in company from English Harbour. In the afternoon, they sighted the high volcanic island of Monserrat, and turned south, running parallel to the west coast of Guadeloupe, so far off that they could only see the top of the island's mountains.

They spent the following day hove to in a brisk trade wind, and in the evening, leaving *Northumberland* on station some twelve miles off Guadeloupe, *Oleander* and *Columbine* began to work their way into the land, towing the boats. At first, the ships moved rapidly, beating against the brisk trade wind, but as darkness fell, they came into the lee of the island and the wind became light and flukey, necessitating frequent course changes and trimming of sails.

Snowden, conscious that *Columbine* had not been in action before, toured the ship with Baker. A meal had just been eaten, and the men not required to work the ship were in its dimly lit interior, waiting, talking quietly and listening to a softly played fiddle. Even in the faint glow of the lamps, the ship, almost new, looked very good, a tribute to Baker's efforts despite his captain's indifference. Some of the men, unsurprisingly, seemed nervous, and Snowden spoke to them at their stations, doing what he could to reassure them. The marines, many of them veterans, seemed more confident, even looking forward to the coming action.

The ship ghosted along before the light land breeze. Standing next to Baker and the Master, Lacey, Snowden watched as the dim outline of the shore grew nearer.

"There's the fort, Sir," said Oliver, who had been standing a few feet away. Snowden and the others peered through the darkness and saw, silhouetted against the faintly illuminated sky, on the top of the headland, the outline of a square building, a blockhouse – or, more likely, the ramparts of the battery.

"So it is," said Lacey, softly, as though the French defenders, more than a mile away, might hear him. "We're just about in the right place, Sir."

"Very well, Mister, bring her to, gently does it."

Without the usual whistles and with hardly a creak, the topsails were hauled aback, and the ship stopped in the water.

Lacey, closely observing the land and sighting against the compass, said, "North-going current, seems to me, at the moment. A knot or so I reckon."

"Man the boats if you please, Lieutenant Baker," said Snowden.

***

Starlight was the only illumination when a runner came aft to where Kennedy was standing with Pascoe. "Bye says he sees the fort, Your Honour," referring to Iris, who had been into Anse à la Barque in his days in a schooner, and was presently standing on the foremast crosstrees.

"Thank you, Appleby," said Kennedy.

"You can see it over there, Captain, I been there myself," said Appleby, pointing.

Kennedy looked to where the seaman was pointing, just off the port bow, and saw the flat outline of ramparts against the slightly luminous sky.

Pascoe said softly to Kennedy, "*Columbine*'s heaving to, Sir."

"So she is, Pascoe. Bring her to, if you please."

The ship was brought round so that the wind was close on the starboard bow, and sail reduced until she was just stemming the current.

Kennedy, against precedent, but following the example set by Snowden, intended to lead the boat party. He was confident that the ship would be in good hands during his absence.

"Very well, Lieutenant Pascoe, you have the ship."

"Aye aye, Sir."

If practice makes perfect, it was not surprising that *Oleander*'s boats were manned quickly and silently. Kennedy had charge of the longboat, *Liberté*, and Luciani commanded *Rosa*, with Ensign Vause of the marines.

With oars wrapped with cloth, almost silently against the faint noise of breakers on the rocky headlands, the boats pulled into the land, towards the narrow mouth of Anse à la Barque.

***

The manning of *Columbine*'s boats was not as accomplished as *Oleander*'s, but the boats, with Snowden in the launch taking the lead, were soon pulling quietly in towards the land. Columbine's launch was a substantial vessel, on whose bows Snowden had mounted a Carronade, but she rowed sweetly enough.

Oliver, steadied by Snowden's hand, was standing on the seat, looking anxiously ahead. The white of the breakers against the dark headland became more visible as the boats left it to starboard. Suddenly, Oliver tensed and pointed.

"I see it now, Your Honour, the beach."

Snowden peered ahead and, as the boat advanced slowly, saw waves gently breaking on a beach at the head of a small bay. "I see it, thank you," he said quietly. In the dim starlight, the boats grounded on the sand. The men disembarked and, under the direction of the petty officers, formed up, marines and seamen in separate lines.

"Very well, West, take the boats back out and anchor just off with the guns trained on the beach in case we have to get back in a hurry."

The Second Lieutenant nodded, "Aye aye, Sir."

Snowden, guided by Oliver, led the column up the steep, rough track from the beach. They passed only one habitation, a small shack, and though a dog barked, no notice was taken of them. Snowden was not surprised. He had spent a disproportionate length of time traversing enemy territory at night, and even in France and Spain there had never seemed to be much enthusiasm for reporting groups of armed men to the authorities. He surmised that the black population of Guadeloupe had no interest in becoming involved in fighting between the French and English and had decided to 'see no evil'.

At the summit of the hill they turned right onto a larger road, and in the darkness Snowden and Oliver almost collided with a man walking along the road in the opposite direction. Snowden, moving with sudden speed, moved behind the man, and in one motion drew his dirk, grabbed the man round the head with his arm covering his mouth, and pulled violently back. He touched the tip of the dagger to the skin of the captive's neck. The man did not struggle.

"*Parlez-vous français*?" Snowden whispered in the man's ear, but there was no response.

Snowden felt a touch on his elbow. "Shall I take him, Sir?" said a voice which Snowden recognised as belonging to Shawcross, Sergeant of *Columbine*'s marines. Snowden thought there was a slight tone of indignation in his voice, as though Snowden, through his act of physical violence, had demonstrated a familiarity with brawling that was not quite proper for a commanding officer.

"Can you speak to him, Oliver?" asked Snowden.

In a low voice, Oliver spoke to the man in the local patois, which Snowden, despite speaking French, could not really understand. The man relaxed.

"He says he was visiting his lady friend, Sir, and was making his way back home."

"Tell him I have some silver coin. If he'll lead us close to the battery, not right up to it, I'll pay him some money when we arrive."

The man, who probably realised in truth that he had no choice, accepted the offer, nodding his head, and the party continued along the road. At the apex of the second bend, their captive stopped and pointed. He spoke to Oliver, who translated.

"He says the fort is just down the road here, Cap," said Oliver. The prisoner spoke again, and Oliver translated: "He says it is only about one hundred yards to the battery." The man, in Sergeant Shawcross' grip, looked terrified, realising perhaps that he was of no further use to the English.

"Shall I let him go, Sir?" asked Shawcross. From the anxiety in his voice, Snowden realised that the Sergeant shared his captive's concern and, influenced by Snowden's reputation, was worried that his commander, knowing that 'dead men tell no tales', was ruthless enough to act accordingly.

Snowden, appreciating that he would have to work to prove his humanity to *Columbine*'s crew, held out some coins to the prisoner, who grabbed them gratefully and, at a shove from Shawcross, took off down the road, back towards the cove.

Snowden looked at his watch, turning it until he could see its face in the dim light.

At that moment there was a violent gust of wind and the heavens seemed to open, rain pouring down on the men. Snowden directed them to crouch behind a rocky outcrop on the left side of the road, and, leaving them behind in Shawcross' care, he walked with Marine Captain Ferrier along the road, which sloped downhill towards the fort at the end of the point of land. He counted his paces, and at seventy he whispered "Get down". They waited, lying on the road, which had turned into a minor river. After a wait of a minute or so, Snowden could not see or hear any activity and so he moved forward with Ferrier, crawling on all fours in the mud. After a few yards he saw the battery, black against the western sky. They stayed where they were for a few minutes, and then Snowden whispered to Ferrier.

"We'll go back, get behind that outcrop where the men are, before *Columbine* starts firing. Bring the guns up and get them trained along the road to the fort. Load them as soon as the rain stops. They'll be useful if we have to beat a retreat."

"Aye aye, Sir." Snowden and Ferrier moved back to where the men were crouching. Soon figures were busy about the guns, and Snowden knew that they would be loaded with grape and ready for action when the squall passed.

***

Close together, *Oleander's* boats, *Liberté* and *Rosa* crept almost silently towards the entrance to Anse à la Barque, which was between two rocky headlands about three hundred yards apart, on which the small swell broke in a smother of white foam. They were quite a way off when Kennedy in the sternsheets of *Liberté* felt the first drops of rain.

Squall!

Kennedy knew that the two boats would become separated in the wind and reduced visibility, so he waved vigorously towards *Rosa*, and as the rain turned into a deluge, Luciani brought his boat close to the stern of *Liberté*, her painter was passed over, and when the wind came, blowing off the land, funnelled directly down the Anse, the two boats were tied together, *Rosa* about thirty feet astern.

It was the stuff of nightmares, trying to make progress in the squall. Kennedy knew that in the rain and wind there was little likelihood of discovery from the fort, and urged the rowers on, but although the men pulled willingly at the oars, the boat, as far as he could tell as he could no longer see the land, made slow progress into the bay. He tried to steer west-north-west, but could only just about make out the compass card, and sometimes *Liberté* lost steerage way and veered off course, and sometimes the painter joining her to *Rosa* pulled the stern round, requiring the rowers to pull harder on one side or the other and occasionally to backwater.

They were going to be late …

Luciani, in *Rosa*, urged his rowers on and tried as far as he could to keep station on *Liberté* so that the painter remained slack, but occasionally the wind overcame his best efforts and the painter tightened, pulling both boats off course. He put a man to stand by the painter, paying it out as it tightened and pulling it in as the strain came off it. The wind slackened slightly as they got further into the cove, and they started to make better progress.

Iris' voice came from the bow of the boat, "Two ships there be, two. One's a man o' war, one's a trader!"

"Yankee, I reckon."

And there they were, startlingly close, tied together alongside a wharf, bows pointing to the sea. The outside ship did indeed look like a schooner and the other one, huge in the darkness, indisputably a frigate – Snowden's *flûte*, *Molene*!

"Hold water!" Kennedy ordered, and the rowers stopped, their blades in the sea, slowing the boat immediately. As *Liberté* lost way, *Rosa*'s painter was hauled in so that her bow was only a few feet from *Liberté*'s stern. When Luciani appeared at *Rosa*'s bow, Kennedy spoke to him, almost shouting to make himself heard over the noise of the squall.

"Luciani, we're late, we must go in immediately."

Before Luciani could reply, the rain to seaward was suffused by a bright orange flash, followed seconds later by the sound of a gun, quickly followed by others.

"Late!" said Kennedy, "Let's go."

"Aye aye, Sir," replied Luciani.

Kennedy heard Luciani say to his rowers, "Give way together, smart, now," and *Rosa* surged forward, heading towards the bows of the ships.

Kennedy gave the same order to his rowers and *Liberté* began to move quickly.

He spoke to Soares at the tiller: "Alongside the wharf" and then "Get her under the schooner's sternline, we'll cut it."

The firing to seaward continued as the boats separated, *Liberté* heading towards the ships' sterns and *Rosa* to their bows. Almost immediately *Liberté* was at the sternline of the schooner, which was bar tight, straining against the wind to hold the ship into the wharf, and Soares worked the boat under the rope until it was resting on *Liberté*'s gunwhale. Above the noise of the squall and between the reports of *Columbine*'s guns, Kennedy could hear the sound of the waves lapping angrily against the wharf and the sides of the ships, and the grating noise as the ships rubbed together.

The hawser yielded to a few soft strokes of a boarding axe, honed to razor sharpness, and as the two ends sprang away in the darkness and the boat moved forwards towards the quay, there came a shout from above them and he saw a man leaning over the schooner's rail. The shout was in English: "Who is that?", the voice American.

That complicates things, thought Kennedy – neutrals. He thought quickly and shouted back, "Royal Navy. Get below, all of you, stay there. Don't emerge till I tell you to," and the man disappeared. He heard shouts from the frigate and then a drum beating, and as *Liberté* passed under the frigate's sternline he saw figures at her rail.

"*Anglais!*" shouted one of them, "*Abordages!*"

The boat bumped heavily on the wharf.

"Steady on, Cox'n!" said Kennedy.

"Thought you was in a hurry, Your Honour," replied Soares, to laughter from the men, his grin visible in the darkness. As Iris scrambled up the wharf, painter in hand, Kennedy shouted, "Pull her in alongside," and hands grasped whatever they could on the wharf, pulling the boat into the wall.

"Give 'em a volley from the wharf, Mr Vause," he shouted.

"Aye, Sir," said the Ensign of Marines.

"Up you go, lads," yelled Kennedy.

***

Aboard *Columbine*, as the boats pulled away ashore, First Lieutenant Baker knew that he was facing the crisis of his career, and relished it.

He spoke to the dim outline of man in a shako standing beside him.

"Master Lacey, take her into the headland if you please."

"Aye aye, Sir."

The topsails were braced round and let draw, and in the gentle land breeze the frigate moved slowly inshore, the land dimly discernible ahead.

"No bottom," reported the leadsman.

"Don't like the look of that, Sir," said Lacey to Baker, gesturing towards the dark bulk of Guadeloupe, where a cloud, rearing above the line of the mountains, was rolling towards Anse à la Barque, but when the squall hit, rain first, and seconds later the wind blowing violently off the land, *Columbine* was ready, the yards manned, men at the halyards and braces. Above the rising noise of the wind in the rigging, the leadsman called, "Ground, forty five fathom." The frigate heeled in the gust, but she was not taken aback. Sail was reduced quickly, the yards braced sharp round, and she was pointed up into the wind until the luffs of the sails trembled.

"Keep her up to it," said the Master to the men at the helm, and the frigate, making perhaps four knots, forged ahead towards the land.

"Thirteen fathom."

"Bring her round, Mister," said Baker to the Master.

"Aye aye. She's about a cable off, I reckon," he replied.

The land was indeed very close as the ship turned to port, bringing her parallel to the land. In the wind and rain, men struggled to reduce sail and back the topsails, bringing the ship nearly to a stop.

"Nicely done, Mister," said Baker.

"Thank you, Sir."

Third Lieutenant Perkins appeared from the companionway with Gunner Forbes. "Starboard guns ready, Sir," he said.

The two men squinted at the shore, shielding their eyes from the wind-driven rain.

"I see the ramparts," said Perkins and pointed.

"Oh yes," confirmed the Gunner, "I see them too."

"Fire the starboard broadside when ready," commanded Baker, "lay the guns very carefully, Mr Forbes."

"I will that" replied Forbes, and he and Perkins went below.

The frigate's guns began firing about a minute later, a slow, aimed, rippling broadside which illuminated the rain with bright orange flashes. Baker saw some of the balls smash into the rampart and the cliffs beneath it. The shore battery did not reply. After the sixth broadside, *Columbine's* guns fell silent.

"Wear the ship, if you please, Mister," Baker said to the Master.

***

Snowden, ashore, lay down in the mud as the ship opened fire. He heard some of the roundshot smashing into the stonework of the battery, and some skipping along the rising ground to where the men were crouched behind the rocky outcrop, the balls tearing through the undergrowth. One broadside, two, three, slow, deliberate ... and then the sixth, as agreed, grapeshot, whistling noisily. *That'll keep their heads down*, thought Snowden, the exultation rising in him, as it always did at the prospect of action.

"Ready, Ferrier?" he asked.

"Aye," said the marine.

Snowden stood and screamed, "At 'em *Columbines*!", heard a whistle blow, and ran along the path towards the fort, slipping and sliding in the mud, pistol – unfamiliar, one of the pair he had taken from *Herault*'s commander's desk – in his left hand, sword in his right, not glancing behind to check that the men were following. At the entrance there was a low guardhouse, and he saw two Frenchmen, probably sentries, crouching behind a wall, sheltering from the frigate's fire. Without slackening his pace, Snowden discharged his pistol at one of them, saw him slump to the ground, and, shouting like a man possessed, ran through the entrance to the fort, onto a level paved area, on its seaward side walled off by a castellated rampart through which long guns on carriages were pointing out to sea and into the Anse. One of the guns had been knocked off its carriage and men were lying or sitting, dazed, around it.

The crews of the other guns were in the process of loading their charges, and they looked round in horror as they heard the British approaching, shouting as they ran. A man appeared in front of Snowden, and he slashed at him with his sword, feeling the blade cut through clothing and into flesh, and then he was on the men at the nearest gun, his sword arm raised ready to strike, when he realised that they had their hands raised in surrender. With a conscious effort he lowered his blade and looked round to see that the crews of the other guns were also in attitudes of surrender.

Captain Ferrier of the Marines came up to him, panting heavily. "My word, Sir, that was quick. They've surrendered, Sir. There's some Frenchies in the buildings, but none of 'em showing any sign of fight. I'm checking everywhere, but I don't think there's any more of them."

"Post sentries on the track. I don't want any to escape."

A French officer limped towards Snowden, offering the hilt of his sword. The fort was theirs – now the work began.

***

Kennedy scrambled out of the boat and onto the wharf, which was wooden and quite wide. He realised that *Columbine*'s firing had ceased, and there was activity on the French ship, which towered above the wharf, enormous, her name, *Molene*, visible on her stern in the diffuse light from the now-risen moon. As a man, one of the Corsicans, Fede, ran with a boarding axe along the wharf to cut the frigate's sternline, Kennedy heard the sound of a window breaking from the ship's stern gallery, saw a musket barrel emerge, fire, and he watched as the man with the axe dropped to his knees.

"Get that swivel up, put some grape through the gallery," he shouted, and the boat's crew hauled the little portable swivel gun onto the dock and dropped it into its wooden mount. There was a volley of fire from *Oleander*'s riflemen kneeling on the wharf, and the remainder of the ship's stern gallery windows exploded in a shower of glass shards. At the other end of the ship, Kennedy could see Luciani's men climbing up from the longboat.

"Right, lads, let's have 'em," shouted Kennedy, and, cutlass in his right hand, at the head of a bawling group of seamen and marines, ran towards the gangway, with Luciani's men running from the bow of the ship. There was firing from the ship, but Kennedy ignored it. He arrived at the gangway at the same time as Luciani, shouted "Up we go, lads," grabbed the stanchion holding up the gangway's handrail, and raced onto the deck.

Behind him, he heard the swivel fire and the cry of men below as its charge of grapeshot flew through the stern gallery and swept along the ship's gun deck. Men from the *flûte*'s crew were gathered on the deck near the head of the gangway, and there was some firing as the English made their way aboard, but there were not many Frenchmen, and as the *Oleanders* behind Kennedy and Luciani raced aboard the frigate, the Frenchmen on deck retreated towards the companionway. The swivel fired again through the stern gallery, and chaos reigned as the men trying to escape from the boarding party on deck were met on the companionway by the ones from below, who were attempting to flee from the grapeshot. The Frenchmen looked at the advancing Englishmen and, almost as one, threw down their weapons.

Kennedy spoke to Ensign Vause: "Keep the prisoners on the deck here. Cover them with the swivel. Get below directly and search the ship. Make sure there's no one below thinking of setting fire to her."

"Aye aye, Sir, I'll do that directly. Sergeant!"

Kennedy heard shouting from the bow of the ship and ran forward. A group of Frenchmen, he thought probably petty officers, had taken cover behind guns and equipment on the fo'c'stle head and were shooting at Luciani and his Corsicans. Before Kennedy got there, he heard Luciani shout something in Corsican and the men rushed forward. The Frenchmen, realising that further resistance was futile, surrendered.

In French, Luciani spoke to one of the men: "Where are your officers?"

The man recognised his accent and his eyes widened in surprise. "You are Corsican?"

"Yes, Frenchman, I am a Corsican, Lieutenant Luciani of the Royal Navy. I ask you again – where are the officers?"

"There are none aboard. They are all ashore – they have gone to the town, I think it is called Basse-Terre. There is an enquiry because the other ship, *Herault*, was sunk."

Chapter 27 – The Yankee

The rain and wind stopped as suddenly as they had begun, and the sun was rising as Kennedy and Luciani, with a party of marines, climbed onto the schooner lying next to the frigate and crossed its deserted deck to the cabin door. Kennedy knocked with the butt of his pistol.

"Open up," he said loudly, and after a pause the door was opened by a tall man.

"Ah," the man said, looking balefully at Kennedy, "George's Navy, interfering with honest trade, no doubt, as usual."

"I am in the King's service, if that's what you mean. Commander Kennedy, HMS *Oleander*, and honest traders have nothing to fear from the Royal Navy."

"George Bentinck, Master of this vessel, *Rosie*, of Baltimore. You've cut my lines, the ship's only made fast with the breast lines to the Frenchie."

"I'll trouble you for your papers and manifest, Mr Bentinck, if you please. Shall we go into the cabin?"

"We shall not, Commander, and I'll trouble you to get off my ship, which is involved in legitimate trade."

"See over there, Bentinck," Kennedy pointed to where a British flag was flying over the fort on the headland. "We have possession of this bay, and, for all I know by now, of the entire island."

The schooner's skipper looked at the fort and nodded as Kennedy continued.

"Look here, skipper, I've just taken the frigate, but we've had several casualties, and I have much to do. Now, we'll go to the cabin and examine the papers, or I'll put you in irons in the hold of the French man o' war you're alongside of" – he said, emphasising the words "*alongside of*" – "while I put a crew aboard your schooner and argue my case before the prize court in Antigua."

Bentinck smiled wryly, swung wide the door, and they went into the cabin. "What was the name of your ship, Commander?" asked Bentinck as they sat at the table in the low room.

"*Oleander*, Mr Bentinck."

"I thought that's what you said. I've heard the name before – were you in Morocco, in Salé?"

"We were there, it seems a long time ago."

"Did you rescue some of my countrymen from the Moors?"

"In a manner of speaking, I suppose we did, Bentinck. Our boats were alongside in the town, and the men took off some Yankees who had been shipwrecked and sold into slavery. Once they were on the ship, there was no chance of the crew giving them up, so our skipper negotiated a price, and we ransomed them. The crew had a whip round, but the skipper paid in the end. We took them to Gib."

Suddenly Bentinck held out his hand. "Commander Kennedy – one of those men was my wife's brother."

***

Outside the cabin, Luciani spoke to Kennedy.

"They got Fede, the bastards"

"I know, Giotto, I'm sorry."

"He was my cousin. The French will pay for it."

Kennedy shuddered slightly. He sometimes felt out of his depth with the Corsicans.

"What are you going to do with the schooner, Ken?" asked Luciani.

"I think we'll have to let it go, Giotto, on the promise it will leave Guadeloupe, but first I'll speak to Snowden."

"Why's that? She's a fine prize."

"She is, but the cargo's been discharged and she hasn't loaded, so we can't say that we caught her carrying contraband. The Admiral told us there's been a lot of anger in America about the blockade, and ships' commanders have been told to act with as much leniency as possible. We've got a fine prize there," – he gestured to the *flûte* – "let's not get greedy. I'm going to visit Snowden in the fort. Get the *flûte* ready for sea directly, Giotto."

Luciani pointed to the British flag flying above the fort. "Give the Old Man my congratulations."

***

Luciani worked to prepare the *flûte*, while Kennedy took *Liberté* to the beach around the headland, past *Columbine* which was anchored just off the land. He saw *Oleander* further out, slowly making her way inshore. He landed in the sandy bay and walked up to the fort, which was a hive of frenetic activity. Boats ran back and forth to *Columbine*, taking the wounded and prisoners off and returning with a variety of stores and equipment. He realised that most of the frigate's crew were either in the boats or ashore, and fervently hoped that the French had no ships readily available to send to Anse à la Barque.

He was greeted by a haggard-looking Snowden, whose clothes were covered in dust. The reason for this shortly became evident when there was a large explosion and a section of the ramparts collapsed, creating a huge dust cloud above a heap of rubble. Men fell upon the rubble, picking up rocks and either carrying them inland or placing them in wheelbarrows, presumably taken from the fort, and adding to the wall or bund which was rapidly taking place on the landward side of the fort.

"It's damned good to see you, Ken. I see you have the *flûte*. What – what was the bill?"

"They didn't put up much resistance, Percy, there weren't many of them, and there were no officers. They were all ashore, an enquiry into sinking of the ship you were in, I believe. Fede was killed though, musket ball, and we have several wounded, but none too seriously."

"Fede was a fine man, related to Giotto I believe. Get the wounded off to *Columbine* directly, Ken, we have an excellent surgeon aboard."

"Thank you, I'll do that. We have several wounded Frogs, some quite bad. Shall I send them as well?"

"Yes, do that. How did you get on, Percy?"

"Froggies were paying so much attention to *Columbine*'s broadside – can't say I blame them, it was pretty impressive – that they didn't notice us until it was too late. The worst scare we had was our own roundshot skipping through the undergrowth – missed us, though."

Kennedy asked, though he knew what the answer would be, "What are you doing now?"

"Fortifying the place – against a land attack."

"I knew it – but why?"

"Because I can, Ken. We did it once before, at Macinhagiu. I don't suppose you've forgotten."

Kennedy grimaced – he knew he would remember Macinhagiu for the rest of his life.

"Come into my office, Ken, we can have a discussion about what I intend to do."

"I will, but I'd like to discuss the Yankee schooner with you immediately."

Kennedy explained that he intended to allow the schooner to leave. Snowden listened and agreed.

"Let him go, Ken – you can make the signal from here."

***

Aboard *Molene*, Luciani looked up as he heard a gun fire on the fort, which was about five hundred yards from the wharf where the ship was lying. The signal was long because, knowing that Luciani did not have a signal book with him, Kennedy had used alphabetical flags. He read out:

Shaking his head, he boarded the American schooner and walked up to Bentinck, who was supervising the replacement of the severed shore lines.

"Morning," he said, "you may leave."

"Thank you," replied Bentinck.

"If it was up to me, you would not be leaving," said Luciani, "but I have my orders."

A gun sounded from the fort and Bentinck looked up and saw signal flags flying from the flagstaff. "Looks like you have another message, Lieutenant."

Slowly, Luciani read the message, as did *Rosie*'s skipper who spelled out:

"F R E N C H F L A G"

"Fancy that," he said with a shake of his head, "you English are devious bastards."

"They are," agreed Luciani, "not at all like us Corsicans."

***

The work making *Molene* ready for sea was progressing well, when Snowden and Baker, accompanied by Vause, boarded the *flûte*.

"Lieutenant Luciani," said Snowden, "I think you've met Baker, premier of *Columbine*."

"Briefly, Sir." Baker held out his hand, which was taken by Luciani. Snowden looked round the ship. "How's the work going, Luciani?"

"Reasonable well, Sir. The rigging is still not fully repaired from the storm damage, and we scarred her a bit when we took her, but with a little more work she'll be ready for sea."

"I'm very glad to hear that. I want to get her away as soon as we can – tomorrow morning if possible. Pascoe's going to take her to Antigua, but he's busy presently, surveying Marigot Bay."

Luciani nodded as Snowden continued, "I want you for a little land-based activity, with the help of Mr Vause. We're getting defences set up on the southern headland, but they're not fully ready, and I'm concerned that there are probably French eyes around us, and word may have got to Basse-Terre by now about what we have done. It is possible that the French might send out a scouting party almost immediately. When you've handed *Molene*'s repairs over to Mr Baker, I'd like to discuss how you might set up a mobile defence using your Corsicans and *Oleander*'s marines."

Chapter 28 – Return to Molene

As the merchant finished speaking, the men in the office of the French naval commander of Guadeloupe were quiet, shocked.

Commander Morel was the first to react. He stood suddenly and said with great force, "I leave, immediately," adding to his First Lieutenant: "come on, Garnier, to the ship!"

"You must wait," said Captain Barcley.

"I cannot," said Morel, in great agitation, "my ship …"

Captain Barcley held up his hand, and said forcefully: "If the fort is in English hands, and an English frigate is in the offing, your ship is either taken, or as good as."

"But she flies the French flag"

"She did this morning …"

"Captain Barcley, I must go to my ship, to see how things are with her. If she has been taken, or is about to be captured, perhaps she could be burned, to stop her falling into the hands of the English. She has a cargo of naval stores …"

"I know, Morel. You may go, but you must have an escort, and you are to be extremely cautious." He turned to an army officer, Colonel Meyer. "Colonel, can you arrange an escort for Commander Morel? It is very urgent."

"I appreciate that, Barcley," replied Meyer, who looked at another army officer: "Major Levy – can you accompany Monsieur Morel? It will be a matter of reconnaissance, to establish what has happened to the fort and to the ships."

"Sir, I will take ten men. We will be ready in ten minutes."

As Levy stood to leave, Meyer said, "Tomorrow morning I will leave for Anse à la Barque with a strong force. Any intelligence you can gather before then will be of prime importance, Major."

***

The road between Basse-Terre and Anse à la Barque ran along the narrow strip of level land that bordered the western shore of Guadeloupe. To the horsemen's left was the bright blue sea, and to their right the hills of the island's interior rose, steep, ravined, covered in bright green forest, impassable, often sheathed in mist, with rainbows appearing and disappearing.

The scenery was, without doubt, beautiful, but *Capitaine de corvette* Morel, whose ship, he believed, was in danger from the English who had captured the fort, was in no mood to appreciate it. The road ran just above the beach, through the settlement of Marigot, and then, in a series of bends, climbed up to the headland on the south side of Anse à la Barque before descending to sea level and continuing along the head of the bay, past the wharf where the ships were moored.

They stopped at the road's summit and Levy signalled for the soldiers to dismount. From the edge of the road, Morel could see the fort on the opposite headland, a British flag flying above it, and from another pole a series of signal flags was displayed. Morel tried, but failed, to interpret the flags. The fort was a hive of activity, men working with picks and shovels and boats running to and from a British frigate which was lying just off the land. Heading slowly into the bay in the light wind was a large schooner with huge raking masts, a British ensign at her main peak.

The road was cut into the slope of the hill, with a stone retaining wall. Morel, standing next to Major Levy, was intent on inspecting his ship, which was partially visible through the trees.

Major Levy turned to a young soldier: "Take a good look at what you can see, Amel, and then back to Basse-Terre, quickly. Tell them: 'Anse à la Barque battery is in the hands of the enemy, and the fort is being reinforced against an attack from the land. There are two British ships ..." He gestured at them, and looked at Morel.

"A frigate and a schooner," said Morel.

"Yes, two British ships, a frigate and a schooner'. Repeat the message, and then off you go, and good luck."

The man repeated the message and turned his horse south, back towards Basse Terre. Without warning, a whistle blew, there was a shot from the woods above them, and Amel, the messenger, clutched at his chest, and soundlessly fell from his horse. Instinctively, the party ran across the road and crouched behind the retaining wall.

Another whistle blew, and, from the bushes on the side of the road opposite the wall a man emerged, tall, good looking, swarthy, but dirty, wearing what seemed to be the remnants of a naval officer's uniform, carrying a bayonetted gun in his hands. Morel watched in horror as the man walked towards him, followed by a group of men with the same guns, who trained them unwaveringly on the Frenchmen. Some wore red coats, and some were dressed as English seamen with wide brimmed straw hats, except for one who wore a shako with a shiny badge with one word, 'Oleander' inscribed on it.

The Frenchmen, pinned against the wall, were helpless. The man in the officer's uniform shouted "hands up!" and then pointed to Morel and said, in heavily accented French: "You, you French bastard, are you in charge?"

Morel recognised the accent - Corsican! Stunned, he could not find the words to reply.

The man turned his head and said casually to the sailor in the shako "shoot the bastard, Tino, and I'll ask somebody else."

"Aye aye, Giotto", said the man, and swung his gun round until it pointed at Morel.

Morel, finding his voice said "Yes, I am in charge. Morel, Capitaine de corvette of the Imperial Navy. Who …?"

"What ship?"

"*Molene*" he pointed towards the head of the inlet.

"Ah" said the man, smiling, "I think not. His Majesty's ship *Molene* has no need of your services."

"You are?" asked Morel, the horror of his circumstances becoming ever clearer "You seem to be Corsican."

"Giotto Luciani, Lieutenant, Royal Navy, and yes, a Corsican."

"Royal Navy! *Bandito*, more like" muttered Morel under his breath.

"I heard that, you French bastard" said Luciani, looking steadily at Morel, "We are about to walk to the fort, our fort, and I can assure you that if you make another remark like that, you will not arrive there."

"You tell him, Giotto" laughed one of the seamen. Morel thought that it was not a pleasant laugh, but said nothing in reply. As they walked along, he caught glimpses of his ship, clearly being prepared for sea. He'd lost his command. Up the hill to the fort they went, where Englishmen, seamen and marines, were working feverishly. Morel saw that a rough rampart of earth and stone had been built, and guns, French guns, were being mounted on it, pointing inland.

Ahead, he saw a group of Englishmen. One of them, a tall man, looking almost like a scarecrow in tattered clothes, his dirty face streaked with sweat, came forward and spoke to the Corsican *bandito*.

***

Pascoe brought *Oleander* to the entrance of Anse à la Barque and anchored. He took the dinghy, the only boat left on the ship, and was rowed towards the beach. As he rounded the point with the battery, he heard a shot from the south, a rifle round. Once ashore he climbed up to the fort, where he was greeted by Snowden and Kennedy.

"Nice to see my old commands, *Oleander* and the dinghy," said Snowden, grinning.

"Nice to see my present command," said Kennedy.

"It seems all went well," replied Pascoe, looking round. "I heard a rifle fire just then."

"Giotto, I expect," said Snowden, "he's with Riley, keeping an eye on the road south. Yes, it all went well, we have gained a fort and a frigate! Pascoe, I have a plan."

"I didn't doubt it for a moment, Sir, you look like you're preparing for a siege."

"Well, Pascoe, not quite."

At that moment they were interrupted by one of the men, a *Columbine*, who had been posted as a sentry on the road leading up from the jetty. He addressed Snowden breathlessly.

"Sir, there's a group of men walking towards the fort. That foreign officer from *Oleander*, Your Honour, with some Frenchmen, prisoners."

A few minutes later, Luciani arrived, his Corsicans escorting a group of depressed-looking Frenchmen and leading several horses.

"A fort, a ship and now some prisoners. My cup runneth over, Giotto," said Snowden.

"Thank you, Sir," replied Luciani. He pointed with his thumb to Morel. "This French ..."

Morel pushed himself forward. "I wish to speak to the commanding officer. I am *Capitaine de corvette* Morel of ..." His voice trailed off.

The scarecrow spoke, in excellent French. "Ah yes, of *Molene*. I fear I have deprived you of your ship, Commander. I am Captain Snowden, Royal Navy," he gestured towards the frigate anchored just offshore, "of His Majesty's frigate *Columbine*."

The British officers watched in amusement as Morel's gaze went from Snowden to the British schooner, and then to Tino's cap badge.

"*Oleander*? And you are Snowden? You were aboard *Herault*! We thought you had died before she sank."

"Luckily not."

Morel drew himself up: "I do not understand what has happened, but, Captain Snowden, it is no disgrace to be captured by you." He looked at Giotto. "As for this man, he seems ..." He stopped as Snowden held up his hand.

"Lieutenant Luciani is an excellent officer, Monsieur Morel, though I am very glad he is on my side. I will hear no criticism of him. Now, I have work to do. I will have you transferred to *Columbine* directly."

As Morel and the other Frenchmen were led away, Pascoe spoke to Snowden: "Sir, your operation would benefit from a landing stage at the base of the cliff. They have built one at Diamond Rock and I've an idea of how we could do it here."

"I didn't doubt it for a moment, Pascoe."

"I presume that at some stage, Sir, we'll have to retreat from this fort – we can't hold it against the entire French garrison of Guadeloupe, and if Villeneuve arrives …"

"That's true, Pascoe, at the appropriate moment I intend to beat a hasty retreat."

"Well, Sir, that's another argument for a landing stage."

"It is, Pascoe. What do you have in mind?"

"A floating one, Sir, supported by barrels, perhaps using timber from *Molene*. If I may, I'll send a boat to *Oleander* for Mr Trimingham and his tools, and I'll get started immediately."

"Delegate to Mr Trimingham, Pascoe, as soon as you can. I'll want you to take *Molene* to Antigua in due course."

Pascoe beamed. "Aye aye, Sir, with pleasure."

"But before that, gentlemen, I have a task for *Oleander*."

"Yes, Sir, what is that?" asked Kennedy.

"Well, do you remember in Corsica, the soldiers marching along the coast road?"

"As if I could forget!"

"Well, from the chart it seems that the road south, to Basse-Terre, the main town, runs along the beach, and there's no way round it. To recover their fort, they'll have to come along it. I've a mind to try out some of these French horses and have a look. Would you care to join me, Ken?"

Chapter 29 – Marigot Bay

Jethro West, *Columbine*'s Second Lieutenant, could not be faulted for enthusiasm. The son of a gentleman farmer, he was well used to working with horses, and he had used the ones captured from the French, with improvised harnesses, to haul two of the guns of the captured French *flûte* to the summit of the headland to the south of Anse à la Barque. As he watched Forbes, *Columbine*'s Gunner, and Captain Ferrier of the Marines carefully supervising the emplacement of the guns, ensuring that they covered the shore road at Marigot, he reflected on how his life had changed since Snowden had appeared. No more weeks of swinging round the hook – once Snowden had taken command, the ship had hardly stopped moving. For the first time, *Columbine*'s guns had been fired in anger, and there had been a shore excursion which had resulted in the capture of not only an enemy fort but also a French *flûte* loaded with stores for Villeneuve's fleet. Prize money! And here he was, not thinking up work to keep the men occupied, but ashore, dragging cannons around with a team of horses, fortifying part of the French West Indies which Snowden had captured. *This was more like it*, he thought.

"I'll go back down for the ammunition, Captain Ferrier," he said.

"Very well" replied Ferrier, and added "Perhaps you should start thinking about how you're going to shift that mortar - Mr Forbes here is keen to get it in position."

They had found a large mortar aboard the *flûte*, and they intended that it should form part of the defences of Anse à la Barque.

***

Pascoe, tired from building what was now universally known as 'Pascoe's Landing', the pontoon supported by barrels which gave access to the headland below the fort, slept aboard *Oleander* for a few hours, and then, when the moon rose and the ship got underway in the light land breeze with her boats towing astern, collected his surveying equipment.

The ship sailed south for about a mile and hove to, not far from the land, off the small settlement of Marigot. *Columbine*'s gig came alongside, and Snowden climbed aboard.

"I've not come to take *Oleander* back, Ken! I just wanted to have a look at the road from the masthead. Perhaps you and Pascoe would like to join me aloft."

Aloft, they could make out the land reasonably well. It was clear that the coast road ran close to the shore, and that there was no easy way round it as the coastal plain was narrow and the land behind it steep and wooded.

After they had returned to the deck, Snowden said, "I think the location is suitable, perhaps not as good as Corsica," – in Corsica, *Oleander* had ambushed a French army column, to devastating effect, as it made its way along a coast road – "but if you get her well inshore we should be able to sweep the road."

"Pascoe's about to survey near the land, Percy," said Kennedy, "and we dropped an anchor three cables to seaward on our way in. It's buoyed, and when we get her settled we'll run hawsers to it, and if the wind fails and we have to leave sharpish, we can warp ourselves out."

"Excellent plan, Ken. I'll leave you to it. I think I'd better get some dispatches to the flagship now. Good luck."

Snowden departed, and for the next hour or so Pascoe, in *Rosa*, carefully surveyed the seabed near the land. As the waning moon rose, *Oleander* was worked further inshore and moored in three fathoms of water, parallel to the beach, about one hundred and fifty yards from the coast road. A long cable, in fact several cables joined together, led to an anchor laid well offshore.

***

As the sun rose, *Molene*, under a tired but triumphant Lieutenant Pascoe, and with a small crew recruited from both *Oleander* and *Columbine*, her sails almost idle in the light breeze, but assisted by *Columbine*'s boats, departed Anse à la Barque and stood directly out to sea.

Three hours later she sighted *Northumberland*. Pascoe hove *Molene* to and went aboard the flagship with Snowden's despatches. Pascoe was confident that the despatches would not come as a surprise to Cochrane – Snowden was capable of careful diplomacy, and knowing the value of keeping the Admiral on his side, had suggested that one of *Northumberland*'s boats with its crew should be kept at Anse à la Barque and that it could be used to take a daily report to Cochrane. He expected that the midshipmen who commanded the boat had returned with glowing accounts of the action ashore, and he was not surprised to see *Northumberland's* men crowding the decks, eager for a sight of the prize.

Cochrane was on the quarterdeck when Pascoe came aboard.

"That is a fine prize, Mr Pascoe," he said, looking at *Molene*.

"She is, Sir, pierced for forty guns. She's a beauty, very nearly new."

"My word, I'll bet she's a flyer as well."

"I think not at present, Sir, she's very heavy laden – naval stores."

"So I understand, though whether we'll be able to get a good price for them in Antigua I don't know."

Pascoe, before he could stop himself, said, "Perhaps we should sell them back to the French."

To his relief the Admiral roared with laughter: "I think Their Lordships might take a dim view of that, Lieutenant Pascoe. By God, Pascoe, that's the second laden frigate your Captain Snowden has taken – he seems to have a golden touch. Come take a glass with me. I know you'll want to be on your way, and I'll not detain you long."

***

Within twenty minutes, Pascoe had *Molene*, with a strong trade wind on her starboard bow, bearing up for Antigua, sixty miles to the north. With her small crew and damaged rigging, he could not set anything more than the courses, but she still sailed very well under her reduced canvas.

My own frigate, he thought, *even if for only a day – what a beaut!*

***

The column that left Basse-Terre before it was light, was led by Major Renaud, an experienced officer who had worked – was working – his way up from the ranks. For a West Indian island, the force at his command was impressive: a column of infantry with mounted skirmishers at its head, and with two guns at the rear, pulled by teams of mules.

Renaud, at the head of the marching men, did not know what to expect. The English had captured the battery at Anse à la Barque, but it was not clear if they were still there and, if they were, whether they intended to stay. Ominously, Major Levy, who had set out on the previous day, had not yet returned.

The column moved slowly on, men from the vanguard occasionally returning to report. The heat was quite intense, and from time to time the column stopped to rest.

Early in the afternoon, Renaud was at the rear of the column, which was proceeding down a steep hill towards the sea. He had ridden back on hearing a report that a wheel of one of the gun carriages was damaged. By the time he had got there, the problem had been overcome, and the gun was trundling forward again. He spoke encouragingly to the men at the column's rear and saw that the front two-thirds of the column had disappeared around a right-hand corner which he knew led along the seafront. He turned his horse and was just about to ride back to the column's head when he heard shots coming from the slope high above the road. A man beside him cried out and fell, and almost simultaneously Renaud felt a tremendous blow to his shoulder and fell from his horse. The last things he saw were the hooves of the mules as they galloped down the hill, trampling his body.

The road along the seafront was separated from the bright blue sea only by a narrow beach of yellow sand, on which small waves broke. As the subaltern at the head of the column rode along it, he saw a ship lying just off the land, quite a small ship. To his everlasting regret he took little notice of it until one of the men marching behind him shouted: "*Le navire, Monsieur – les Anglais*!"

With his heart suddenly thudding in his chest, he looked towards the ship, and saw that a huge flag had broken out at her masthead, and was flapping lazily in the light breeze. An English flag. Behind him, from the wooded slopes above, he heard musketry, and shouts, and from the top of the headland between him and Anse à la Barque, the sound of cannons, followed by the thudding of hooves as the vanguard galloped back along the road.

Ambush, he thought. He heard a drum beat aboard the ship, whistles blow and the man behind him shouted again: "The ship …"

She was very close to the shore, perhaps a hundred and fifty yards away, and he watched spellbound as men swarmed up her masts, guns slung over their shoulders, and others emerged onto her fo'c'stle, pulling covers from two huge bulbous-looking cannons, whose gaping black mouths seemed to be pointing directly towards him. He had heard of those guns – the English called them 'smashers'. He had only time to shout "Down!" and throw himself off his horse before they fired, one after the other, sending grapeshot whistling towards the land, into any of the soldiers who had been too slow to get down on the ground. His horse, miraculously unhurt, galloped off up the road. Men on the masts of the smoke-wreathed ship shouldered and aimed their muskets, but there was a shouted order, a whistle blew, and they did not fire. The gun crews finished reloading the smashers and swivelled them round back towards the shore.

A man on the ship's fo'c'stle shouted through a speaking trumpet: "Surrender – *Capituler.*"

The subaltern knew he had no choice. He took off his shirt, stood and waved it above his head. For a few minutes he sat on the road, unable to move, horrified by the groans and shouts of the wounded. He watched dully as two boats filled with marines set off from the ship, and started when a shadow fell over him and a voice with a strong Corsican accent said from behind him: "Are you the officer in charge?"

He looked up and saw a tall handsome man, dirty and unkempt, wearing the semblance of a naval officer's uniform, carrying an unpleasant-looking gun with fixed bayonet on a sling over his shoulder. A pair of men dressed as English sailors accompanied the man, as well as a young officer, possibly a marine, dressed almost as disreputably.

"No, the Major is in charge, he is at the rear of the column."

"The Major is at the rear of the column, but he is no longer in charge."

"You mean …?"

"Yes," said the man cheerfully, patting his gun, from whose muzzle smoke wreathed "as the English say, 'dead as a doornail'."

The subaltern groaned. "Who are you?" he asked in a shaky voice.

"You Frenchmen keep asking me that. I am Giotto Luciani, Lieutenant in the Royal Navy, and you, *Signore*, are my prisoner."

"He's not a *bandito*," said one of the men behind him, laughing.

The marines landed and the boats drew off, the guns in their bows pointing at the land. The subaltern saw that the disproportionately large gun on the bigger boat was a small Carron, and that the smaller boat, ironically for him, was called *Liberté*.

The marine officer came up to Luciani: "Sir?"

"Disarm them, weapons in piles, officers and warrants to be kept, rest can clear off. Take the guns and stores with us if we can. If not, spike the guns and fire the stores."

"Aye aye, Sir. The wounded?"

"Leave them, we'll take them off in the boats."

A few of the French soldiers dropped their muskets and ran, but most stayed to be disarmed.

***

Crouched behind the tarpaulin-covered port Carron on *Oleander*'s fo'c'stle, Kennedy watched as the vanguard of horsemen trotted past the ship moored just offshore, apparently oblivious to her menace. A few minutes after the skirmishers had passed, he saw the front of the column appear around the bend at the end of the shore road. They were marching slowly, headed by an officer on a horse. Through his glass he could see the man's face clearly, a surprisingly young man to be in command of such a body of men. His mind wandered for a moment – *what was that lad doing here, risking his life to protect a few wealthy planters?*

The officer was only a cable's length from the ship when Kennedy gave the order: "Colours," and looked aft to see *Oleander*'s huge battle ensign break out at the main peak. He nodded to the Bosun, who blew his whistle. A drum sounded and men who had been crouching or lying on the deck, concealed from the land behind the bulwarks surmounted by the hammocks in their nets, stood up, the sharpshooters climbing the rigging, rifles slung on their backs, the gun crews rushing to the Carrons on the fo'c'stle, ripping away the tarpaulins that hid them from a casual observer.

Almost simultaneously, he heard the roar of the guns on the headland astern, and rifle fire from Luciani's men on the hill behind Marigot. Ashore, the column had lost its cohesion, as men rounding the bend pushed at their colleagues in their eagerness to get away from the snipers behind them.

Kennedy saw the officer on the horse turn and stare at the ship and shout something, and turned to the Gunner, who was sighting along the barrel of the port Carron, adjusting the elevation screw: "Mr Trott, aim a little high if you please, there's no need for a massacre. Fire as you bear."

"Aye aye, Sir."

Trott carefully adjusted the gun's elevation and pulled the lanyard. The Carron roared, throwing itself back on its little trolley. He moved to the starboard smasher, which fired almost immediately. Kennedy saw French soldiers fall and blew his whistle.

"Cease fire," he shouted, "Cease fire."

He picked up his speaking trumpet, pointing it at the young officer: "Surrender, *Capitular*, Surrender."

He saw the officer wave a white shirt. "Easy work, Mr Trott."

***

Snowden, at the gun emplacement on the southern headland, watched the drama at Marigot unfold below him – the vanguard wheeling back as the cannon beside him fired, the distant sound of Luciani's rifles and the subsequent collapse in the French soldiers' discipline, and finally the fearful discharge of grape from *Oleander*'s Carrons.

As Snowden swung himself up onto his horse he turned to *Columbine*'s Second Lieutenant: "Good work, Mr West. Signal for *Columbine*'s surgeon to repair aboard *Oleander*. I think there will be employment for him. I am going down to the road."

"Very well, Sir," replied West, but Snowden had already spurred his horse towards the road to Marigot.

Chapter 30 – Basse-Terre

Men had begun to straggle back in the dark, exhausted, some wounded. They had been interviewed by Colonel Meyer, the French military commander of Guadeloupe, and Captain Barcley.

At the end of the interviews Meyer turned to Barcley: "A disaster, Barcley, a complete, horrible mess."

"You were not to know ...," replied Barcley.

"Twice we have been ambushed, walked right into it. *Oleander*, repeating what she did in Corsica. Duval says that the famous Snowden died aboard his ship, but *Oleander* is here, and if she is not commanded by Snowden, there must be an equally formidable commander. The people in Martinique have a British stronghold on Diamond Rock, which so angers the Emperor, and now we in Guadeloupe have one at Anse à la Barque. The Emperor himself ordered that Snowden must be eliminated, and now he's here. We have no choice, we must immediately inform Ernouf."

Ernouf was the governor of Guadeloupe, the man responsible for brutally suppressing the rebellion of the island's former slaves, who, having been granted their freedom during the Revolution, had fought bitterly against Napoleon's re-introduction of slavery. Sitting in General Ernouf's office, Meyer and Barcley related what had happened.

When they had finished, Ernouf gave them a shrewd look. "What are we to do, gentlemen?"

"The first thing we need, General" replied Barcley, "apart from cool heads, is reinforcement. We have men to defend the forts, but they are garrison troops, as we have seen, not really suited for offensive operations. We need first-class soldiers, and above all we need ships to deal with *Oleander* and the British frigate. Villeneuve has brought plenty of ships and troops, and now is the time to use some of them. We must report honestly to Villeneuve, tell him what has happened and request reinforcement. The matter will be taken out of our hands, perhaps, but we cannot help that. If we are not honest, the truth will soon emerge, and it is better if he hears it from us."

"I agree, Sir," said Colonel Meyer.

"You are right, gentlemen," said the General. "With your assistance I will write an urgent despatch."

***

Snowden had spent most of the day in *Columbine*'s launch. They had left Anse à la Barque in the relative cool of first light, but there was not much wind in the shadow of Guadeloupe, so the men had rowed for a considerable portion of the trip to *Northumberland*, stationed some twelve miles north-west.

Snowden was welcomed warmly aboard the flagship by Cochrane.

"I believed I should come and report in person, Sir," said Snowden.

"Quite right, Captain Snowden. Thank you. I had a report yesterday from Lieutenant Pascoe who was on his way to Antigua with that fine prize. A most promising young man, I believe."

"He is an excellent officer, Sir."

Cochrane skimmed over Snowden's report and looked up.

"It seems, Snowden, that you've been having a very interesting time ashore, with excellent results, it appears."

"Thank you, Sir. In essence I am only repeating what I have done before."

"You do yourself down, Snowden."

"Thank you, Sir. I have a suggestion which I think may be of interest."

"A suggestion, Snowden, or one of your fully formed plans?"

Snowden smiled: "I suppose the latter, Sir. Here it is ..."

***

Oleander left Marigot in the afternoon, carrying the wounded under the care of Surgeon Dawson, and the French officers who had been made prisoner. Morel and Levy, allowed to walk freely on the deck, had watched as the British ship was worked out to sea. Morel had seen Kennedy, the ship's Commander, nod to the Master and say 'if you please, Mister', heard the Bosun blow a short blast on his whistle, and watched as the ship was warped out of the bay on the long anchor cable and the sails set with hardly a word spoken, the only sound apart from the creaking of ropes being, to Morel's astonishment, a fiddler playing *Ça Ira* to encourage the men at the capstan, the sailors singing along lustily to the chorus.

He had turned to the Corsican, Luciani, who had changed by some subtle process from *bandito* into an obviously highly competent sea officer. "*Ça Ira*?" he asked.

"I am as astonished as yourself. You will have to ask an Englishman."

As Snowden had suggested, as soon as the ship was settled on her course, and was moving slowly in the light and variable winds in the lee of Guadeloupe, *Oleander's* armament was exercised. The Carrons on the fo'c'stle were fired, then the broadside, and finally there was rifle practice, the men shooting at bottles thrown overboard. Some of the men, especially the Corsicans and marines who had been using rifles for a long time, had become expert marksmen, and bottles exploded into fragments as rifle balls found their mark.

The French officers, who had been allowed on deck to exercise, watched the performance, grimly appreciative. To the crew's cheers, Kennedy stepped forward and said in a voice pitched to overcome the noise of the wind and sea: "The moment we have been waiting for – seamen against marines."

The crew cheered again as two men carrying rifles stepped forward. "For the seamen, Lieutenant Luciani, and for the marines, Sergeant Riley." There was a burst of applause.

"The chief bandito" said Morel to Major Levy as Luciani stood casually on the deck, his rifle in both hands "not the duty of an officer, I think, shooting muskets."

Levy saw Luciani test the temperature of his gun barrel by touching it with the back of his fingers. "Have you not noticed, Morel," he said "that the guns they are firing are rifles, not muskets."

Morel watched as a marine threw a bottle high in the air, and as Luciani, seemingly with all the time in the world, shouldered his rifle and, apparently without sighting along it, shot the bottle out of the air, to cheering from *Oleander's* crew.

"He may be a *bandito,*" said Levy to Morel "but he can certainly shoot."

Sergeant Riley stepped forward, a seaman threw a bottle, and Riley, similarly unhurried, shattered it.

The contest continued until Luciani missed his third bottle, and Riley hit his, prompting wild cheering from the marine contingent and catcalls from the sailors.

"Is this discipline?" asked Morel "can they run their ship like this?"

"I have never seen anything like it, I admit" replied Levy "it is a demonstration of supreme confidence, arrogance, I would say."

***

At first light next morning *Oleander* was hove to off Basse-Terre, the main town of Guadeloupe. As the sun rose, with a white flag flying at her mainmast, Kennedy took the ship into the roadstead, passing close to a departing local sloop, which went through violent manoeuvres to avoid the British schooner. Kennedy was dressed in his best uniform, and the officers and men were smartly turned out. He fired a gun, and, after a few minutes he heard an answering gun from the fort above the town, and saw a white flag break out.

Oleander anchored just off the town, and almost as soon as the sails were furled, a boat approached under a white flag, and a French naval officer climbed aboard. He looked at the marines and seamen drawn up on the deck, and then walked to where Kennedy and Luciani were standing.

"I am Captain Barcley, commander of naval forces in Guadeloupe."

"Commander Kennedy, Royal Navy." He pointed to an immaculately dressed officer, "this is Lieutenant Luciani."

"The famous Corsican" said Barcley, and then said, correcting himself, "perhaps not *the* famous Corsican, but famous enough. You were mentioned by the men that returned from Marigot, Luciani."

Luciani nodded "Favourably, I trust." Barcley looked at him, but did not reply.

"Will you accompany me to the cabin?" said Kennedy "Lieutenant Luciani, you have the ship."

In the cabin Barcley asked: "The purpose of your visit, Kennedy?"

"We wish to repatriate the men who were wounded yesterday. We have an excellent surgeon aboard, but he believes the men would be better off ashore. We also have some captured officers who we would like to release on parole."

"How many men do you have aboard?"

"Twenty five, with wounds of varying severity."

"May I visit them?"

"Of course."

***

Barcley stayed aboard as, in an operation supervised by Surgeon Dawson, the wounded were lowered into French boats, and taken ashore. When the transfer was complete, Barcley spoke to Dawson "Thank you for the care you have shown our wounded, Mr Dawson" Dawson nodded, and Barcley turned to Kennedy: "your ship, Kennedy, is very famous."

Kennedy nodded: "You are right, we have seen a good deal of action."

"How long have you been in her?"

"Since she was new."

"And Captain Snowden, he is famous as well."

"Justly so, in my opinion, Monsieur Barcley."

"Even our Emperor knows of his exploits."

"So I have heard."

"Is he aboard *Oleander* now?"

"No, he had other pressing business, as you can imagine, at Anse à la Barque. However, he requested that this letter be delivered to you. Would you care to read it in the cabin?"

Barcley read, with growing incredulity and indignation. When he had finished, he looked at Kennedy and said: "Commander Kennedy, are you familiar with the contents of this letter?"

"Somewhat familiar."

"It is a damned outrage, Kennedy, impudent. Admiral Cochrane tells us that Captain Snowden has captured part of Guadeloupe, and in the interests of humanity he warns the French military to leave the island. The French leave Guadeloupe! Are you aware, Commander, of the strength of France in the West Indies? There is a huge fleet at Martinique, carrying thousands of soldiers. Did you know of that fleet?"

"We know very well of Villeneuve's fleet, I saw it first in the Mediterranean a few weeks ago, from this very deck, and the other day we watched from the summit of HMS" he emphasised the initials "*Diamond Rock* as the ships arrived at Martinique. Impudent or not, Barcley, you have been warned."

Barcley stood and jammed his hat on his head, "I will depart now, Kennedy. I thank you for your hospitality, and for the humane treatment of our wounded and the release of the officers."

As they watched the French captain being rowed away from the ship, Dawson said to Kennedy: "That man didn't seem happy, Ken."

"He wasn't happy, Grant," replied Kennedy, "not at all. He'd just been given an ultimatum, a ridiculous demand, that the French should abandon Guadeloupe completely."

"And what was his reaction? Derision, presumably."

"No! To my astonishment, Grant, he took it seriously."

"Why?"

"He is frightened of Snowden, or at least the idea of Snowden!"

Chapter 31 – Interlude

Admiral Villeneuve, in command of the Combined Fleet of French and Spanish ships anchored in Fort de France, Martinique, had been ordered by Napoleon to take Diamond Rock, *'that symbol of insolence at the doorstep of Martinique'*, and the island's governor, Villaret de Joyeuse, had forcefully urged him to action.

Villeneuve was not about to make the same mistake as Admiral Missiessy, who had broken out of Rochefort and led his ships to the Caribbean earlier in the year. Missiessy, whose fleet included a 120-gun three-decker, four 74s and three frigates with transports carrying 3,500 troops, had been explicitly ordered by Napoleon to take *Diamond Rock*. He had not done so, returning to France after a few desultory attacks on British possessions, incurring the anger and contempt of the Emperor, who had written to the Minister of Marine:

'I am choked with indignation to learn that he did not take the Diamond ... I should infinitely have preferred him to lose a ship of the line, than he should fail to rid Martinique of that hump. I want him made aware of my anger ...'

***

Colonel Meyer's trip in the small sloop had started badly. Standing out to sea from Basse-Terre, Guadeloupe at first light, they had been horrified at the unexpected sight of HMS *Oleander* sailing into the roadstead. It was only after the sloop had put about and had crept close under the guns of the fort that they noticed that the British ship was flying a white flag. The sloop's voyage to Martinique was postponed until the purpose of *Oleander*'s visit was ascertained, and so it was not until early afternoon that the trip southward was resumed.

The sloop stood well off from the British island of Dominica and arrived at Fort de France, Martinique on the morning of the next day. Colonel Meyer was informed that Admiral Villeneuve was at the command post on the headland overlooking Diamond Rock, in company with Villaret de Joyeuse, General Lauriston, commander of the troops brought from France on Villeneuve's fleet, and the Spanish Admiral Gravina.

From the post on Diamond Head a compelling vista was unfolding. Across the narrow strip of sea, the Passe des Fours, which separated it from Martinique, stood Diamond Rock, rising abruptly from the blue sea, impossibly steep, its base fringed with breakers, green vegetation clinging onto the almost vertical slopes.

An officer handed Meyer a glass. He focused it and the detail of HMS *Diamond Rock* swam into view. He could see a wooden landing stage with a boat raised on davits, and a wall running between two batteries just above sea level. At the top, a British flag was flying, and the barrels of guns, big guns, protruded from their emplacements near the summit. He wondered briefly how the British had managed to get the guns from their ships to the summit, but he had been at Calvi, and remembered how Nelson had brought guns from his ships up cliffs and along mountain paths so that they commanded the citadel and forced its surrender.

The guns on the Rock fired occasionally, and a French ship that was sailing slowly between the Rock and the mainland fired back. She was a big ship, a two-decker, probably a 74, and there was another similar ship beating up to windward on the other side of the Rock, clearly with the intention of joining her sister. Accompanying the 74s were smaller ships, a frigate and an assortment of sloops. All of the ships were towing boats.

He handed the glass back to the officer, who took him to where Admiral Villeneuve stood with a group of senior officers, watching the ships manoeuvre.

"Colonel Meyer from Guadeloupe," said the aide, and withdrew.

"I am sure this will be good news," said Villeneuve, as he took the dispatch from Meyer.

"I am afraid not, Sir …"

Chapter 32 - Decisions

The discussion took place in *Columbine*'s cabin on the day *Oleander* returned from Basse-Terre.

"So, we riled Froggie up, Ken?"

"We did, Perce, proper riled, he is!"

"So, what will they do now?"

"They will have to come after us, or they will end up with a *Diamond Rock* in Guadeloupe. Boney won't like that."

Snowden paused. "He won't, will he? I don't think they can leave us alone, and their opportunity to get rid of us is now, with Villeneuve's fleet here."

"Can we hold them off?"

"Not a determined attack, not remotely, unless we are considerably reinforced, and that's not likely to happen."

"Shall we just abandon the place? After all, we've demolished their battery, taken the *flûte*. We're very definitely ahead. On the other hand …"

"Quitting would perhaps be the prudent thing to do, Ken, but I infer from 'on the other hand' that you think we can perhaps do a little better than that, and I agree. As I said, the French will have to do something about us – the officers we had prisoner told us that Boney was very cross about *Diamond Rock*. If Villeneuve has to report that, while his fleet was here, the English took part of Guadeloupe and he didn't do anything about it, well, I think Monsieur Villeneuve's naval career, and possibly his life, would be in some jeopardy!"

"What would you do if you were the French, Percy?"

"I'd think I'd move quickly. They can't be entirely sure that we won't reinforce Anse à la Barque, bring in more troops and use it as a beachhead to take the island. They can't afford to give us time. At the moment, they have large numbers of troops carried by Villeneuve's fleet. They must attack the *Diamond*, but that can't occupy many of them for long – we know Maurice doesn't have enough water to hold out for more than a few days. Now, they can't afford to break up their main fleet, in case Nelson catches up with them, so they won't send the big ships here, unless all of them come."

"They can't send the whole fleet, Perce."

"No, of course they can't. The ships will need repairs and re-victualling, and they can only do that in Fort de France. They can't all anchor here – it's too deep, and they can't keep station in the light variable winds. They will probably think that they need ships though, to deal with the threat of *Oleander* firing onto the coast road."

"So they'll bring frigates."

"I think they will, Ken, but it is really almost a complete guessing game. I mean, for example, they could go round the north of the island, but there are not really any good landing places to the north, and it's unlikely that their soldiers are practised in boat work. They could land the troops at Pointe à Pitre and march them over the island, but it's pretty mountainous, and it would be a hard slog for their troops, after months on the ships, and the French told Dawson that there was a lot of sickness amongst the troops."

"Could they land the troops at Basse-Terre and bring them along the coast road, like they did before, but land a smaller body just north of us and attack from the north as well? They'd need two frigates and perhaps a transport."

"I think that's most likely, Ken, but perhaps one of the frigates will approach from the north. Now, they're bound to have people watching us before long, from the south if not from the north, so if we're going to do anything, we should do it quickly. We'd better go off and speak to Cochrane. He's very experienced, and he has some pretty smart officers who are worth listening to."

"Behold a new man – *Captain* Snowden – who suddenly thinks other people are worth listening to!"

"I said 'listening to', Ken, not necessarily doing what they say!"

***

Snowden and Kennedy were both present at the meeting in *Northumberland*'s great cabin which finalised the plan. As Snowden had hinted, *Northumberland*'s captain was an intelligent man and his input was useful. As the meeting broke up, Cochrane took Snowden aside.

"Be damned careful, Snowden. We don't want to get too ambitious – remember what happened when that fool Jameson tried to make a name for himself."

"As if I'd forget," said Snowden, "we won't do a Jameson, Sir."

***

On 27 May, the attack on *Diamond Rock* began. The attacking force was enormous, including two 74s. Colonel Meyer could not help but be impressed by the spectacle taking place below him – men attempting to land on the Rock, and eventually succeeding, the British retiring to higher levels. It was only a matter of time, Meyer realised, before the *Diamond* surrendered through shortage of water or ammunition.

Villeneuve knew this as well, and was able to give some time to planning the operation to clear the English out of Anse à la Barque. He realised, all too acutely, that there must be an operation, and it must be done quickly. Given time, it was possible that the British beachhead might turn into another *Diamond Rock*, with huge forces necessary to remove their presence before it became a springboard for a British invasion of Guadeloupe. General Lauriston, the commander of the troops on Villeneuve's fleet agreed, as, with less vehemence, did Villaret de Joyeuse, the governor of Martinique.

"Swift and decisive action, gentlemen, is what is needed in this situation," declared Villeneuve. "Two frigates will be required ..."

***

Albert Duval, formerly commander of *Herault*, but now Second Lieutenant of the 74 gun ship *Intrépide*, watched as the frigate *Didon* sailed into Fort de France roadstead, signals flying from her masts.

"She's from France. Orders, without doubt," said Captain Infernet, *Intrépide*'s commander, in his rough Provençal accent, watching as a boat was lowered from the frigate. "Napoleon kicking Villey's arse."

***

Admiral Villeneuve, from his command post above *Diamond Rock*, was not cheered by the sight of *Didon* arriving from the Atlantic, giving the *Diamond* a wide berth before turning and beating back up towards Fort de France. He had a dread of receiving orders from the Emperor, which were often couched in insulting terms, and he expected that the despatches that the frigate carried would not make for easy reading.

The problem, he knew, at heart was the condition of his fleet. The Revolution had decimated the Navy's officers, and many experienced men had been removed or even guillotined, to be replaced either by officers from the merchant marine or by men promoted from the lower ranks. Some of these men were fine seamen, but the Navy had lost a great deal of expertise. France built excellent ships, probably the best in the world, but they spent most of their time in port, and neither the officers nor men had practice at handling or fighting their ships. In contrast, the ships of the Royal Navy were almost continuously at sea, and the ships, though battered, were constantly repaired and kept sea and battle worthy. The English seamen were veterans, used to handling their ships in all weathers, their fighting skills and spirit honed by constant drills and skirmishes. It seemed to Villeneuve that he was leading amateurs against professionals. Additionally, Villeneuve's ships were beset by sickness, especially amongst the troops.

When the messenger arrived, Villeneuve was sitting in his command post with General Lauriston. The despatch, when he read it, caused him to lose the power of speech for a moment, and he wordlessly passed the paper to Lauriston, who read it, his face paling.

Villeneuve, recovering, said hoarsely, "Nelson passed Gibraltar on 10th May. He must be nearly in the West Indies by now."

***

On 2 June, with Maurice and his men driven almost mad by thirst, HMS *Diamond Rock* surrendered.

Chapter 33 - Counter Attack

The soldiers that were landed at Basse-Terre on Guadeloupe for the attack on Anse à la Barque had been embarked at Toulon on Villeneuve's ships several months previously. Sickness was prevalent, and morale indifferent. The column was to be led by Colonel Juppé, an efficient if uninspiring leader who had come out from France with Villeneuve. Because Juppé had not previously served in Guadeloupe, Colonel Meyer was accompanying the expedition. After disembarkation, the men spent a couple of days at Basse-Terre exercising, and then set out northwards.

The column was arranged so that there was artillery near its front and rear. Juppé had carefully listened to the accounts of the survivors of the previous column, and to the officers who had been aboard *Oleander* as she had delivered them to Basse-Terre. They had determined that the weapons on *Oleander*'s fo'c'stle which had caused so much devastation recently at Marigot, and previously in Corsica, were Carrons, which had a limited range, much less than the long artillery pieces equipping the column. A frigate, *Nymphe*, was to sail parallel to the column on the coast road, to protect it against attack from the sea, and another, *Persephone*, was to sail north around Guadeloupe and land a smaller diversionary force on the beach at Bouillante, about three miles north of Anse à la Barque.

The first sign of trouble came just to the south of Marigot. From ahead, they heard small arms firing, and shortly afterwards one of the vanguard's horses came galloping back, its lifeless rider trailing behind with his foot tangled in a stirrup. Meyer winced at the sight. Shortly afterwards, several of the other horses returned, riderless.

"There's a bridge just ahead, Juppé, over a little river. I expect they'll have done something there."

"That boy who came back on their ship said that they had a band of riflemen, sharpshooters, led by a Corsican."

"We have our Corsican, Juppé, and it seems they have theirs. I was in Corsica myself, Meyer, and this whole thing reminds me of fighting there. Never far away from the Royal Navy, and Corsican marksmen taking pot shots."

With extreme caution, a lieutenant with several soldiers went forward to investigate. There was more firing and some of the soldiers returned, without the lieutenant.

"There's a bridge ahead, Sir," said the sergeant, "but it's down, blown up, and there's a wall across the road. A low wall, Sir, and they're firing from behind it. Devilish accurate, Sir. The river's in a big ditch - a ravine, Sir, a nasty obstacle."

"Can we flank them Sergeant?" asked Juppé.

"I don't know if we can, Sir, it would be the devil of a job to get round through the jungle."

"We'll have to bring the guns up, Sir, to get rid of them."

"Thank you, Sergeant," said Juppé.

Darkness was approaching and they had little choice but to halt the column for the night, a night that few of them would forget. They lit fires and the men started to cook their rations.

***

In the darkness, aboard *Columbine*'s launch just off the beach at Marigot, Second Lieutenant West whispered to the Gunner, "There it is, Mr Forbes, a campfire. I know the distance from here to the bridge is five hundred yards. I'll try and estimate the range to that fire. Give me a light, here, thank you."

West looked along the compass face, and then worked with ruler and dividers on a sketched chart for a few minutes. "Looks like the range is six hundred and twenty yards."

"Aye, Sir," said Forbes. He consulted a hand written table on a piece of paper, and made small adjustments to the Congreve rocket launcher, while West worked at the anchor lines until the boat was pointed exactly at the campfire ashore.

Forbes was as confident as he could be in his rockets, a weapon only recently adopted by the Royal Navy. They were generally considered to be inaccurate, but he had worked very hard to produce the best rockets he could. The moulds for the propellent were as good as the carpenter could make them, and he had carefully weighed the powder. The sticks were straight, their dimensions exactly as specified, and the weight of the completed rockets was as it should be. He'd made a good many of them in preparation.

"I think that's dead on, Guns," Said West, and the Gunner squinted over the boat's bow towards the shore, seeing that more fires were now burning. "When you're ready."

***

Colonel Juppé was sitting on a camp stool, looking forward to his dinner, when there was a loud explosion, somewhere in the woods further inland, and he heard shrapnel tear through the leaves. After a few seconds there was another one, and then another. He looked up and saw a fiery trail arc through the sky from the direction of the sea.

"*Fusée*, Rockets!" he shouted as one burst on the road in an explosion of flame and whizzing balls.

"The fires, extinguish the cooking fires!" he shouted, and the call was taken up down the column. Soon the fires were out, but the rockets continued.

"They have the range, Juppé, we must move back along the road," said Meyer.

As another rocket exploded in the trees near where they were standing, a Major, Perrin, came up to them.

"Sir, there are casualties."

"Perrin, we must fall back along the road, out of range."

"Yes, Sir. Sergeant!"

Discipline did not break down, but the retreat along the road in the dark was not the French army's finest moment, although the rockets had stopped. They kept walking for about a mile, until there was a clearing in the trees, which extended to both sides of the road. Pickets were set and the men settled down. They lit small fires, shielded from the direction of the sea by tents, the soldiers began to eat, and casualties were attended to.

"The rockets come from a ship," said Juppé, an edge of anger in his voice. "The frigate, *Nymphe,* should be protecting us against attack from the sea." He paused for a moment and added: "The men are not ready for this, I fear, after months cooped up on the ships."

"There has been little wind," replied Meyer. "When we've seen the sea from the road, it has been flat. The island is a barrier to the wind, and it is often calm on the west coast. We have undoubtedly moved faster than the ship. You are right about the men, but there are many veterans among them, and there was no panic earlier."

Juppé was just about to turn in when there was a blood chilling scream from the perimeter of the camp, and then another from the other side of the clearing. He saw muzzle flashes, and heard gunfire and the cries of men.

He yelled "To Arms", heard orders shouted, and the call of a bugle. Men ran around, bumping into each other, cursing, as they struggled to dress and take up their weapons. There was more gunfire, but eventually the soldiers were organised into lines, fairly ragged lines, and formed a square. It was a rather irregular formation, but nevertheless it was a formation, and when gunfire was again seen from the perimeter, a volley was fired towards it by the men kneeling in the first rows.

***

From the boat, Lieutenant West saw the campfires go out.

"They're probably moving away, back along the road." He said to Forbes, "how many have we got left?"

"I reckon they are, Sir. Ten remaining."

"Let's give 'em a couple more, Guns, and then call it a night. I'll turn the boat a little to starboard, and I think we should increase the range a little, say another couple of hundred yards."

After two rockets had been fired, they waited silently in the boat, but saw and heard nothing. They retrieved the anchors and rowed slowly north, back towards Anse à la Barque. After a few minutes, West heard, behind them, the sound of musketry.

"Oars," he ordered, and the boat stopped and lay quietly.

"Did you hear that, Forbes?" he asked.

The Gunner clearly had, as he was pointing in the direction he thought the shots had come from.

West, grateful for Forbes' presence of mind, quickly sighted along his compass. "Just about south-west." West had been warned that the column ashore might have a naval escort, but he was young and enthusiastic, and he did not hesitate. "Give way starboard, backwater port."

The boat swung rapidly round, and when it was heading in the right direction he called, "Oars, give way together, lively now," and the men settled into a steady but fast rhythm. Standing in the boat, he heard a few isolated shots and then a ragged but sizable volley.

"That sounded like a lot of muskets to me," said the Gunner.

"And to me," replied West, "and just inland of us. Let's have the light."

He worked rapidly with his chart and the instruments.

"I'm assuming they're going to stay near the road."

"Bound to," replied the Gunner.

"Let's say seven hundred yards, Mr Forbes. I'll keep the boat lined up with the oars."

"Seven hundred yards it is, Sir," said the Gunner, moving forward "Let me know when she's on the line."

***

After the second musket volley, with no fire returned, Juppé was beginning to hope that whoever had attacked them had either been hit or had fled. The first soldiers who had been killed, it seemed, had been victims of men who had come out of the woods carrying cutlasses. An eyewitness, one of the sentries who had been near the first man killed, said that the attackers were black men.

"Maroons," said Meyer to Juppé, and then, explaining, "there was a rebellion here a couple of years ago, before I arrived, a very nasty affair when we re-established slavery. There are people, Maroons they are called, escaped slaves, I don't know how many, who live in the forests. They have no love for us, and I think they are taking the opportunity ..."

He did not finish his sentence, for the night to seaward was lit by a rocket trail and the projectile blew up in the forest nearby, accompanied by the now-familiar patter of balls flying through the leaves.

"Where the hell is the Navy?" shouted Juppé.

***

Nymphe's commander, Captain Durand, listening to the musketry ashore, watched as a rocket crossed the sky, exhausted its fuel and arced towards the land, its progress marked by a glowing red ember, and exploded in a flash of light, followed by the sound of the blast. He hammered the rail in frustration. *The damned fools in the Army, letting the column get so far ahead of us*, he thought.

The first rocket attack had been launched from a ship or boat several miles north of where *Nymphe* was lying becalmed, but this second attack came from a ship or boat – *boat*, he thought, *unless there was more than one rocket-launching vessel, it must be rowed* – much closer to his ship.

He shouted, "Watch for the next rocket launch, try to see the boat."

There was another 'whoosh' and they saw, briefly, on the starboard bow, illuminated by the flame of the rocket, the outline of a ship's boat, a big one.

"A boat only," he said to the First Lieutenant, who was sighting along the compass.

"Yes, Sir"

Durand moved to the rail, where, in the dim starlight, he could see his ship's two boats towing alongside.

"You saw it, the English boat?" he shouted down to the Second Lieutenant in the cutter.

"Yes, Sir."

"Course is east north east" said the First Lieutenant "into the land."

"Away the boats," ordered Durand, and the two boats, phosphorescence flashing around their oars, pushed off from the ship and rowed away.

***

The Gunner was just setting up the third rocket when the man at the stroke oar of the launch said quietly to West: "Sir, I heard something. Over there." He pointed out to sea, holding his arm steady.

"Quiet, everybody," said West, and the boat's crew sat still, tense, listening in the almost complete darkness. Suddenly, out to sea, distinctly French, a voice shouted an order, followed by more voices, and noises, familiar noises.

"A ship," hissed West to the Gunner, who had joined him in the sternsheets. "They're getting a boat away. They're after us."

They lay quietly for a few more minutes.

"I see it," said the stroke oarsman.

West moved to the side of the rower and looked along his arm to where he was pointing, and suddenly he could see the outline of a ship, a big ship, a frigate, her sails hanging limply from her yards, startlingly close. He could not see the boats she had launched, but knew that they must have seen the flames from the rockets and would be heading towards them.

West was young, and reckless, and the night was very dark, illuminated only by the stars peeking through the clouds.

"Give way together, lads, easy," he commanded, and headed out to sea, away from the land. After a few minutes he said, "Oars" and then, as the boat glided to a stop, "Quiet now, men, look and listen." Astern of them, several hundred yards away, they could hear the passage of boats, more than one, but he could not tell how many, rowing fast.

And there, just behind them, was the French frigate, visible against the sky, becalmed, sails slack, occasional orders and answers clearly audible.

"Guns," he said, quietly, "how many …?"

"Three," replied the Gunner, adding musingly, "a frigate, becalmed with all her sails set. What a target!"

"Let's get in closer," said West.

The noise of the frigate's boats faded away, but the sounds of the ship grew lounder and more distinct as they approached. She was easily visible now, high above them in the darkness, silhouetted against the sky. West's heart was thudding so loudly that he was surprised that the whole boat's crew could not hear it.

He stopped the boat when he could stand the tension no longer.

"I'll line her up, Guns," he said, as the Gunner went forward to attend to his rockets.

"When you're ready," whispered West, conscious that his voice was shaking.

There was a loud 'whoosh' and the first rocket flew off towards the frigate, its trajectory almost flat, trailing flame. It briefly illuminated the ship as it flew low over her, cartwheeled as it hit something aboard, and then exploded with a deafening bang in the silence of the night.

"Too low," said the Gunner, and bent to his firing frame, making adjustments. The second rocket missed the ship altogether, flying close to her foresail, but the third, the third! Hit the sail full on, hanging there, spitting fire, until it exploded.

West sat mesmerised by the spectacle as the sail, the lowest one on the foremast, burst into flames, huge flames, with sparks flying vertically in the still air. The ship became alive with noise and shouting, but the flames spread rapidly, igniting the fore topsail.

"Sir," said the Gunner urgently, "time to go."

They saw no more of the frigate's boats. West supposed they had returned to the ship to render what assistance they could, but the trip back to *Columbine* was one he would never forget: the enormous flames on the frigate's burning mast illuminating the faces of the rowers with blood-red light, the "Oohs!" from the men as some spar or rope fell burning into the sea or onto the deck of the ship, making West think of a firework display he had watched as a boy. Before long, the land breeze sprang up and they set the sails, the boat moving quietly towards Anse à la Barque.

***

Admiral Cochrane was relaxing in *Northumberland's* cabin. He heard whistles blowing and the sound of the ship coming to life when a young midshipman was shown in by the steward.

"Captain's compliments, Sir, there's rockets being fired near the shore."

Cochrane went on deck and saw for himself the fiery parabolas of the rockets. They could see the flash of the explosions as the rockets landed and faintly hear the sound of the explosions.

Captain Tobin saw Cochrane approaching and touched his hat. "I've got the ship underway towards the firing," he said "Snowden's up to something!"

"He's always up to something, Tobin. We know he was expecting a French advance on Anse à la Barque, perhaps the rockets are associated with that."

"Quite likely, Sir"

As the 74 sailed quietly into the land, the rocket fire stopped. For two hours or so all was quiet, but then more rockets were fired onto the land, as *Northumberland* came to a stop due to lack of wind.

"I'll get the boats out," said Tobin his voice betraying his eagerness, "we might make a bit of progress."

After another pause, they saw rockets fired on a flat trajectory, a few miles ahead, and then flames, huge flames, clearly coming from a ship.

"My God," said Tobin, telescope to his eye, "unless I'm very much mistaken, that's a frigate with her foremast on fire. It must be French."

"You're correct, I believe," said the Admiral. "The French would not be firing on the land, and as far as I know they don't have the Congreve rockets. But what's firing – *Columbine, Oleander*, or one of their boats?"

"If it's a boat, it must be a plucky fellow in her, to attack a frigate."

The French ship blazed, and after a while the wind returned and *Northumberland* began to overhaul her boats, which were left towing astern. When day broke, she was close to the land, perhaps a couple of miles off, and clearly visible, quite close, was the ship that had been on fire.

"It *is* a French frigate, by God," said Tobin. "Her foremast's down." He took his telescope from his eye and turned to Cochrane: "Pretty burned around the bulwarks near the foremast. Damned lucky the whole ship didn't catch fire."

***

The first rocket fired at *Nymphe* had come without warning, and for a few moments Captain Durand seemed to have completely lost the power of speech, and indeed of movement, as the rocket hit a coaming and flew around the deck, hissing, in a shower of flame and sparks. The explosion that followed was not large, but Durand felt a ball whizz past him and heard other men call out, wounded.

"Sir," shouted the First Lieutenant, "Sir," shaking Durand out of his reverie.

"Quarters!" he shouted. "Bow chasers ready, fire at the rocket launcher when ready."

A second rocket rushed overhead, completely missing the ship.

"Get that bow chaser *ready*," he shouted, with great urgency in his voice.

He saw the third rocket coming, from the moment it left the launcher, its flame briefly illuminating a ship's boat. *His frigate, under attack from a ship*'s *boat, it seemed ridiculous*. He watched in horror as the rocket hit the foresail almost at its centre, spun wildly and exploded. The sail, which was dry as there had been no rain all day, burst into flames.

"Shall we cut the foresail halyard, Sir?" asked the First Lieutenant.

"No, keep the fire off the deck for as long as we can. Flood the magazine." He knew that down below, in the interior of the ship, men would fetch water from the pump in buckets and wet the powder room.

"Get the mainmast sails off her, cut them free and drop them on the deck. Keep everything wet." Men rushed aloft, bearing axes, and before long he heard chopping, and sails began to fall. Others threw buckets of seawater over the decks, but around the foremast their efforts were thwarted by the flaming debris falling from above. The topmast came down, with a roar, trailing burning ropes, and men fought to damp the flames. The deck was a horrible tangle of fallen sails and rigging, illuminated by the red glow of the flames engulfing the foremast. Men struggled to get the sails free of the yards and, as soon as they were free, to throw them overboard. At some time during this nightmare, Durand realised that there were no more rockets.

***

By the time morning came, the fire was out and the ship was safe. Durand was on the quarterdeck, discussing how they could get the frigate underway with the First and Second Lieutenants and the Bosun and Carpenter. The foremast was still standing – for now – but was in imminent danger of collapse.

"We must get some temporary shrouds on that foremast," said the Bosun, "that's the priority. If ..."

He was interrupted by a shout: "Sail on the port beam."

Durand and the men around him looked up and saw, to their horror, not more than two miles away, her sails shining in the light from the rising sun, a two-decked warship heading directly towards them.

"A 74," said Durand.

"That's all we need!" said the Bosun.

The First Lieutenant studied the approaching ship with his telescope. "English colours," he said, "guns run out, boats towing."

Durand knew that there was no possibility of his 38-gun ship winning a fight against the English 74. Under normal circumstances the frigate *Nymphe* would probably have been able to run away from the English 74, but she was completely disabled, unable even to turn.

Durand looked away from the approaching ship to the men around him. "Gentlemen, we are unable to fight the ship. We cannot save her, so we must save the crew. We will abandon ship. Have all the boats launched."

The shore was close and the wind light, so the boats were able to ferry a good proportion of the crew ashore before the British ship came within range and opened fire with a bow chaser. The shot bounced across the water and across the frigate's bow. As the huge 74 backed her topsails with the obvious intention of positioning herself behind *Nymphe* so as to be able to rake her end to end, Durand gave the only command he could.

"Strike the colours!"

Chapter 34 – Aftermath

Snowden's intention was not to hold his improvised fort, but to annoy the French as much as possible while minimising his own casualties. His forces were much smaller than the French, but he had managed to deploy his men and armaments in such a way that a successful attack on the beachhead, if it was defended strongly, would require considerable French resources, resources that could only come from Villeneuve's fleet.

He was fairly sure that the French would send an attacking force from Basse-Terre in the south, but he also knew that an attack from the north would be possible, though this would mean that the French would have to land men and guns on a beach rather than on a wharf, and, despite the light winds, a northerly swell was finding its way around the northern extremity of Guadeloupe, making the surf run quite high on the beaches on the west side of the island. The French knew about *Columbine*'s presence, so they would not attempt to land too close to where she lay off Anse à la Barque.

When a signal from the headland on the south side of the Anse was seen, Snowden rode over and, almost as he arrived, heard the familiar sound of rifle fire – contact with the enemy. The French did not appear on the coast road at Marigot, so he assumed that Luciani had delayed them at the demolished bridge. He returned to the improvised fort at Anse à la Barque as night fell, only to return to the south as Congreve rockets were fired from *Columbine*'s launch and landed amongst the campfires visible on the road. Standing nest to Marine Captain Ferrier, he saw the French campfires extinguished and heard the faint sound of voices and equipment as the French withdrew.

"They are returning back along the road," said Ferrier. "Magnificent work from West and your '*bandito*', Sir."

"Preparation, Ferrier, that's the key to it."

"I agree, Sir."

"Still no attack from the north," said Snowden.

"It will come," replied Ferrier.

"I believe it is very likely" replied Snowden, "but there are not many good landing places north of us, especially with this swell running. *Northumberland's* closer inshore now, keeping watch, and Kennedy's taking *Oleander* on a cruise northward at first light."

Later in the night, Snowden watched and listened as musket fire broke out on the road south, first individual shots and then ragged but large volleys. The French were clearly being attacked, but Luciani's orders were to retire after attacking the French at the blown-up bridge. The only attackers Snowden could think of were the Maroons, people like Oliver and Andre who had escaped from slavery and lived in the forests.

Snowden did not know of the presence of the French frigate, which had crept slowly north in the night, so West's attack on her came as a surprise. Snowden saw the rockets fired from *Columbine's* launch, their trajectory almost flat, and then the blaze on the frigate's foremast, starkly illuminating the rest of the ship. He expected the entire ship to catch fire, but the blaze gradually died down. He was beside himself with anxiety, wanting to take *Columbine* and capture the enemy frigate, but knowing that if he did, he would leave the fort without cover and the means of evacuation.

As dawn lightened the sky, he was joined by a jubilant West. "Did you see it, Sir?" he said, without preliminaries, "the Froggie frigate?"

"I certainly did, West! Good morning" said Snowden, "you've had quite a night of it! It seems that you and your launch have considerably damaged the enemy. My congratulations."

"Thank you, Sir," replied West, "Mr Forbes is an artist with the Congreves! When I saw that frigate, becalmed, I realised we would probably never have such an opportunity again." There were cries from the men around them, and he paused and turned his head: "Sir, look, out to sea."

In the brightening daylight, they saw *Northumberland*, the sun reflecting on her sails, making her way towards the crippled frigate, whose boats, heavily laden, were ferrying men ashore from the frigate.

"They're abandoning her, Sir," said West, "amazing. I've defeated a frigate with a ship's launch!"

Snowden, realising that *Northumberland's* diversion close inshore to take the frigate, south of the Anse meant that the approach to the north would not be covered, replied distractedly: "So you have, West."

West, unabashed, continued: "We're off again directly, Sir, soon as the men are fed. Forbsey … er, Mr Forbes, the Gunner, wants to have a last look at the mortar on the beach."

But Snowden had turned, and was issuing orders.

***

"She's struck, by God," said Captain Tobin to Admiral Cochrane, and then, "My compliments to the First Lieutenant, I wish to speak to him directly."

A midshipman ran down to *Northumberland*'s lower gun deck, and minutes later, the First Lieutenant appeared.

"Sir," he said and then, looking forward, "she's struck."

"She has indeed, Mr Ratcliffe," said Tobin, "you've little choice with no sails and a 74 bearing down on you. If you please, take the launch and the gig and take possession of her. We'll pass a hawser to tow her off directly. The sea breeze is coming up, so we'll have to be smart about it."

"Aye aye, Sir." Ratcliffe hurried off, giving a stream of orders.

***

As the day broke, Kennedy took *Oleander*, towing *Liberté*, north, close into the shore so as to keep the wind – 'within two pistol shots of the land' was the advice given in the most widely used pilot book. Without Luciani and the shore party, the ship was undermanned, and Kennedy was tense, realising that, as the French had attacked from the south, there was a good possibility that they would do the same from the north, and that with *Northumberland* engaged elsewhere, the enemy could have arrived unobserved.

As they sailed slowly along, the sea breeze, blowing towards the land, increased as the island warmed. He sat on a stool and ate the breakfast that Cox the steward had brought him, burgoo, oatmeal liberally sweetened with molasses. Around him, the crew were doing the same, chopping bananas and mangos onto their burgoo, laughing, exchanging banter. Despite his anxiety, as he drank his coffee, he was conscious of the great beauty of the island, the forest-covered mountains with mist on their peaks, the sea bright blue with flying fish escaping from unseen predators below, and the green vegetation ashore.

About three miles north of Anse à la Barque, they rounded a headland and were able to look into the Bay of Bouillante, a wide bight with a low rocky beach. Though they were on the west side of the island, protected by the land from the ocean waves, enough swell was making its way round the north of the island to make the shoreline white with surf.

Behind the headland, moored parallel to it, just off the beach, was a frigate, a big French frigate. She was rolling in the swell, and boats were alongside, into which men were climbing. On the frigate's decks, soldiers were drawn up, waiting their turn in the boats. There were boats near the beach, attempting to land men through the surf.

"Rather them than me, " said Spurling, *Oleander's* Master, pointing, and Kennedy saw that one of the boats, a heavy launch perhaps thirty feet long, had got herself broadside to the surf, and men in the water were trying to stop her surging back and forth in the waves, "I can't make out how this northerly swell gets right in here."

As the drum beat to quarters, and whistles blew, Kennedy called out "Mr Appleby," and when the Master's Mate appeared, gave him a hastily scribbled note, "take *Liberté* and get this back to Captain Snowden. Have a good look round before you go, in case there are any questions. I'm going to see if I can disrupt this landing a bit, and then take *Oleander* north and wait for the frigate in case she comes out. It's in the note."

"Aye aye, Sir, best of luck."

"And to you, Appleby."

Oleander slowed briefly, to allow Appleby and his men to board *Liberté*, and the boat was soon on its way south, back towards Anse à la Barque.

The French frigate was perhaps three-quarters of a mile from *Oleander*, which was making five knots. *Nine minutes*, thought Kennedy, as the men ran barefoot and silent to their stations.

He spoke to the warrant officers around him: "We're going to try to get directly ahead of her and rake her with the smashers, see if we can cut some of her rigging. Hello, she's seen us." He pointed to the frigate, which was encumbered by the boats alongside which were crashing into each other, despite the booms rigged to keep them apart. As they watched, a long gun barrel which had been suspended above a waiting boat was unceremoniously dumped into the boat with considerable force. Men who had been climbing over her sides jumped into the boats, which set off for the shore.

Spurling, the Master, looked up from his work on the navigation table.

"How far to the frigate?" asked Kennedy.

"Three cables length," replied Spurling.

Four minutes, thought Kennedy, and called up to Iris at the foremast crosstrees: "Clear, Iris?", referring to the condition of the seabed.

"Can't see nothing, Mr Kennedy, sand and grass I reckon. Frigate's all excited though. Mans aloft, getting sail on."

"Guns ready," reported Trott, "I'm going up to the fo'c'stle head."

"Get straight back to the deck guns once you've fired the smashers, Trott" said Kennedy to the Gunner as he ran forward, and then to the Master "Helm hard down on my mark, Mister, when we get past the frigate."

"Aye aye, Sir."

Spurling turned to the quartermasters at the wheel: "You heard that. One cable" he said to Kennedy.

One minute.

Kennedy said to Spurling "Helm up a little, so the port smasher bears". The ship turned to starboard, heading into the land, as Kennedy drew his sword and held it over his head. The frigate was close now, her bowsprit high above the low-built *Oleander*, men aboard her peering over the rail, while others frantically hauled on ropes, trying to get the ship under way. *Too late, Froggie,* thought Kennedy.

"Bearing now!" shouted Trott from the fo'c'stle.

Kennedy yelled "Fire!" and brought his sword down.

The port Carron on the fo'c'stle fired, sending grapeshot over the frigate's bow, its trajectory probably too high to hit the men on deck, who had sensibly decided to lie down, but Kennedy saw cordage part aloft, and the foretopmast stay unravel and then part, to cheers from *Oleander's* crew. He saw the men from the port smasher, its work done, run to the starboard broadside guns.

"Down your helm," ordered Kennedy, and the men spun the wheel. As soon as she turned, the starboard Carron fired, sending shot over the frigate's deck and into her rigging. For a moment, Kennedy thought he had misjudged it, and the ships would collide, but *Oleander* swung clear, her rigging passing within feet of the frigate's jib boom, which, with its stay to the masthead parted, was on the point of cracking, bending down towards the sea.

"Starboard broadside," yelled Kennedy, and as *Oleander* surged past the French ship, her long deck guns fired, one by one, sending more shot into the frigate's rigging in the hope of disabling her. The frigate, though, was no slouch, and her bow guns returned fire.

"Her broadside's obstructed by the boats alongside" said Spurling, ducking as a roundshot screamed overhead, "luckily for us."

Oleander had now turned and was heading north-west, out of the bay, moving at about five knots. Kennedy looked back at the frigate, which, despite the jib boom dragging in the water, and the wobbling foretopmast, had succeeded in setting some sail. She was now almost broadside on to the onshore sea breeze, and soldiers were pushing their way into the boats.

"He'd be better off staying at anchor," said Spurling, reviewing the scene, "he'll have her ashore if he doesn't mind out." And then, "No he can't, her cable's parted. Grapeshot must have cut it."

As *Oleander* steadied on her course, away from the frigate, with the intention of blocking the French ship's path northwards, the frigate, despite her damaged rigging, clawed off the land, men working frantically on her deck and aloft.

"Good man" said Spurling, appreciatively, studying the French ship, and then "smartly handled" as she tacked, heading north west, out of the Bay.

***

They heard the distinctive roar of *Oleander's* Carrons almost at the same time as Appleby arrived in *Liberté* to report to Snowden in the fort. Snowden knew what it meant even before he read the note – Kennedy had found the French to the north.

"Signal *Columbine* to get under weigh, and that I'm about to join," ordered Snowden, and to Appleby, "Take me to *Columbine*."

The ship was already moving as Snowden climbed aboard.

"Mr Baker," he said to the First Lieutenant, "there's a French frigate, a forty gunner, in Bouillante, about three miles north."

"I heard the Carrons, Sir. Kennedy's got a nerve, if he's attacking a frigate with his schooner!"

"Yes, Baker, he's not short of nerve!" He slapped the rail: "Let's get this thing moving."

"My pleasure, Sir," said Baker, smiling.

***

The French frigate sailed out of Bouillante Bay, hard on the wind, against the sea breeze, the wreckage cut away, and men working to repair the damage. *Smart work indeed*, thought Kennedy.

The lookout shouted, "On deck there, *Columbine*'s under weigh."

Kennedy looked up and saw the British frigate's sails to the south. Even damaged, the French ship was a fast sailer, and she was making good progress north east, out to sea. She couldn't catch *Oleander*, but Kennedy realised that unless she was slowed in some way, *Columbine* would not be able to overhaul her without leaving Anse à la Barque unsupported. The only means of interfering with the Frenchman's escape was *Oleander*. *Three miles*, he thought, Columbine's *three miles away. half an hour at best, we have to stop the Frenchman for half an hour.*

"Mr Spurling," he said, "we have to get athwart the Frenchman, get some more shot into her rigging, slow her down if we can. Let fly the topsail sheets briefly, and signal ENGAGE THE ENEMY MORE CLOSELY."

Kennedy hoped that the French commander would see the signal and believe that there was another ship, apart from *Columbine*, within sight.

"Aye aye, Sir."

Kennedy walked over to where Gunner Trott was working to ream out the touchhole of a gun. "Mr Trott, load with bar and chain, I want to have another try at damaging the Frenchman's rigging."

They tacked the ship so that the wind was on *Oleander's* port quarter, and waited, tensely, across the course of the French frigate. Her commander, aware of *Columbine* astern of him, clearly realised what *Oleander* was trying to do. He bore away a little, and *Oleander* reduced sail to keep across him. He tried bearing up, with a similar result. With minute alterations of course and speed, Kennedy tried to shepherd the French frigate so that she was hard on the wind and could only turn to starboard, away from the wind.

The French frigate was perhaps half a mile away when she fired her bow chasers, but the guns' elevation was too low, the shots falling harmlessly into the sea between the two ships, to derisive cheering from *Oleander*'s crew, who waved their hats insultingly. Four more times she fired, three missing, but one shot tore into *Oleander*'s hull, on the waterline, amidships, with an enormous crash, sending spray over her decks.

A carpenter's mate ran up shouted "Hole on the waterline, Sir", and dashed back down below. The French frigate was close now, so close that Kennedy could clearly make out the individual men on her decks.

"Steady, lads," shouted Kennedy, and then "Starboard broadside - Fire!" Oleander's guns fired on the uproll, through the French ship's rigging. Without waiting to see the result, Kennedy said: "Tack her now, Mr Spurling, get that shot hole out of the water."

For a moment, the schooner hung in irons, directly into the wind, but then, as she always did, she came round, went onto the other tack and started to make way. *Oleander* was fast out of stays, and her crew, honed to perfection, got the sails drawing immediately, but, Kennedy realised, they were too late – the frigate was overhauling her as she gathered way, and her devastating broadside would soon bear.

"BELOW" he shouted, "EVERYONE BELOW EXCEPT GUN CAPTAINS. LIE DOWN." Men ran for the companionways.

For what we are about to receive, he thought, *may the Lord ...*

There was a shout from forward – "Her mizzen!" – and he saw the frigate's mizzen mast slowly collapse, hitting the rail on its way down, even as her broadside fired.

"Starboard battery, fire," he shouted, and as *Oleander's* puny guns returned fire, he was aware of balls hitting the ship, of splinters whizzing and men crying, but when the smoke cleared, *Oleander* was still sailing, her sails and rigging intact. In contrast, the French frigate was almost stopped, the mizzen mast and sails dragging alongside, men working with axes to cut it away.

He looked astern and saw *Columbine*, less than a mile away. The Carpenter approached. "What's the damage, Mr Trimingham?"

"That Frenchman throws quite a weight, Sir. Four holes in the hull, Sir, some broken frames. The first one that hit's on the port waterline, and now we've got three on the starboard side. We're making water, quite bad, no chance of keeping ahead of it until we get patched up. I'll get over the side in a chair to work from the outside, but if you could keep her upright for now I'd be grateful."

"I'll do what I can, Chips."

"Deck there, I see *Northumberland*, just coming round the headland, she is."

***

From *Columbine*'s deck, Snowden watched in a state of extreme tension, with Baker by his side, as Kennedy interposed *Oleander* between the French frigate and the open sea.

"My God," said Baker, as the frigate's mizzen mast came slowly down, "that'll slow her down." And then, as the French ship fired her broadside at *Oleander*, "Poor bastards".

Snowden watched, appalled, as balls struck the side of his old ship. By the time *Columbine*'s bow chasers were within range of the French frigate, the massive sails of *Northumberland* were clearly visible astern. Snowden knew that the French had seen her too and must realise that resistance was useless. The French ship, her mizzen mast missing, foretopmast and jib boom missing, could not sail close to the wind and she was gradually being pushed into the land. There was no possibility of her being able to claw off. Suddenly, her helm was put up and she headed for the shore.

"Going to beach her, by God," said Snowden to Baker, and almost immediately the French ship grounded, some men clambering over her sides and swimming for the shore, others sliding down ropes from the bowsprit and landing almost directly on the beach.

"Shall we fire on her, Sir?"

"I don't think we will, Baker. There can be almost nobody left aboard her, so there's no point. We don't want to damage her any more, it will only reduce her value. The danger is that they set her on fire. Take Perkins and the launch and the gig, go and secure her, quick, now."

***

Columbine was moored fore and aft so that she was parallel to the beach, not far from the grounded French frigate, and *Northumberland* slowly worked herself into the Bay of Bouillante, where she moored similarly.

"Signal from flag, Sir," reported Fisher, the young midshipman, interrupting Snowden, who was gazing fixedly at *Oleander*, "You're required to repair aboard *Northumberland*. She's sending a boat."

"Very well, Mr Fisher, thank you. Reply to *Northumberland* and ask her to pick me up from *Oleander*."

Snowden turned to the Fourth Lieutenant who was standing nearby. "Atkinson, pass word to Mr Dawson and Chips, they're to accompany me in the yawl to *Oleander.* They're to take their tools and as many mates as possible to render assistance. You have the ship, Mr Atkinson."

***

Oleander had anchored, but she was obviously lying low in the water, and Snowden could hear the familiar monotonous rhythm of her pumps as they approached. Trimingham, dangling over the side in a chair, was attempting to nail a lead patch over a splintered hole, gasping for breath as the ship's rolling ducked him underwater. "We'll be with you directly, Chips," shouted Snowden as the boat passed, and the carpenter waved his hammer in reply without turning. Snowden climbed aboard *Oleander*, saw that the quarterdeck was empty and immediately went down the companionway. Kennedy, and the crew, those that were not ashore, were working to keep the ship afloat, pumping, shifting cargo, hammering nails into patches.

Kennedy turned as Snowden touched him on the shoulder. "How are you doing, Ken?" he asked.

Kennedy started and turned "Been better, Perce!" he said through a mouthful of nails.

They heard a boat arrive alongside, and men, some of them carrying tool chests, poured down the companionway. "Looks like *Northumberland's* sent some bodies." Snowden remarked, "You'll be all right now."

But *Oleander* had suffered grievously from the French frigate's broadside. Thanks to Kennedy ordering the men below before the frigate's broadside struck, no men were killed, but several from her small company had been wounded, some seriously, and the ship's hull had been damaged, with ragged holes, and broken frames.

"I have to leave you know, Ken, the Admiral calls."

Kennedy waved distractedly, and turned back to his work.

***

As Snowden was piped aboard the flagship, the Admiral came forward to meet him, a smile beaming on his face.

"Splendid work, Snowden, absolutely splendid."

"Thank you, Sir."

"And Kennedy, in *Oleander*, stopping that frigate."

"He did very well, Sir, and not a man killed. Got them all below before the frigate fired her broadside."

"Thank God for that."

"*Oleander's* leaking, but Kennedy's got plenty of men and gear now, he'll be able to get her to Antigua."

Cochrane nodded, smiling: "Three frigates, Snowden, what a cruise!"

"Well, Sir, only two until we get that one off the beach, but what a difference a 74 makes!"

"It certainly does, when you're up against frigates" replied Cochrane, and then looking at the beached frigate said: "She'll come off almost by herself when the sea breeze goes down."

Snowden nodded. Despite his reputation for risk taking, he was at heart a cautious man, a man who would wait until the cards were stacked in his favour. His success was essentially due to his ability to seize the opportunities that he either made, or came his way, while at the same time recognising risks and carefully evaluating them before taking action. The handling of the frigate in the action against *Oleander* had convinced him that the French had at least one highly competent commander, and he did not relish the prospect of recovering the frigate once the enemy became organised enough to protect her from the land.

"As long as she doesn't bump too hard on those rocks and start a plank."

"Swell's not so bad as it was earlier." A gust of wind blew through the open stern windows.

"There's the trade coming back," said Captain Tobin. As the land cooled, the sea breeze which blew near the coast dropped, and the north-east trade wind, coming over the mountains and blowing offshore, reasserted itself. They felt the great ship heel slightly, and from the deck they heard shouts.

Tobin stood up. "I'll go on deck and see what's going on."

"What's next, Snowden?" asked the Admiral "there's a good deal of unfinished business ashore."

"There is, Sir. I don't think the people that have just landed here will represent much of a threat – they probably left most of their arms behind on the frigate, but judging by the campfires last night there was a pretty significant force advancing from the south. They've been annoyed by Luciani, no doubt, and by the rockets last night, but we can't hold the fort indefinitely against them, and I believe it is best for us to get out as soon as we can. If you've no objection, Sir, I'd like to take *Columbine* back to the Anse, and make the necessary arrangements directly."

The Admiral, a veteran of shore operations, paused before replying. His rank was far in advance of Snowden's, but in reality, he knew that this was Snowden's operation, and that Snowden was, as politely as possible, giving him his orders. Cochrane was a clever man, an astute politician, and appreciated that Snowden's success would reflect positively on him.

"I shall bring *Northumberland* back to the Anse as soon as I have the frigate" he said, "to cover the retirement. I will ask Tobin to make sure all the boats are prepared."

"Thank you, Sir, that would be most welcome. If you'll excuse me, I'd best get back to my ship."

"Once again, Snowden, thank you, but we must be very careful not to incur any losses after our success."

As Snowden walked onto the deck, his sleeve was grabbed by an exultant Tobin.

"There's the French frigate, Snowden, come off by herself. My word, Percy, you've certainly livened things up!"

Snowden looked, as the French frigate, lightened by the departure of hundreds of men, responded to the offshore wind and drifted towards the sea. He saw his own frigate, which was directly in the path of the abandoned French vessel, set her topsails and heave in her bower anchor cable.

"Indeed, Tobin, she seems to be eager to volunteer for His Majesty's service."

Tobin reflected for a moment and said, smiling "Well, Snowden, it seems that on the plus side *Columbine*'s taken a frigate, but on the negative side you're down by a kedge warp."

Snowden laughed: "It's a trade I'd willingly take, but the kedge's on a grass line, so no loss." A grass line was made of coir, not as strong as conventional ropes, but it floated, and so *Columbine*'s kedge anchor could be easily recovered from a boat.

"I'm going to put our Second aboard the prize, Snowden, if you've no objection, and get her to Antigua as soon as possible. She should be able to sail if she's carefully handled, and Keyes is a good seaman."

Though Baker, *Columbine's* First Lieutenant, was already aboard the prize, Snowden wanted him back in *Columbine*, and did not object. "Very well" he said, "I'm going back to the fort."

Chapter 35 – Besieged

They had seen, out to sea, fire illuminating the sky. A man climbed a tree to get a better look, then came to report to Colonel Juppé.

"It's a ship, Sir. The sails are on fire."

"That's our naval support gone, I think, Meyer," he said to his fellow colonel.

When the dawn broke, bringing almost immediate daylight, Juppé and Meyer forced their way through the woods until they had a view of the sea. Just off the land they saw the French frigate, her foremast a smoking ruin. Boats, crowded with men, rowed towards the shore, and others, empty, returned to the ship.

"They're abandoning her," observed Juppé, fascinated by the sight – "Why? She is merely damaged."

"That's the reason," replied Meyer, pointing to where a huge ship, flying a British ensign, was making her way towards the crippled frigate. "A 74, if I'm not mistaken." He paused, "A frigate, even one that was not disabled, could do nothing against such a ship."

Juppé felt despair wash over him.

"May I suggest, Juppé," said Meyer, "that we get going quickly. The 74 will be engaged with taking the frigate and probably towing her away. The coast road at Marigot will be impassable if the English station that ship just off the land."

Juppé realised he was right, and the column got moving directly after breakfast had been eaten. They stopped on the road where the first rocket attack of the previous night had taken place, and a large party of skirmishers went cautiously forward, moving through the woods at the side of the road. The English rifles fired with murderous accuracy from the wall across the road, but the veteran French soldiers did not retreat this time, instead taking cover and returning fire, advancing towards the enemy, tree by tree. After fifteen minutes or so, the English, clearly realising that they did not have the manpower to stop the French, broke away from their positions behind the wall across the road and disappeared into the woods.

A messenger was sent back, and shortly afterwards the column halted just short of the fallen bridge and Colonel Juppé came forward with Meyer.

"We can get the men over that, slowly," said Juppé, looking at the ravine in which the river ran, "but I'm not sure about the guns or the …" He stopped speaking as they heard a distant bang. Both men, experienced soldiers, knew immediately what it was, and that they had fallen into a well-prepared trap.

"Mortar!" shouted Juppé, "Down!" as the bomb landed in the trees near where the troops were waiting and exploded in a hail of shrapnel, which tore through the undergrowth. As men got back to their feet, rifle fire came with deadly accuracy from the woods ahead of them. A man fell, but the French skirmishers knelt behind trees and returned fire, though their muskets were outranged.

There was another bang and a further explosion in the woods, closer to the road this time. Juppé had had enough. "They've trained the mortar on the road near the bridge," he said to Meyer, and then turned and shouted: "Fall back along the road."

"I'm going to see if I can spot the mortar," yelled Meyer, as the troops, who needed no further urging, made their way back along the road, lying on the ground as they heard the mortar fire.

Meyer pushed his way forward through the undergrowth until he had a view of the coast. He saw a puff of smoke come from a clump of trees near the beach and heard the thump of the mortar as it fired. The shell arced through the air and landed near the road with a terrific explosion. A ship's boat lay just off the land, the large cannon in her bow trained on the shore.

They've set that up well in advance, he thought, *we can't take it quickly, not without naval support.* He heard rustling in the woods in front of him and out of the corner of his eye saw a figure move between trees. The man, a black man, raised a musket to his shoulder ...

***

Luciani, lying behind the rough earthen wall across the road, ducked as the first mortar round exploded in the woods. *Good shooting,* he thought – the practice they had had over the last few days had precisely targeted the mortar on the road, with Luciani spotting for Gunner Forbes, who had laid it with his usual precision. *Columbine*'s marines were manning the weapon, under Forbes' direction.

After the third mortar round, he peered over the top of the wall and saw what he knew was a senior officer getting to his feet and clearly ordering a retreat. Another officer, probably a colonel, made off into the woods. With cold deliberation, Luciani put his rifle to his shoulder, and, resting the barrel on the wall, carefully aimed at the officer on the road and gently pulled the trigger – *for Fede,* he thought, as he reloaded, watching the man collapse. A junior officer went to the man lying on the road, lifted up his head and then gently laid it back down.

You should have run away, you French bastard, thought Luciani as he shot the second man. Riley's rifle fired, its muzzle pointing around a tree at the side of the road, and another French officer fell. The combination of mortar fire and sniping was too much for the men at the front of the column, who retired back along the road.

A black man emerged from the woods behind Luciani, a musket carried carelessly in one hand and a bloody *something* in his other, which he waved at the Corsican. Luciani returned the wave as the man disappeared back into the woods.

"Was that ...?" said Riley.

"I don't know what you call it" replied Luciani. He stopped reloading his Baker and gestured towards the top of his head "the hair."

"A scalp" said Riley "he was waving a scalp."

"Scalp" repeated Luciani "my English word for today," he thought for a moment: "Nobody likes the French."

Luciani had sent his report back to Snowden, and he was resting by the side of the road with the men, eating the fruit they had bought from the escaped or freed slaves who lived in shacks nearby, when Lieutenant Ferrier, the commander of *Columbine's* marines, arrived on horseback. In the last few days, working closely together to prepare the ambush, Ferrier and Luciani had formed a close relationship.

"Ah" said Ferrier, reining in "the chief *bandito* and his men."

"Compliment accepted, Ferrier."

Ferrier dismounted, and signalled for Luciani to join him a few yards from the men. "I've come from the fort, Giotto, we're clearing out."

"Clearing out? I thought we were just getting started."

"So did I, but I think Snowden wants to quit while we're ahead. And, Giotto, we're very far ahead" he briefly brought Luciani up to date.

"Well," said Luciani, "I see what you mean. We certainly do seem to be well in credit, and if the Old Man says its time to go" he shrugged "he's probably right."

"Best of luck" said the marine, "I'm going down to the beach to show the Navy how to load a mortar into a boat."

A horseman arrived at the fort with a despatch from Luciani, and after Snowden had read it, he went with Kennedy to *Northumberland*, where they were warmly greeted by Admiral Cochrane and Captain Tobin. Cochrane, whose recent career had not been rewarded with great success, was almost light headed with joy, and he went so far as to embrace Kennedy.

"Well done, young man," he beamed, "you can be sure that I will favourably mention you in my report."

"Thank you, Sir."

Snowden said, "Sir, I've just had notice from Mr Luciani, *Oleander's* second, who has been ashore ..."

"We've heard all about Lieutenant Luciani," said Tobin, "the *bandito*!"

"He seems to be a highly effective officer," said Cochrane, "though perhaps rather unconventional in his approach. I'd like to have him to dinner, he must be a most interesting man. He's going in my report as well, you may be sure of that."

"Well, yes, Sir, Luciani is interesting, and he's an experienced fighter ashore. It but it seems from his despatch that the French column that had been approaching from the south has been stopped at the bridge. Luciani says that both of its senior officers, Colonels, are dead, and indeed that he took care of one of them himself – he's a deadly shot with the Baker. Luciani thinks that the column is not likely to advance further today, and unless it gets naval support, it may even return to Basse-Terre."

"Does he, by God!"

"He does, and that is also the opinion of my marine officer, Ferrier. It seems that Mr West's rockets ..."

"Mr West, indeed," said Cochrane "and his rockets – another one for the despatch."

"Yes, Sir, Mr West, in combination with the sniping and the mortaring, to say nothing of the death of two senior officers, has sent them back in some disorder. Apparently, the Maroons have been attacking as well, Sir."

"Have they! Well, Snowden, what do you want to do now? I'm still for pulling out, while we have the opportunity, before Villeneuve turns up and ruins everything."

"Yes, Sir, with your leave, I'll go ashore and supervise the dismantling of the fort."

Chapter 36 – Abandoned

Snowden went ashore, and the work of dismantling the fort commenced. Guns were spiked and thrown over the cliff into the sea, and some were filled with sand and shot, and blown apart. Supplies were taken off by boat from Pascoe's Landing. In the middle of the activity, a marine came up to Snowden.

"Begging your pardon, Your Honour, but there's a black man here. He keeps saying '*Capitaine*' and I think he'd like a word with you, Sir."

"Very good, thank you. Please bring him to me."

He shouted to where the former slave Oliver was working and beckoned him over.

"Oliver, can you translate for me?"

"I will do my best, Sir."

"He's a Maroon, Sir," said Oliver, after listening to the man's story, "their captain. He's been fighting the French. He says they killed several Frenchmen in the column. What he wants, Sir, are weapons, muskets and ammunition. He says he can make good use of them against the French. I think he's right, Sir."

Snowden thought quickly. "I don't think I can give you any weapons, Sir."

Oliver translated, and the Maroon became disconsolate.

"But it is always possible that some things will be overlooked when we leave."

The Maroon looked at him in hope as Oliver translated.

"In particular, we may overlook things in that storeroom there." Snowden indicated its location by a nod of his head.

The man smiled and said, "Thank you, *Capitaine*."

***

By dusk, the fort was abandoned. The last act, after lowering the flag and chopping down the flagpole, was the demolition of Pascoe's Landing.

The British squadron that left Anse à la Barque was ragged but triumphant. *Oleander* was in the van, patched up, her leaks under control. The French frigate, *Persephone*, that had lost her mizzenmast to *Oleander*'s fire, proceeded under her own canvas, a stumpy mizzen mast having been hastily rigged to give balance. *Northumberland* towed the *Nymphe*, the frigate with the burned foremast, and the undamaged *Columbine* kept to the rear of the squadron, under very reduced canvas to avoid overrunning the towed frigate. At first, the ships were in the lee of Guadeloupe and progress was very slow, but their speed suddenly increased as they neared the northern tip of the island. The sixty-mile trip northward to Antigua, close hauled in the fresh trade wind, was slow but uneventful, and the ships arrived in English Harbour at noon on the following day.

***

At the start of the French attack on HMS *Diamond Rock*, the weather was unusually hazy, and the British lookouts on the northern headland of St Lucia, twenty miles to the south, could not see the Island. Some of the French ships preparing to attack *Diamond Rock* were driven south by an unusual combination of wind and current and passed close to St Lucia, where they were seen by the British lookouts. Unfortunately, at least from the British perspective, haze prevented the lookouts from observing the ships as they returned north, and General Brereton on St Lucia assumed, wrongly, that Villeneuve's fleet was heading south, and word to this effect was sent to all the British islands, generating a great deal of concern.

On 4 June, Nelson and his fleet arrived in Barbados, to be told that Villeneuve had been seen heading south, and was likely by now to be in Trinidad. Nelson immediately sailed south, but soon realised he had been misled, and turned north, cursing General Brereton.

***

The British had not evacuated the fort at Anse à la Barque too soon, for on 6 June Admiral Villeneuve and his fleet left Fort de France in Martinique and headed north on their way back to Ferrol in northern Spain. On their way, they stopped at Guadeloupe, in Basse-Terre roadstead, and learned the news of the attack on Anse à la Barque and the loss of the frigates. The troops were re-embarked and the fleet lost no time in getting underway, but when they passed Anse à la Barque, the English had gone. The party sent ashore to investigate found nothing but wreckage and broken guns, and was fired on by musketeers hiding in the undergrowth, who, unusually for the Maroons, seemed to have no lack of ammunition.

Chapter 37 – Baltimore

They had seen no land since they had departed from the Gironde nearly a month before, but that morning, as dawn broke and the day slowly brightened, it was clear that a landfall was imminent. The coast was close – after nearly a month at sea, they could smell it, and land-based birds flew around them. The brilliant blue of the Gulf Stream had faded, and the water was now a murky green.

A providential break in the clouds at noon on the previous day had allowed them to get a good shot of the sun, so their latitude was reasonably well established, but the overcast nights had prevented any lunar observations for several days, and their longitude was only an educated guess. In the light wind, they hove *Payoff* to and sounded, the French Admiral Morlaix and *Payoff*'s American skipper, Captain Molineux, standing next to the Bosun as he retrieved the sounding lead. ,

"Six fathoms," said the seaman, examining the base of the sounding weight, which had been armed with tallow. "Sand and broken shell."

Molineux, Morlaix and the Mate, who had just joined them, all took a pinch of the sand, feeling it between their fingers.

"It's pretty much the same, hereabouts," said Molineux. "We'll get her sailing and keep our eyes skinned. Let's have some grub." He turned to the Mate: "You have her, Mister."

The ship had been well provisioned in France, and so the breakfast, supplemented by fish which had been caught the day before, was ample. "Well, Odile," said Molineux, "the trip's nearly over. Are you looking forward to America?"

"I'm certainly looking forward to seeing Dominique and Jacques, and I'm sure America will be most interesting."

"And you, Morlaix?"

"I'm eager to see the family, and America too, of course. I'm sure it has changed a good deal since I was last here."

"There's certainly been considerable progress in the last twenty years or so."

"But at the same time, I've enjoyed being at sea again."

"It has made such a difference to him," said Odile, "working the ship and taking a watch. He no longer seems to be a cripple, and it has done him much good to be away from the war, from the responsibility. It seems to have been years since he smiled, and now he hardly stops grinning."

"Well," said Molineux, "it's not every day that we have such a useful passenger – not in fact since we carried your daughter and her husband. Dominique even became expert at taking the lunars, she could find her way round *Bowditch* with the best of them. And she wasn't afraid of a bit of pulley hauley, either. And how have you liked the voyage, Odile?"

"I've liked it pretty well, thank you. I've had an opportunity to reflect and, as you know, to write. To my surprise I've not much missed the politics, the backstabbing, though," she looked at the skipper, "sometimes the conversation is not as scintillating as it might be – I think I have heard enough discussions of bilge pumps to last a lifetime."

"I'm sorry for my rough and unsophisticated ways, Odile, but that pump was a very important topic for a few days, not that she leaks much of course, tight as a ..."

There was a shout from above: "Land!"

Suddenly, the cabin was empty.

***

The land was low and indistinct, but there seemed to be little doubt of its identity to the men on the ship.

"Cape Henry," said Morlaix to his wife, pointing to a dark line on the horizon, off the port bow, "at the southern tip of the Chesapeake."

"How can you tell?" asked Odile. "It looks like a smudge to me."

"Well, everything adds up – the noon sight yesterday, the dead reckoning from the last lunar sight, the depth and colour of the sea. And of course, Molineux is a Chesapeake man, and I've spent a bit of time here too."

During the American Revolution, Morlaix had been a master's mate in the French Royal Navy, and his ship had been involved in the battles of Cape Henry and the Chesapeake, when they had stopped the British Navy's attempt to relieve General Cornwallis' army at Yorktown. Once back in France, politicised by his experience of the American Revolution with its Enlightenment ideals, Morlaix had been a delegate to the States General. As a Breton, he had naturally become a founding member of the Jacobin Society, and had taken an active part in the Revolution. He had met Odile, a passionate revolutionary, and a woman committed to intrigue, at the height of the Revolution. The purging of so many officers in the French Navy had meant that there were opportunities for men from the lower decks, especially men with ambitious and well-connected wives, and Morlaix's promotion had been rapid.

Payoff passed close to Cape Henry, and, disdaining the services of a pilot, over the next two days made her way slowly up the busy Chesapeake, working her tides in the light winds, until she came to the thriving port of Baltimore.

Although they had travelled to America on the personal orders of Napoleon, and Morlaix was a serving officer in the French Navy, he and Odile preserved the fiction that their visit to America was a private one, solely with the object of visiting their daughter, and they made no contact with the Americans at an official level.

They stayed in a hotel in the bustling town, and sent a letter to their daughter, care of the DuPont Company at Brandywine Creek, about eighty miles away by road. Morlaix was astonished at the development that had occurred since his last visit.

"Fifteen years since I've been here," he said to Odile, "and the place is hardly recognisable. So much progress. If only we French devoted as much of our energy towards industry as we do to war."

"We have no choice," replied Odile, "the whole world is against us."

It was their habit to leave the hotel for long walks, and, several days after their arrival, with the hope that there would be a letter from Dominque unspoken between them, they returned to the hotel.

"Visitors for you," said the hotel owner, smiling and pointing to the lounge.

A sensation like an electric shock ran through Odile as she heard, from behind her, a familiar voice say, "Good afternoon, Mama." She turned to see her daughter framed in the doorway, her husband, Jack Stone, behind her, both smiling broadly.

***

That evening, after dinner in the hotel, Morlaix said, "You asked earlier, Jacques, how I was able to obtain leave to come to America."

"Yes, I did, and you didn't answer me, or at least gave me an evasive reply."

"The reason we are here, Jacques, is because of your employer."

"Monsieur du Pont?"

"Yes. It is a matter of gunpowder – powder for the French forces in the West Indies."

Morlaix saw Jack's eyes narrow. "Could you explain what you want to do?"

"The supply of powder for the military and the navy in the West Indies presently comes from France. That is a long way, and the ships that take it, besides the weather, have to contend with the British Navy. It is thought that a supply from America would be more secure, and I am ordered to inspect the works and, if satisfactory, secure a supply. I hope that this will not cause friction between us – your employer supplying His Majesty's enemies."

"It has that potential, Monsieur Morlaix, certainly," said Jack.

Dominique interjected, "I don't think there will be any repercussions, father, because I don't believe Monsieur du Pont will sell powder to France."

"And why is that, Dom?"

"Do you know of his history?"

"A little, but please tell me why he will not want to sell his powder to France."

"Very well. Briefly, he was very close to his tutor, Antoine Lavoisier …"

"Lavoisier, that was a disgusting thing that was done," said Odile. "What a loss for France, and indeed the world."

"Yes, Lavoisier went to the guillotine, as you know, father," said Dominique, "and du Pont and his father barely escaped. If Robespierre hadn't been killed …"

"The upshot is," said Jack, "that du Pont has a deep dislike of the Revolution, and I don't think he's likely to sell gunpowder to France."

"But we have our Emperor now," said Odile, whose political ideals had metamorphosed from ardent Jacobinism to support for Napoleon. "Surely he will change his mind."

***

The next morning, a letter arrived at the hotel from du Pont, addressed to 'M Morlaix'.

"Du Pont has invited us to Brandywine Creek to stay in his house," said Morlaix after he had read the message. "I'll reply, accepting the invitation, and I think we should depart for Brandywine as soon as we can."

Chapter 38 – Du Pont

In the boat from Baltimore to Elkton, at the north-east extremity of the Chesapeake, Morlaix and Jack sat together on the deck. "Jacques," said Morlaix, "I would like to tell you what I have been doing in France recently."

"Please do."

"It concerns your friend, Percy Snowden."

"I read recently about his activities."

"Did you?"

Jack, whose pacifism did not entirely negate his enthusiasm for his friend's activities, said, "Yes, it was extensively covered in the newspapers, probably exaggerated, but ..." Jack smiled. "Capturing a frigate with his schooner, raiding ashore in the Gulf of Lions, taking all that Spanish gold. As I say, probably exaggerated, but he did have great success in Corsica as well last year, didn't he? He sent me a pamphlet about Corsica, written by a 'British Tar' – Percy's not one for false modesty. He must have put Boney's nose well out of joint." He looked at Morlaix. "Sorry, I didn't express that very well, Admiral Morlaix."

Morlaix cleared his throat, smiling "However you put it Jacques, it did annoy the Emperor. Very much."

Jack said, "Oh ..."

"And Napoleon, personally, asked me to do something about it."

"Oh, I see. And presumably you did do something?"

"Yes, I did. I laid a trap – on the Canal du Midi."

"And did you spring the trap?"

"Yes, I did, very successfully, but I did not catch Snowden. I don't think Snowden was behind the raid, it was much too clumsy, but his schooner was involved in making a diversion."

"And the schooner, his *Oleander*?"

"Got clean away."

***

They were met at the house at Brandywine Creek by Madame du Pont, who told them that her husband was not available – a crisis in the factory, she explained – but he would be pleased to entertain them to dinner later. Declining the invitation to rest in their rooms, they went with Jack and Dominique to their house.

"Much smaller in scale than Monsieur du Pont's," explained Dominique, as they went through the front door into the main room.

"It is still comfortable, Dominique!" said Odile, "very pleasant. When I remember what your father and I had at your age ..."

"You have made up for it now," said Jack, remembering the Morlaixs' elegant town house in Paris, and the pleasant villa, of which he had heard much, near Agen in the south.

Morlaix went with Jack to the engine house where the Admiral was introduced to Abel Shawe, the engineer in charge of the works: "Monsieur du Pont ordered an engine from Boulton and Watt in England, Admiral Morlaix, but the company has so far been unable to obtain the necessary licence to send it to America. In the end, we decided to attempt to manufacture an engine ourselves."

"You remember me talking to you in Paris about my time in Portsmouth with Robert Fulton," said Jack, "the American inventor?"

"I remember it very well, and as you know I have met Fulton myself."

"Well, Fulton is very interested in steam engines."

"He ran one on the Seine," said Morlaix. "The first one sank, but the second was a great success."

"Well, Fulton told me a great deal about steam engines. At the time I knew him, he was negotiating for the purchase of an engine with Boulton and Watt, and he had a great deal of information about their machines. As a result, I know something about the machines, and I'm helping Abel with building this one. We have decided to start with a small-scale engine, half the size of one of Mr Watt's."

"Yes, Admiral, he's been very helpful," said Shawe. "The main problem with building an efficient steam engine, in my opinion, is making the cylinder to actually be cylindrical. An unfinished iron casting won't do, it's too rough and the steam leaks past the piston. Jack knew that B and W had used a boring bar to solve this problem, and he built one himself. It worked very well." He pointed to a ladder. "Climb up and have a look for yourself ..." He looked at Morlaix's wooden leg. "I do beg your pardon, Admiral."

Morlaix smiled. "I think I will have to forgo the inspection of the cylinder for now. Your engine, even if it is only a scaled-down version of one of Watt's, is certainly very impressive. It seems to be nearly finished."

"It is close to completion," said Jack. "It bars over smoothly – but we're having trouble getting hold of enough copper to finish the boiler."

***

"They seem very happy," said Morlaix to his wife as they dressed for dinner. "Jack's work with the engine is very impressive."

"I think they are going to do well in America," replied Odile. "It is the place for people like them."

"It certainly seems to be. As for my own mission …"

"What about it?"

"I think Dominique and Jacques are probably right. I think if du Pont was favourably disposed towards selling powder to us, he would have met us earlier, in a business setting."

"But you have not yet told him what we want. He no doubt thinks that we are here merely to visit Jacques and Dom."

"That is possible, Odile." He saw her open a small box on the dressing table. She walked towards him, holding up his Légion d'honneur decoration.

He raised his hand. "No, Odile, I don't want to wear that tonight. Shall we go?"

***

The du Ponts had invited Jack and Dominique, and Odile was pleased to see that the du Ponts seemed to hold them in high regard. The dinner was good, and Monsieur and Madame du Pont were excellent hosts. The conversation was mostly about France. Odile, in her usual sparkling way, gave an account of the political situation, and Morlaix described how he had organised the response to Snowden's raiding activities.

Du Pont looked at him keenly: "And of course, Morlaix, after that success the Emperor decided that you, his most successful naval man, should retire on holiday to America."

"He had become very tired, Monsieur du Pont," said Odile, rather defensively.

"I'm sure, Madame Morlaix," said du Pont, with perhaps a hint of sarcasm. "And what, Morlaix, is your view on the likely outcome of the war?"

"As a naval man, du Pont, I can't be very hopeful. The Emperor has a huge army in the Channel ports, Boulogne mostly, but they can't get across to England unless we defeat the Royal Navy, or at least have local supremacy. Unless the English make some dreadful mistake, that will not happen, and I'm not even sure that once landed in England, Napoleon would have the easy victory he imagines. They have made considerable defensive preparations in recent years. And then there is Lord Nelson, whose purpose is not just to defeat our fleet, but to annihilate it."

"But Napoleon will have the rest of Europe, even if he doesn't succeed with England."

"With England undefeated, blockading our ports, fighting against us on land and subsidising our enemies, I do not think that he can win in the long term."

"Talleyrand is of that opinion as well," said Odile. "He says that Napoleon has been so successful in war that he believes all problems can be solved by war. Talleyrand thinks we must negotiate a settlement from a position of strength, and negotiate soon."

Du Pont looked thoughtful, but turned to Jack.

"Shall we speak of something more cheerful, Jack Stone?"

"I would be happy to do that, Monsieur du Pont."

"How is your engine progressing? I have not had time to get to the shed recently."

***

After dinner, du Pont asked Morlaix to join him in his study. When they were seated and had glasses of brandy in front of them, du Pont said, in French, "The answer is no, Admiral Morlaix."

Morlaix smiled. "To what question, du Pont? I was not aware that I had asked one."

"Well, then I will ask it for you: 'Monsieur du Pont, will you supply powder for the French military in the West Indies?'."

"You are very perceptive, du Pont. I was in fact intending to ask that question. May I ask why you have declined this opportunity? I suppose because of your treatment at the hands of the previous government."

"That is part of it, certainly."

"But I can assure you that the accession of the Emperor has changed all of that. Order and law have been restored. I have no doubt that you would be welcomed with open arms if you returned to France."

"I have no intention of returning to France. I cannot forget La Force."

Morlaix winced. He knew that du Pont had been imprisoned with his father in La Force prison, the site of a notorious massacre.

"And I cannot forget Lavoisier. No, I will not sell powder to the French military."

"I understand your feelings, du Pont, and I speak as a former Jacobin, but you hinted that there was an additional reason for your refusal to deal with France."

"There is, Morlaix. Around these parts, and especially in Philadelphia, there are many businessmen who are Quakers. Do you know of the Quakers, Morlaix?"

"I have heard of them, certainly."

"Perhaps they're stronger in England than they are here, but nevertheless I count several among my friends, and, well, in some ways their philosophy is easy for me to accept as a Huguenot, and, I hope, as a humane man."

Morlaix nodded. He believed he knew what was coming.

Du Pont continued, "The Quakers have influenced me, Morlaix, very much, and the issue that exercises them above all is the question of slavery. You want powder for the military in the West Indies, and I will tell you why I would not sell it to you, not even if you were the only customer standing between me and ruin. The Revolution did some horrible things, dreadful, as you know, but it did do at least one good thing – it freed the slaves on the plantations. You spoke of Napoleon bringing order, but part of the order that he brought was to restore slavery to the West Indies. Can you imagine that, Morlaix, enslaving people who had only just been freed? And the way that it was reimposed was bloody, cruel in the extreme. Influential Englishmen are against slavery, and I expect that before long they will abolish it. The English Navy, against whom you would use my powder, is led by Lord Barham, a fervent abolitionist. No, Admiral Morlaix, I will not send powder to the West Indies."

Morlaix nodded. "Your decision does you great credit, Monsieur."

"Thank you, Morlaix," du Pont sighed. "Can we change the subject? Another glass?"

***

"So you see, Odile, there's no possibility of du Pont supplying powder – our mission is entirely in vain," said Morlaix, as they sat in their comfortable room. He thought for a minute or so and then added, "I suppose we should think soon of returning to France. I must say that the prospect does not appeal to me very much."

"Nor me, and I don't believe we should think of returning just yet."

"Why's that, Odile?"

"I mentioned at dinner that I had spoken to Talleyrand."

The Admiral smiled "You did, but I assumed that you were just indulging in a bit of name dropping."

"As if I would!"

"It has been known."

"I'm sorry I didn't tell you this before, but our foreign minister would like us to take a house, perhaps in Philadelphia or New York – he left the location up to us – and do what we can to influence the Americans to be favourably disposed towards France."

Morlaix grinned. "Will that not undercut our official representative?"

"Leave that to me," said Odile.

Chapter 39 – The Dockyard

Molene, the captured French *flûte*, had been in the dockyard at Antigua for some time, her cargo discharged, to be stored in warehouses. Some had been requisitioned by the Navy and some was due to be sold at auction. It would not fetch as high a price as it would have done in England, but *Molene* herself was valuable, a fine ship, nearly new.

Pascoe, who had brought *Molene* to Antigua after her capture in Guadeloupe, was still nominally in command, though with the ship awaiting repairs, there was little for him to do. He knew that command of a commissioned frigate would only be given to an older man and that he would not retain her when she was accepted into the Royal Navy.

Just after she was commissioned, *Oleander*, the first Bermudian-built schooner destined for the Royal Navy, had been subjected to scientifically conducted trials in the North Sea. The trials, in which Pascoe had been enthusiastically involved, had measured the ship's performance in various conditions, using instruments for determining quantities such as the ship's speed, her angle of heel and the strength of the wind. Pascoe had distilled these results into a book of tables which could be used to ensure that the ship was sailing with the optimum sail configuration for the prevailing conditions.

For some time, he had been thinking of ways to improve the performance of ships, informed by his experience not only of *Oleander* but of commanding *Daisy*, a lateen-rigged Moroccan xebec. He had been making sketches of what he called a 'sliding keel', which would extend a vessel's draft when she worked to windward, and in the dockyard in Antigua, with *Molene*'s carpenter's workshop and tools at his disposal, he had made a model of his invention, using some light cedar wood which Mr Weedon, the dockyard's superintendent, had found for him. Pascoe believed that the sliding keel showed great promise and thought that he had overcome the difficulties of strengthening the ship's hull to accommodate the loads from the keel. He could not wait to show it to Snowden and Kennedy.

Despite its poor reputation with Navy men – Nelson had called it a 'dismal hole' – Pascoe had enjoyed his time in Antigua. As well as his model making, the island's merchants had been free with invitations, and his fellow officers were not averse to the occasional carouse. He was anxious, though, to rejoin *Oleander*, and was overjoyed when he saw her leading Cochrane's squadron into the harbour, though, as she came closer, he could see that she had suffered. Her hull seemed to be covered in roughly applied patches and her reduced canvas and slack rigging seemed to tell of more serious damage.

Amazed, he watched as he saw that the squadron included two fine frigates, both with rigging and mast damage, flying British ensigns over French ones. *More prizes*, he thought, and then, *am I entitled to prize money?*

Perhaps he should really have reported to Snowden aboard *Columbine* first, but as he swung himself aboard *Oleander*, Pascoe felt as though he was coming home. From the deck he looked round and his earlier impression was confirmed – she had been knocked about.

"What happened?" he asked Luciani.

"Ken decided to take on a frigate, Pascoe. I don't fully know the details, as I was enjoying a run ashore at the time, but she got a broadside."

"What frigate?"

Luciani gestured over his shoulder with his thumb towards one of the prizes. "That one, *Persephone*. As you can see, it ended well."

"And your run ashore?"

"That also went very well."

"And the other frigate, the one over there?"

"*Nymphe*. Lieutenant West, Second of *Columbine*, set her foremast on fire with the Congreves, and *Northumberland* took her."

"And the fort, at Anse à la Barque?"

"Abandoned it, in good order. Your landing stage was very useful."

***

Northumberland was short of water, which was difficult to obtain in Antigua, and she sailed almost immediately to replenish her supply in Dominica. The dockyard in Antigua did not have the capacity to work on the two damaged French frigates, it was already working to ready Molene for service in the Royal Navy, and had other work in addition. Snowden's orders were to remain in Antigua until the two prize frigates and Oleander were made temporarily ready for sea, and then to accompany them and *Oleander* to Bermuda.

On the second night, Snowden hosted a dinner party for the officers of *Columbine* and *Oleander*. It was a festive and occasionally riotous occasion.

"How are *Oleander*'s repairs going?" Snowden asked Kennedy.

"Well, not too bad. They only have to get us to Bermuda for the repairs and paying off."

"Seems to be the end of an era, Ken, *Oleander*'s era. And now she's to be paid off. It feels a lifetime ago since we commissioned her in Bermuda."

"My God, Percy, so it does, but the dockyard work is not all that extensive, and she'll be on her way with a new crew before too long." He looked solemnly at Snowden. "It will soon be the second era of *Oleander*. Or perhaps epoch. What do you think young Pascoe - intellectual that you are – epoch or era?"

"He's not going to answer you, Signore," said Luciani, nodding towards Pascoe, whose head was resting in his arms on the table. "I think he's not intellectual at the moment, in fact he's asleep."

***

For several hours next day there was considerable tension in the British base. The French fleet had been sighted in the distance between Antigua and Monserrat, and ships, the few that there were, and shore defences were made ready, but it soon became clear that the enemy was not interested in Antigua but was heading, almost certainly, towards Europe.

***

On 12 July, Nelson's fleet arrived in Antigua. Snowden, to his surprise, was signalled to repair aboard *Victory*. Hurriedly changing into his best uniform and with the boat crew as smartly turned out as could be managed at short notice, he made his way to the towering three decker, where he was piped aboard.

Nelson's flag captain, Hardy, met him. "His Lordship wishes to speak to you, Snowden. Please follow me."

When they went into the great cabin, Snowden was shocked by the Admiral's appearance. He was pale and gaunt and looked impossibly tired – *there's a man that needs some leave*, thought Snowden.

Nelson looked at the young captain before him and thought *there's a man that needs some leave.* "Ah, Snowden," he said, "thank you for coming, please be seated. I've read Cochrane's despatch in which he speaks very highly of you. It seems a long time, doesn't it, since you took me on that tour around Toulon in your schooner. A memorable occasion, especially with your beautiful *bandita* aboard!"

He slapped the edge of the table with the despatch: "You're responsible for the only bit of good news I've had for a while. We've been on this damned ship for two years, have we not Hardy, doing nothing except chasing Villeneuve?"

"We have, My Lord," said Hardy, a large, healthy-looking man, so different from his commander.

"And you, Snowden, you've been having a very active time of it. It has done us good to read of your exploits. I'm glad to see you have your post – you've already done remarkable work with your frigate, and I'm sure you'll do more in future."

"Thank you, My Lord."

"Well, as I said, it's been damned good to hear of your exploits, and I wish you success. Now, if you'll excuse me, I have business to attend to."

Snowden turned to leave, but Nelson said: "you seem dreadfully tired, Snowden, please think about taking some rest." He made a note on his blotter.

"My Lord," said Snowden.

***

"Is he well, Hardy?" asked Snowden, as they emerged onto the quarterdeck.

"As well as can be expected, Snowden. He is a very worried man, he feels that the fate of England is in his hands, and, as he said, he's been aboard this ship for two years, chasing our friend Villeneuve, and now we've missed him again. He just wants to bring the French and Spanish to battle, and to go home."

"It's extraordinary that he found the time to speak to me like that, Hardy."

"Hardly, Snowden, you have done very well and have brought Nelson some much needed cheer." Snowden returned to his ship, wondering.

Chapter 40 – The Weary Chase

When Nelson's fleet had arrived in Barbados on 4 June, after a fast trip across the Atlantic, they had found the island in uproar. A mistaken report from General Brereton of St Lucia stating 'it was apparently clear that the enemy had gone south' from Martinique had reduced Barbados' inhabitants almost to a state of panic, which lasted until Nelson arrived, when the mood changed to one of wild optimism. Nelson read the report and immediately sailed south.

The fleet's arrival in Trinidad on 6 June was somewhat farcical, as, due to a mistake in signalling, Nelson's fleet was believed to be French and forts were destroyed and guns spiked on their approach. Finding that the French had not been in Trinidad, Nelson anchored for the night and in the morning made his way back north, along the chain of the Lesser Antilles. In Grenada, the governor told him that no attack had been made on his own island, or on St Lucia or St Vincent, and it was here that the frigate *Jason* found him, with a report that Villeneuve had been seen from Dominica, his fleet heading northward.

Increasingly convinced that Villeneuve and the Spanish Admiral Gravina were, as Nelson said, "pushing for Europe, to get out of our way", he continued north, anchoring in Antigua on 12 June, where he was told that the French fleet had passed the island a few days previously, without making any attempt to attack the British naval base. The French were almost certainly heading back to Europe, but the question was – where? Nelson agonised over the decision, but eventually decided that Villeneuve's Combined Fleet would most likely head for the Strait and return to the Mediterranean and Toulon to support Napoleon against the Austrians. Believing that if he was wrong and the French made for a northern European port, the Western Approaches to the Channel were sufficiently guarded by Admiral Cornwallis's squadron, Nelson decided to head for Gibraltar. The French had a start, but the British fleet sailed much faster than the French and, if he had guessed right about the destination of the French, he might catch Villeneuve in the Atlantic. On 13 June the troops that had been embarked at Barbados were sent ashore and Nelson departed Antigua for Gibraltar, sending the fast brig *Curieux* to England with dispatches.

Nelson was wrong, and when he arrived at Gibraltar, he realised he had missed Villeneuve. Heading back out into the Atlantic, he searched for the French, until a few days later an American merchantman told him that Villeneuve had passed to the north and was undoubtedly heading for the northern Spanish port of Ferrol.

Nelson had not set foot ashore for nearly two years, and frustrated, sick and exhausted, with leave overdue, he sailed in *Victory* to England.

Chapter 41 - Eastwards

From the deck of *Intrépide*, Second Lieutenant Duval watched the coast of Guadeloupe slide past, impossibly green, with rainbows shining in the mist on the forested mountain peaks. Shortly after the despatch that the frigate *Didon* had brought from France, the fleet had departed Fort de France in Martinique, stopped briefly at Basse-Terre, Guadeloupe, to collect the soldiers, and was now off Anse à la Barque.

Duval, who had the watch, saw the signal from the flagship and backed the 74's topsails, almost stopping the ship in the light wind. *Intrépide*'s commander, Captain Infernet, watched Duval from the weather side of the quarterdeck and, when the manoeuvre was complete, beckoned the Second Lieutenant over to him.

"You handle her well, Duval," he remarked.

"Thank you, Sir."

"Another debacle," said Infernet, pointing towards the land. Duval knew more or less what was coming and did not much care for it. Sickness was rife, the mood in the fleet was not good, and some of the ships' captains were almost openly insubordinate, none more so than Captain Infernet.

"The English took our fort, seized three frigates and routed a column of infantry, and then retired, without a finger being laid on them. And what have we done – we," he gestured around him, "with all these ships and thousands of soldiers? We've captured Diamond Rock, HMS *Diamond Rock*! And they only surrendered because they had run out of water. And if it wasn't for Joyeuse insisting on it, Villey would not even have tried that."

"Yes, Sir."

"And now we're going back to Europe, almost without a shot being fired at the English." He paused. "There's nothing wrong with Frenchmen, Duval, our army is feared throughout the world, but our Navy ..."

Infernet's diatribe was interrupted by the sound of musketry from ashore. He threw up his hands: "An ambush. I hope it's nothing worse. Watch for signals from the flagship, Duval, I'm going to my cabin."

***

The French fleet passed Antigua, the headquarters of the British, but just off the island a British fleet of merchant ships was sighted. It turned out to have a very small escort, and morale was temporarily improved by the capture of the fourteen merchantmen, carrying valuable cargoes, though Villeneuve was visibly shocked when one of the merchant commanders told him that Nelson had been in Barbados only a week previously. Abandoning the idea of any attack on Antigua, Villeneuve headed for Europe.

A few days later, a sail, a brig, was sighted far astern of the convoy. A fast frigate was despatched to investigate, but the brig turned and ran. It reappeared the next day, venturing closer, and one of the seamen recognised her as *Curieux*, a fast ship which had been cut out of Fort de France by the British and was now in the service of the Royal Navy. At the approach of a frigate, *Curieux*, handled with extreme smartness, hauled her wind and set her course north-west.

"Off to report us to England, no doubt," said Infernet, "discovered by our own ship."

***

The voyage of the Combined Fleet across the Atlantic was slow and the ships were encumbered by a huge number of sick men, something else that provoked the scorn of *Intrépide*'s commander, who told Duval that 'everybody knew' that the English ships hardly ever had a sick man aboard. Duval was not sure that this was true, but the French fleet had been impressed by the care given to the wounded Frenchmen aboard HMS *Oleander* before they were put ashore at Basse-Terre.

Captain Infernet, though, kept his ship in good order, and, despite his rough manner, was a humane and popular commander. His son, who was only ten years old, was signed on as a midshipman and was a favourite of the men.

The orders were for Ferrol, in the very north-west of Spain, by chance where *Intrépide* had been built. At Ferrol they were to join with other French and Spanish ships and then to sail northwards to join Admiral Ganteaume's Brest fleet. It was known that Nelson's fleet was only a few days behind and that the Royal Navy in England would be forewarned of the French and Spanish fleet's arrival by HMS *Curieux*.

Duval did not really enjoy serving aboard *Intrépide*. He had had independent command - only of a *flûte*, it was true, but nevertheless a substantial ship - and it was hard to go back to obeying orders, to being a small part of a great machine, and, he thought, *a great machine that had no purpose*. The ship that had rescued him, *Molene*, had been taken by the English and her commander, his friend Morel, had been taken prisoner. Villeneuve's fleet had captured *Diamond Rock*, but apart from that - nothing - *all these ships and thousands of soldiers*, he thought.

***

The Combined Fleet continued eastwards, towards Ferrol. The passage was slow and uncomfortable, the weather often bad, the ships straggling and sometimes falling out of the sight of the flagship. Though they took some small ships, there were many sick, provisions were scarce, and morale was low. The sight of the smallest merchant ship would provoke a flurry of signals from the flagship – inevitably provoking the scorn of Captain Infernet. "Frightened not only of Nelson, but by the *very idea* of Nelson!" he remarked.

On 30 June, the ships passed north of the Azores, and at eleven o'clock on 22 July, about a hundred miles west of Cape Finisterre, the *Indomptable* sighted eleven ships ahead, and frigates sent to reconnoitre reported that there were in fact twenty two. Villeneuve had met the British.

Chapter 42 – Cape Finisterre

Curieux reached Plymouth on 7 July, after a fast passage of 24 days from Antigua, far outpacing Villeneuve's Combined Fleet. Captain Bettesworth drove post haste to London and met Lord Barham, the First Lord of the Admiralty, on the 9th. Barham, though he had never commanded a fleet and was nearly 80 years old, was an able man, with an excellent grasp of strategy. He realised the implications of Lord Nelson's despatches and Captain Bettesworth's conclusion that Villeneuve was heading for Ferrol in northern Spain. Ferrol was an important naval base, and it was known that there were ten enemy ships of the line there.

This was a moment of great danger for England. Barham, realising that the French and Spanish could potentially form a great fleet and sweep up the Channel to cover Napoleon's invasion barges, reacted masterfully in concert with another able officer, 'Billy Blue', Admiral Cornwallis, commander of the Channel Fleet.

Forewarned, a sizable fleet under Sir Robert Calder was assembled and stationed about a hundred and twenty miles off Cape Finisterre, with the intention of intercepting Villeneuve on his way back from the West Indies.

Astonishingly, given the vagaries of weather and timing, the strategy worked.

***

Aboard *Intrépide*, Duval had the watch. The weather was foggy, with a light breeze fitfully blowing from the west-north-west. *Intrépide* was moving slowly, and Duval had his work cut out to keep station in the straggling fleet. Realising that he was overhauling *Formidable*, Duval was absorbed in taking in the royals to slow the ship, when the bell sounded for noon. He handed the ship over to the Third Lieutenant and was making his way aft to write up his log when a gun sounded from a distant ship, and then another, and Captain Infernet ran on deck.

Log forgotten, Duval stood with the Captain and the other officers as more guns sounded and a signal broke out on Villeneuve's flagship, *Bucentaure*, dimly visible in the mist just ahead of *Formidable*. The officers peered closely at the flags, whose colours were dulled by the poor visibility, and then at each other.

"That's it, then," said the First Lieutenant, "the English are between us and Ferrol."

"We will have to fight," said Infernet.

Duval stayed on deck to assist as *Intrépide* was manoeuvred to form the required fighting line, the fleet tacking in succession. Infernet, fine seaman that he was, handling his great ship with delicacy and precision. At about two in the afternoon, as the ship was established in her place, Duval went below to his battle station, the lower gun deck. In the gloom, he was greeted by the Gunner, Samson.

"Ready, Monsieur Samson?"

"As we'll ever be. We've not enough men to be fully manned, though some of the sick have come out to help."

"That's to their credit, Samson."

"It is, Sir, though some of them can hardly stand! What's the situation topside, Sir?"

"Weather's thick. We got a glimpse of the English, though, before it closed in again. There's a lot of them – I don't know how many – in between us and Ferrol."

"They've been waiting for us, then?"

"I think they have, Samson. You remember we were spotted by *Curieux*, so it would be strange if they hadn't prepared."

"Is it Nelson?" the Gunner asked – a question that had been discussed by the officers on the quarterdeck since the enemy had been sighted. Nelson was held in almost superstitious awe by the men of the French fleet, the victor of terrible battles in which the French had suffered such disastrous defeats, and who had pursued them with such relentless energy since they had left Toulon.

"We don't think so, Samson. Nelson would be overtaking us, not standing in our way," replied Duval.

"Let us hope you are right, Sir."

Their conversation was interrupted by the distant sound of guns, muffled but seemingly coming from ahead, followed almost immediately by the order to 'run out'. As the ports were opened, grey light washed into the gun deck, suddenly relieving the darkness as the men heaved at the tackles, sliding the guns outboard.

The Gunner looked along the lines of cannons, at the men standing by them, at the smouldering matches and piles of shot, and cried, "Ready, Sir!"

"Lower gun deck ready," Duval shouted up the companionway.

They heard another broadside from ahead, closer now, and then the sound of another, followed, unnervingly, by the distant sound of cheering.

"I was at the Nile, Sir," said Samson, grimly, "where the English cheered like that."

He handed Duval some oakum and the Second Lieutenant stopped up his ears, moved to the ship's side and climbed round a gun to look out of the port. The fog was thick, and he could only just make out *Formidable* ahead. Suddenly, on an almost parallel course to leeward, a ship appeared, a 74, and with a start Duval realised that she was flying a huge British ensign – *a battle ensign*, he thought, *this is it*. There was a bugle call from above and the order "As you bear", and Duval drew his sword, crouching beside the gun. The British ship came on, her yards braced round, guns run out, and Duval could see men on her deck, waiting, as he was. Duval looked aft and saw the gun captains sighting along the barrels of their cannons, tense and expectant.

When he was sure that the gun next to him was sighted on the enemy, Duval stood up, moved away and brought down his sword, shouting "Fire!"

He watched as the match was brought down to the touch hole and the nearest gun fired, deafeningly, throwing itself back against its breech rope, followed at irregular intervals by the remaining port battery. The air became thick with reeking smoke as the men reloaded their guns. Holding up his hand to stop the gun closest to him being run out, he clambered round it, the metal warm to his touch, and looked out of the port. The English ship was still there, much closer, apparently undamaged. *Intrépide*'s port lower guns were firing as quickly as they could be reloaded now, their crews reinforced by the men of the idle starboard battery. He walked along the deck in the smoke, occasionally patting a man on the shoulder or making encouraging gestures, the noise incredible, despite his stopped ears.

He was aware that the English had still not fired, and when he looked out of a port, he saw that the enemy 74 had closed the gap between the two ships. Holes had appeared in her sails, but her speed seemed undiminished. She was very close now, the black circles of her gun muzzles huge and menacing, all seemingly pointed at him. Without warning, her forward lower gun fired, followed at intervals by its fellows, and he ducked hastily back into the ship as he felt balls strike the oak of *Intrépide*'s hull and heard splinters whizz through the air. Men screamed and a gun was hit, toppling over on its carriage, trapping a crew member underneath its iron barrel. Duval heard himself yelling, urging the men to reload and fire. The English ship's rate of fire was tremendous, much faster than anything Duval had imagined was possible, and men in the gun deck were hit by balls or splinters.

As suddenly as it had started, the fire from the English ship stopped, and Duval looked out of a port. The fog was impenetrable and there was no sign of the enemy.

"Cease fire!" he shouted, "Cease fire!", and eventually *Intrépide*'s lower guns fell silent. He ran over to where the Gunner was supervising the lifting of the toppled cannon.

"I'm going on deck for a minute," he shouted, "to report."

He ran rapidly up the companionway and onto the quarterdeck, where Infernet stood, surrounded by a group of petty officers, reporting damage. Spars had fallen, and men were employed cutting at the rigging. The fog was now so thick that the ship seemed to exist in a white world of her own.

Infernet saw Duval coming and raised his eyebrows enquiringly, listening as Duval quickly reported on the condition of the lower gun deck.

"Minor damage up here, Duval, spars and some casualties from the grapeshot. The fog has stopped the action for now, but we may blunder …"

His words were cut short by a shout from *Intrépide*'s stern, and they looked up to see a ship appear, out of the fog, an English ship, heading towards them on a converging course.

"Back you go, Duval," shouted Infernet, and Duval slid back down the ladder to the lower gun deck. The capsized gun had been righted, but the man underneath was dead. Duval shuddered.

"There's another one coming," he shouted to the Gunner, "from astern."

The Gunner nodded, and they moved to the quarter gallery, where the enemy ship he had seen from the deck, another 74, was intermittently visible through the swirling mist, overhauling *Intrépide.*

"Give her the quarter battery," ordered Duval.

Intrépide's quarter guns fired, and then her broadside, but the English ship came relentlessly on, not deigning to reply until she was beam on, very close, when she began to shoot, deliberately, but with extreme rapidity, the balls ploughing into the French ship's hull, turning the gun deck into a scene of terror, full of smoke, splinters, screams and the report of guns. There was a great crash nearby, and Duval heard and felt the passage of a ball close past his head and saw the Gunner disintegrate into a bloody mess of flesh.

And then, suddenly, it was over, but Duval would never forget the next few hours of horror on the lower gun deck. The wounded were carried away, the dead pitched unceremoniously over the side through the gun ports, and repairs were made to the pumps, an urgent matter as the ship was leaking. He was aware from time to time that Captain Infernet was there, encouraging him, and gradually, slowly, some semblance of order was restored.

At about six o'clock in the evening he went on deck. Fallen spars had been cleared away and the ship was under full sail. It was still foggy, and though he could see *Formidable* ahead, there was no sign of the British.

"We live to fight another day," said Infernet.

***

So ended the Battle of Cape Finisterre. Eventually, the fleets sighted each other, but there was no eagerness on either side to re-engage. Admiral Calder seemed overly concerned about protecting two prizes which he had taken, prizes that turned out to be useless, and was anxious to rejoin the Channel Squadron. The battle, 'Calder's Action' as it became known in England, was initially thought to have been a success, but eventually it was considered that Calder had missed an opportunity to destroy the Combined Fleet. Calder was subsequently recalled to England to face the court martial he had himself insisted on, doing his cause no good by selfishly pleading with Nelson that he should travel home in the *Prince of Wales*, his own ship, rather than a frigate, thus depriving the British side of a 98 gun ship at Trafalgar. Calder's court martial was held after Trafalgar, which changed the perception of what was expected of British Admirals, and he was severely reprimanded for 'not having done his utmost to renew the engagement'.

***

Villeneuve, who was puzzled by the disappearance of two capital ships in the fog – ships that had been captured by the English – likewise showed no enthusiasm for re-engaging, and headed for Ferrol. Napoleon was furious. Villeneuve's cruise to the West Indies had been a monumental, wasted effort, the only result being that his ships were full of sick and wounded men, short of provisions and low in morale. As a final blow, the north-easterly wind meant that they could not fetch Ferrol, and eventually anchored in Vigo Bay, a hundred miles south.

Emerging from Vigo on 1 August, Villeneuve took his fleet to Ferrol. On 13 August the fleet departed, intending to head north to join the fleet at Brest and eventually to force the Channel. Mistaking a small group of British ships for the Channel Fleet and having been fed misinformation by a Danish merchantman, Villeneuve turned south and entered Cadiz. The threat of invasion from Napoleon's army was over.

Chapter 43 – Respite

The convoy – it was more a convoy than a squadron, consisted of *Oleander* - patched up so that she was seaworthy enough to reach Bermuda as long as no really heavy weather was encountered - the two French prizes, *Persephone* and *Nymphe*, and *Columbine*. The decision about whether the prizes would be refitted in Bermuda or sailed back to England for overhaul would be decided in Bermuda, depending on the availability of the yards there.

Manning the prizes for the voyage from Guadeloupe to Antigua had been simple, given the resources of the force that had attacked Anse à la Barque – *Northumberland* alone had nearly eight hundred men in her crew – and the distance involved – only about sixty miles.

The trip to Bermuda was entirely different. It was much longer, about a thousand miles, and the winds that the ships were likely to encounter were not as reliable as the trades. The manpower available was very much less and would have to come mostly from *Columbine*.

Pascoe, who Snowden trusted implicitly, would command *Persephone*, and First Lieutenant Baker, rapidly earning Snowden's respect, would take *Nymphe*. Baker would be assisted by *Columbine*'s Third Lieutenant, Perkins, and Pascoe by Second Lieutenant West. The prizes were to be manned by the minimum possible number of midshipmen, petty officers and ratings, and Snowden hoped for fair weather and the absence of enemies.

He was sitting in his cabin with the Purser, going over accounts, when Surgeon Dawson was shown in.

"If I may have a word with you in private, Captain," he asked.

The Purser stood to leave. "Excuse me, gentlemen."

"What is on your mind, Grant?"

"You, Percy. I'm concerned."

Snowden was sufficiently self-aware to know what Dawson was concerned about. His head ached and he felt weak and exhausted, tired beyond measure. He thought back to Nelson's remarks.

"Tell me."

"I won't tell you, I'll ask. How do you feel?"

"Fine, not too bad at all." The Surgeon looked sharply at him, and he reconsidered his words. "Very well, Grant, if you must know, I'm just about all in. It's not rational, but I'm dreading the trip to Bermuda. I keep thinking about the reefs, the state of the other ships."

The Surgeon paused, as though carefully framing his words: "You've had a few head injuries, I believe."

Snowden thought, “Yes, I have, I’ve been unlucky in that way. The blast at Maguelone didn’t actually injure me, but it had a bad effect, and I seem to be very sensitive to the sound of guns now. And my time in the dinghy – I have nightmares about it – and sometimes I even think of it during the day. I wish *Oleander* wasn’t carrying the damned thing around on her davits – it sets me off when I see it!”

“Percy, you weren’t recovered from all that when you abandoned the sinking ship, and since then you’ve been almost constantly in action, in a state of high tension.”

“I always feel drained after action, but I admit this is worse, much worse.”

“It’s bad, Percy, but there’s a cure for it – rest.”

“No rest for me at the moment, Grant. I’ve got to get the prizes manned, and …” He paused as Dawson held up his hand.

“The officers and men are well trained and experienced. They know very well what to do. At present, Percy, you are surplus to requirements. I have spoken to Mr Weedon …” Weedon was the Dockyard Superintendent.

“That rascal! Says he can’t work on the schooner or the frigates.”

“You know very well he can’t, Percy, his dockyard is very small, and he has a backlog of important work, including commissioning *Molene*.”

“I suppose that may be true, but what about him?”

“You know his house on the hill, behind the dockyard?”

“Yes, I know it.”

“He’s agreed to put you up there. It’s very quiet, breezy and cool. Just what you need. To paraphrase Cromwell, you are doing no good here – in the name of God, go!”

Snowden went, as ordered.

***

The Weedons’ house was as advertised, breezy and cool. For four days Snowden relished the quiet family life, enjoying rest and dinners with Weedon and his wife, who were excellent hosts. The headaches receded and he began to sleep soundly at night, undisturbed by nightmares.

One afternoon, starting to feel slightly bored and not wanting to outstay his welcome, he borrowed a horse and set off towards Antigua’s main town, St John’s, on the north-west side of the island. He dined at Smith’s Tavern, and was soon engaged at cards with several seemingly prosperous men. At the end of the evening, Snowden was down, but he had enjoyed himself greatly, despite the rather obvious questions from some of the players about the prize money he had accumulated.

On the second evening, he lost again, rather more heavily. As he got up to leave, one of the players, Stephen Hocking, the player who had won most, glanced at his fellows.

"Will you be joining us tomorrow evening, Snowden?" Hocking said, slightly too eagerly. "There's a ball at the court house and you're very welcome to play with us there. We usually play for slightly higher stakes."

"Thank you. Yes, I'll see you tomorrow, gentlemen," said Snowden "I look forward to retrieving some of my money." D*ear little lamb*, he thought.

***

The ballroom was brightly lit and the whirl of women and men in brightly coloured clothes almost dazzling. Snowden made out several officers from his own ship at the dance, but made no effort to speak to them, instead moving towards a room at the back where tables had been set up.

"Ah, Snowden, good evening," said Hocking. "We hoped you would come. Will you have a drink?" He glanced at his fellows with a barely suppressed grin.

"Lemonade only, thank you," replied Snowden, who had been warned off alcohol by the surgeon, and who anyway made it a rule not to combine drink and cards. When the drink arrived, accompanied by glasses of rum punch for the other players, Snowden surreptitiously sniffed his lemonade and realised that it was liberally spiced with rum. He set it to one side and play began.

Snowden's technique, honed to perfection over years of practice, solitary to begin with, followed by a successful card-playing career, was to make full use of his remarkable memory for cards, his ability to read the faces of his opponents and to exploit to the full the hand that was dealt to him. *Much like battle*, he thought, *and like in battle, opponents could be defeated when confidence of success clouded their judgement*. Drink circulated freely, but Snowden stuck to his almost untasted lemonade. After an hour or so, he began to win – not all the time, but he won more often than he lost, and his winnings began to mount. After two hours, the pile of coins on the table at his elbow was very sizable, and he knew that the mood on the table was turning against him. It was time for him to leave.

"So soon?" asked Hocking, looking at Snowden's glass. "You haven't drunk your lemonade."

"No," said Snowden, "I was not as thirsty as I thought I was, and of course lemonade like that often makes me dizzy."

Hocking smiled grimly, "You're a close one, Snowden, that's for sure," and Snowden wondered if he intended to make trouble.

He heard a familiar voice behind him "Well done, Sir," and looked round for the first time since he had started playing and saw West standing behind him with Luciani and several other officers. Snowden was not surprised to see that Luciani, who was smiling broadly, had his arm around a woman's waist, and even less surprised when Hocking said, in a much more pleasant voice, "Goodnight, Captain, and I wish you a pleasant evening."

"You're an evil looking crew," said Snowden to the officers, as he got up to leave, "Thanks."

***

Prize money, or 'head money' if the prize was an enemy warship, was divided in a complex way between ships and their complements. If an individual ship took a prize, and the prize was deemed legitimate - 'condemned' - the money would be divided amongst her people and her station's commander. Ratings received a much smaller portion than the ship's commander and officers, but if the ship had been successful, a sum sufficient to change their lives. *Oleander*'s previous cruise had been very successful – she had captured, almost undamaged, *Blonde*, a large French privateering frigate with a valuable cargo, and had intercepted a consignment of gold destined for the French Navy. The small size of *Oleander*'s crew meant that the money would be divided amongst fewer men.

However, there could be considerable delay between the taking of the prize and the payment of prize money, and there were frequently legal disputes. At Kennedy's prompting, they had taken *Blonde* into Plymouth, where Snowden's local connections and legal representation would expedite a fair return, but it was still a lengthy process. The gold, which had been taken to Gibraltar, was a different matter altogether, and it would undoubtedly be years before *Oleander*'s crew would be rewarded for its capture.

The delays and legal disputes, difficult enough for officers like Snowden to overcome, could prove insurmountable to ratings, who were sometimes cheated out of their money by unscrupulous agents for small advances. Snowden believed that *Oleander*'s crew, largely Bermudian, were especially vulnerable as they would have even less opportunity to make their case than Englishmen. He knew that some captains, especially the wealthier ones, paid their crews' prize money in advance, and, while he was resting, he had determined to do the same if he could.

Weedon, who had lived on Antigua for some time and was well connected, arranged for Snowden to meet a banker in St John's. The banker, after considerable discussions and much notarising of bills, had agreed to advance money to Snowden.

Kennedy had disbursed this money to *Oleander*'s crew, assisted by *Columbine*'s Purser, who kept a meticulous record of the proceedings, obtaining each man's signature or mark as he received his money.

Two days after his card game, Snowden, headache gone and feeling immeasurably better, stood on *Columbine*'s quarterdeck, watching as Third Lieutenant Perkins took the ship out of English Harbour, at the head of the convoy for Bermuda.

Chapter 44 – Bermuda

The ships were all fast sailers, but progress towards Bermuda, a thousand miles to the north, was stately rather than rapid. *Columbine* was in fine fettle, well worked up, but she was not fully manned, having sent nearly a third of her crew into the two prizes. The French frigates were seriously undermanned, with just enough men to sail them, but not to fight in any meaningful way, and *Oleander*, though almost fully crewed, was still weakened by her broken frames. In Antigua, the ships' carpenters had temporarily doubled them, but a proper repair required the attention of a dry dock, and until they were repaired properly, her sail-carrying capacity was reduced.

Throughout the passage north, the weather had been clear enough to allow them to obtain good sights of sun and stars, and several of the ships carried chronometers. They were certain of their position, but Bermuda, a low island fringed by reefs, stretching for miles out to sea, on which the swells of the Atlantic broke in ceaseless fury, was not a place to approach in the dark, and so on the afternoon of the sixth day, about forty miles south of the island, the ships hove to for the night. Early in the morning the three frigates proceeded into the harbour of St George's, where word spread quickly that *Oleander* was about to return, and when she came into the harbour, dressed overall with signal flags, and flying a long paying-off pennant, her band playing *Ça ira*, a considerable crowd had assembled on the quayside. There were cheers from the crowd, but the ship had been away for a long time and Snowden knew that this enthusiasm would be tempered with apprehension, as relatives waited for news of their loved ones.

***

In the evening, after a rather difficult meeting with Bermuda's naval Superintendent – who claimed to be much overworked – Snowden walked by himself to where *Oleander* was lying alongside the wharf and looked at the ship, damaged but still beautiful with her huge raking masts and graceful lines, returned to the place where she had been built. Memories flooded back, so many memories, overwhelming. The desperate fight against the corsairs, Julia White emerging from the cabin carrying a bloodstained cutlass, and there, hanging on davits on her stern, the dinghy …

From the shadow of *Oleander's* mainmast, Kennedy watched Snowden as he stood, deep in thought, on the quayside, and when he saw Snowden wipe his eyes he called out, "Percy!"

Snowden started, jerking his head towards the sound of the voice.

"Ken, I didn't realise there was anybody there."

Kennedy walked along the gangway and joined Snowden on the wharf.

"Are you all right, Percy?"

"I believe I am, Ken, I was just thinking ..."

"I know, Percy, we've done a lot in her."

"It seems almost like a dream."

"Would you like to come aboard? Take a glass? There's still some of that Corsican wine, and I think I can find a bit of biscuit."

"I'd like that very much, Ken."

Historical and Geographical Notes

Although the main events in the book are fictitious, I have tried to make them historically plausible by fitting them into the well-documented campaign that led to the Battle of Trafalgar in 1805. There was a real battle at Anse à la Barque in 1808, part of the British capture of Guadeloupe, but it was dissimilar to the action I describe. Several of the ships mentioned in the book were real, including *Curieux*, (featured on the front cover), *Intrépide* and *Northumberland.* Although *Northumberland* was stationed in the West Indies at the time of the book, I have taken liberties with her movements.

The geography of the West Indies has not changed much since Snowden was active there, and I think that my descriptions, based on cruising there in my 40 foot yacht, are accurate. Anse à la Barque is now a peaceful anchorage, but the remains of a fortification on the northern headland, with broken French cannons scattered in the undergrowth, are a reminder of its violent past. Today, Grand Cul-de-Sac Marin in the north of Guadeloupe is almost unvisited by cruising yachts, but small boats still travel along the Salt River which connects it with the Petit Cul-de-Sac Marin in the south of the island.

Diamond Rock is steep, windy and intimidating, and anyone who sails past it cannot fail to be impressed by the Royal Navy's achievement in fortifying the island, less than a mile from Martinique. The feats of seamanship and *ad-hoc* engineering required to hoist heavy guns from the deck of an anchored ship to the summit, using only the power of the wind and human muscle, are astonishing.

Men from HMS *Diamond Rock* really did capture the French colonel of engineers, but without assistance from Luciani and in less dramatic fashion. A French-speaking lieutenant, aided by a former slave, talked their way into the man's bedroom and abducted him.

The north-east trade wind still dominates life in the Lesser Antilles, and the passage between Guadeloupe and Dominica is as boisterous as it was when Snowden crossed it in *Oleander*'s dinghy. The remains of fortifications in the West Indies are highly evocative, perhaps none more so than those at Prince Rupert Bay in Dominica, restored through the efforts of Dr Lennox Honeychurch.

Monsieur du Pont really did manufacture gunpowder at Brandywine Creek, and the DuPont Company, grown beyond recognition, still has its headquarters there.

When considering the battles for possession of the West Indies, I always think – why? Why did the French and British care about these islands, especially Britain, whose economy was changing, expanding beyond imagination as a result of the Enlightenment and the Industrial Revolution? The British were already reluctant to commit British troops to their defence, raising the West Indian Regiments against the protests of the planters. I think, perhaps, that the Islands were not really what was being fought over and were almost incidental to the great struggle being fought in Europe, merely convenient stages for fighting what was, until about 1914, referred to as the Great War.

A glossary and photographs of some of the places featured in the book are available on my website:

www.paulwestonauthor.com

About the Author

Paul Weston's (www.paulwestonauthor.com) writing is informed by his career as an engineer and entrepreneur. An apprenticeship with the BP Tanker Company was followed by several years at sea on tankers, offshore oil support vessels and ferries. He started and ran Weston Antennas, designing, manufacturing and installing large satellite earth station antennas. As a mechanical engineer he worked for Siemens, and has several patents to his name.

He has been sailing since childhood, initially in the family's converted fishing boat *True Vine,* and in his teens crossed the Atlantic in a home designed and built 26 footer, and in his twenties raced to the Azores and back on another 26 footer. He owned *Mitch*, a 31 foot Mitchell Sea Angler, for over twenty years, and during an intermittent four year voyage with his wife Sally, took the boat to the Mediterranean and back by sea, river and canal. They have now reverted to sail, and own *Kim*, a 40 foot aluminium lift keel yacht which they bought in France and have sailed via Spain, Morocco and the Canary Islands to the West Indies.

Books in This Series

Paul Weston Historical

Maritime and Naval Fiction

Weymouth Bound – When Apprentice Jack Stone's first ship is captured by the French, he determines to survive, and do what he can to frustrate a French scheme to strike at the heart of the British establishment

Not by Sea – Napoleon's army is blockaded in Boulogne. Thwarted by British sea power, he entrusts an alternative scheme to the brilliant Captain Morlaix.

Cape Corse – Lieutenant Snowden RN in his fast Bermudian built schooner, *Oleander*, is sent to the Mediterranean to support a dangerous and delicate operation which could materially support the defeat of Bonaparte.

Gulf of Lions – In a secret mission to support the Spanish opposition, Snowden takes *Oleander* on a wide ranging cruise from Brittany to Spain, France and Morocco.

Diamond Rock – Captain Snowden, in his frigate *Columbine*, and Commander Kennedy in *Oleander*, carry out a daring operation on the French island of Guadeloupe.

My website, www.paulwestonauthor.com, gives background information on the novels.

Illustrations

The Author's Boat in Anse a la Barque

Diamond Rock from the Author's Boat

Printed in Dunstable, United Kingdom

77568576R00111